T0349923

MIDNIGHT
AT THE
HOUDINI

MIDNIGHT AT THE HOUDINI

DELILAH S. DAWSON

DELACORTE PRESS

Text copyright © 2023 by D. S. Dawson
Jacket art copyright © 2023 by Aurelie Maron
Chapter opener frame art by wabeno/stock.adobe.com

All rights reserved. Published in the United States by Delacorte Press, an imprint of Random House Children's Books, a division of Penguin Random House LLC, New York.

Delacorte Press is a registered trademark and the colophon is a trademark of Penguin Random House LLC.

GetUnderlined.com

Educators and librarians, for a variety of teaching tools, visit us at RHTeachersLibrarians.com

Library of Congress Cataloging-in-Publication Data is available upon request.
ISBN 978-0-593-48679-5 (trade) — ISBN 978-0-593-48680-1 (ebook)

The text of this book is set in 11.3-point Adobe Garamond Pro.
Interior design by Cathy Bobak

Printed in the United States of America
10 9 8 7 6 5 4 3
First Edition

For Sleep No More and the McKittrick Hotel,
where I finally found that secret wardrobe door
that led me somewhere magical.
Fortune favors the bold.

1.

The night is perfect and glorious and sparkling, too beautiful to be real. Like magic.

Anna is ten years old, and this is the fanciest birthday party she's ever attended. The castle-like home's sprawling grounds host a miniature Ferris wheel, unicorn rides, a cotton candy machine, and a stage, all surrounded by twinkling lights and spotlights twirling into the indigo clouds. She was invited not because she knows the birthday girl, but because her dad's latest hotel is a huge success, the most popular hotel in Vegas, and because her family just moved into a similar mansion down the street, leaving their old three-bedroom ranch behind. Her dad is over by the pizza ovens, surrounded by smiling strangers desperate to be his friend.

Anna is very much hoping to experience something similar.

It's early summer, and next year, she'll start at a new private school with . . . well, basically all the girls at this party. Anna looks around, nervously fusses with her tiara. The elegant invitation looked like it came straight from Cinderella's castle, and it proclaimed this to be a Princess Party. Anna has therefore dressed up as a princess. Her mom insisted on a professional fitting for her dress, which has a huge skirt with rainbow layers of tulle, as well as an updo and makeup appointment at the salon. Anna's mom is taking their recent change in status very seriously, and Anna wants to impress her new classmates, so she went along with it.

She doesn't see any kids her age, though—just the adults on the patio and dozens of little kids running everywhere, shouting, trailed by frazzled nannies. Following the sound of a booming pop song, she ends up at a pool so big her old house could've fit inside it. There are grottoes and slides and a diving board and a DJ. Two large groups of kids around her age cluster in tight circles on either side of the pool, girls on one side and boys on the other. Anna is closest to the boys' side, and there's one boy, with perfectly floppy blond hair and ice-blue eyes who's so beautiful she thinks he must be a movie star. He's the leader, the one all the others are clustered around, and he looks at her with curiosity.

Anna puts on her best, most confident smile and says, "Hi."

"Hi," he says back.

Someone gasps, and the girls sashay over to the boys' side of the pool, circling Anna like wolves and clutching drinks that look alcoholic but surely aren't.

"Are you flirting with my boyfriend? At my birthday party? Josh, was she flirting with you?"

Anna freezes and realizes she's made a huge mistake. The birthday girl is furious with her. No one else is wearing a princess dress, a tiara, or even a token touch of celebration.

Tank tops and short shorts with heeled sandals are the unspoken dress code. The girls remind her of matching gingerbread cookies, their hair in flat, smooth shades of honey and gold and their skin deeply tan. They wear makeup—fake eyelashes, shiny lip gloss—like they're in high school, not fifth grade. The boys look athletic and untouchable, and now that Anna has been singled out, they too stare, silent and judging.

"We just said hi," the beautiful boy says with a shrug. "No big deal."

Anna is frozen in place, knowing in this moment that everything about her is wrong. Her dress, her face, even her unlightened hair. All the kids stare at her with secondhand embarrassment or outright hostility. In the silence, as they wait to see what Anna will do, one girl cackles behind a manicured hand.

"I'm Anna Alonso. My dad is Daniel Alonso. We RSVP'd—"

"Oh, so your dad has that tacky new hotel. My dad made me invite you. How old are you? Like, six?"

The birthday girl's mouth twists in a mocking smile. There are more cackles and titters. The girls openly glare at Anna, look her up and down, and she wants to die. She should not have agreed with her father's request to come. She should not have allowed her mother to doll her up like a baby. She should have begged her older sister, Emily, to come. Everyone likes Emily, and Emily knows how to fit in. If Emily was here, Anna wouldn't be the object of mockery. Emily wouldn't let anyone speak to Anna like that. Maybe she would've told Anna not to wear this stupid dress.

But no. Emily was mad at Anna and ignoring her, and now Anna's reputation is ruined before she's even set foot in school.

The twinkling lights fade away. The scent of popcorn goes rancid. The night is dizzying now, huge and threatening and intolerable.

Without answering, Anna turns and marches away from the vicious girls and untouchable boys posing by the perfect pool.

"So embarrassing," a girl says behind her.

"So immature," says another.

"Oh my God, if that was me, I would move."

Anna won't turn around, won't let them see her cry. She stomps past the squeaky Ferris wheel that no one is riding. She gives a wide berth to the unicorn rides, noting that the ponies' horns have elastic straps and their manure looks like any other manure. She sidesteps hired princesses in ball gowns with visible zippers, sweat smearing the heavy makeup around their wigs. There must be a corner of this enormous yard that offers some escape from the wretched girls and their cruel whispers.

There. She spies a gazebo in a far corner.

It's wrapped in lights like a fly in a spider's web, like everything else, but half the bulbs are out, leaving a convenient slice of shadow. Anna slides onto the bench, her skirt catching on the rough wood, and sighs in relief, slumping down so that no one will see her and do that horrible thing adults do where they ask in a singsong voice what's wrong.

The tears won't wait any longer. They pour out, and she scrubs at the glitter on her cheeks, the bubblegum-pink lipstick on her lips. She would yank down her hair, but she knows it's held in place by a thousand bobby pins and a gallon of hair spray.

Her hands come away smeared with black and pink and iridescent glitter.

Oh no. She's still got to walk out of this party next to her father. She's a complete mess, and he's going to be furious at her for making him look bad. Her job here was to present well and make friends—he made that perfectly clear—and she is an enormous failure.

"Pick a card, any card."

Anna looks up, tears streaming and snot bubbling, to find a magician standing there.

Or, more accurately, a man with white hair dressed like an old-fashioned magician, right down to the dusty tailcoat and tall black hat. Anna is certain that the girls would have horrible things to say about him, so maybe that's why he's also in this dark corner of the yard. She looks back toward the pool, terrified that the other kids will see her talking to what amounts to a clown.

With an aggrieved sigh, she selects a card from the perfect fan he presents. "Am I supposed to look at it?"

The man smiles through his curling white mustache. "Of course. One of us needs to know what it is!"

Hiding the card behind her hand, Anna turns it over. It's the queen of diamonds, but instead of the usual harsh-faced royalty drawn in stark lines of red and black, there's an elegant yellow canary wearing an ornate gold crown and surrounded by branches with delicate white blossoms. The intricate illustration is pressed into the thick paper, and the card feels old and important.

"Now put it back in, wherever you like."

Anna wants the magician to leave and let her be miserable in peace, but she knows he won't go away until the trick is over, so she shoves the card into the fan in a different place from where she took it. The magician shifts the queen back into the deck and moves the cards this way and that, shuffling and ruffling them, stacking them and cutting them and causing them to fly from one hand to the other like a line of ducklings. An hour ago, this trick would've been intriguing and exciting, but right now, Anna only sees useless practice and trickery.

She realizes with dull finality that magic isn't real and never was.

"Is this your card?" The man holds up a card with a white rabbit—the king of hearts—and Anna shakes her head.

"How about this one?" He holds up another canary card. The king of diamonds—close, but no cigar—and again, Anna shakes her head. The magician deflates a bit and stares down at his cards as if they've somehow betrayed him. "They must be feeling stubborn today," he mutters as if to himself before looking up at her brightly. "Do you have any encouragement for them, maybe give them a tap for luck?" He holds out the perfectly stacked deck in both hands, as if offering her a beautifully wrapped gift.

Anna glances around to make sure none of the vicious girls are nearby. "You can do it, buddy," she says softly, staring at the neat stack of cards. She taps the top one, and it sticks to her finger. When she turns it over, it's the queen of diamonds. "Wow. Good trick." She pastes on a smile and holds out the card, hoping not to hurt the magician's feelings. "Thank you."

But he doesn't go away. He takes her card and puts the deck

away in his jacket and cocks his head. He's an unusual sort of man; he should seem very phony, like everything else about this party, and yet there's a heaviness to the cloth of his jacket, a subtle shine to his hat. Somehow, he seems more real than anything else here.

"Not a believer, eh?" he asks.

Anna shakes her head, and he leans in, conspiratorial.

"But I bet you'd like to be."

She shrugs. Her feelings are too complex and private and new to explain to some random man paid by the hour to walk around a spoiled brat's party.

"You know . . ." He reaches into one sleeve and pulls out a brightly colored handkerchief, and then another and another, dozens of them piling up at his feet. "We think we know what's possible, but the role of the magician is to prove otherwise."

Anna feels a new wave of tears threaten. "It's all fake," she mutters. "All of it."

The man has run out of handkerchiefs, and his white-gloved hand cups the last one as if he's caught a firefly. He holds his closed fist out, palm down.

"What if I could make you believe?" His tufty white eyebrows shoot up.

"You can't. But thanks for the trick." Anna looks away, hoping he'll take the hint.

"Ah, well. Can't blame an old man for trying. Enjoy the party." He opens his hand and the last handkerchief flutters to the ground. With a tip of his hat, he walks away.

When he's gone, Anna looks down at the heap of handkerchiefs he's left there—crimson and goldenrod and emerald and indigo, rich and silky—a mess someone else will have to clean up, once the party is over. She decides to scoop up the whole mass of them and toss them in one of the conveniently placed garbage bins before one of the other kids notices the motley pile, but when she stoops to gather the handkerchiefs, that last one catches her eye. It's all balled up, snowy white, different from the others in size, shape, and texture. And she's fairly certain it dropped with a heaviness it shouldn't possess.

She glances around to make sure she's still alone before plucking up the white handkerchief and undoing the knots. Nestled within is an earring, a simple golden hoop.

Anna goes still, every hair on her body rising, her feet numb and her hands shaking so hard she nearly drops her prize.

Three days ago, she lost one of Emily's earrings, a special gold hoop her sister had received as part of a pair for her fifteenth birthday. In those three days, Anna's beloved older sister and best friend, usually kind and sweet and doting, has not spoken a word to her. She was supposed to come to this party and help Anna make friends. She refused.

The past three days have been the three worst days of Anna's life—and that was before tonight. If Anna gives Emily this earring, this earring that inexplicably matches Emily's missing earring exactly, then perhaps her sister will talk to her again. It can just be a small mistake instead of a huge one.

She carefully knots the handkerchief back around the earring and shoves it deep into her dress pocket. She stands on the edge of the gazebo, scanning the huge yard, but she doesn't see the magician anywhere. She wants to thank him, for all that she's not sure how to say it, how to be grateful without acknowledging that what he's shown her cannot be explained away by logic.

She hides in the gazebo until it's time to go home.

She looks up at the night sky, at the twinkling stars, wishing that wishing really worked.

She tells her father she had a lovely time and the girls were nice.

She gives the earring to her sister.

Emily forgives her.

Anna tells herself that magic isn't real.

She tells herself it doesn't pay to believe in childish tricks. She tells herself to grow up.

She tries to forget the magician.

She fails.

2.

The night is perfect and glorious and sparkling, too beautiful to be real. Like magic.

Max is ten years old, and he has finally found his way to the party he's always dreamed of seeing.

Overhead, crystal chandeliers sparkle, spilling their light onto a throng of dancers clad in grand ball gowns and swooping robes and sharp black tuxes. They wear masks in every shade of the rainbow, their eyes twinkling from the shadows as they turn and spin and dip to a dizzy waltz. Max has wanted to come here for a long, long time, and he finally found a way in. He is the only child here, and he hopes no one will notice.

He steps into the room, shiny black shoes clicking on the tile floor, and resists the urge to fiddle with his carefully tied bow tie. After thorough consideration, he visits the buffet first, sampling the cakes and pastries and cheeses and fruits, tucking little sandwiches into his jacket pockets and gorging on strawberries dipped in a chocolate fountain. He inspects the punch but knows full well that he can be whisked away just as easily as he was allowed in and must show respect for this place. He would like to ask someone to dance, but is quite simply too overwhelmed to find the words. Now that he knows there is dancing here, he'll learn the dances, and when he comes back, he'll know better.

Wiping sweet lemonade from his lips, he drifts toward a curtained niche, one of many set into the ballroom walls. Within the niche, a magician cuts a woman in half with a gleaming silver saw as the crowd gasps. The next niche reveals an automaton that can play chess, and different members of the audience take turns moving a piece and waiting to see what the clever wooden boy with the painted freckles will do next. Again and again, he silently curtails every attempt to best him. Another niche holds a séance, complete with a spectral woman's head floating in a crystal ball as a tambourine shakes somewhere nearby. Each one of the many niches reveals some marvelous new trick or exhibit, things the boy has read about but never witnessed. The crowds part politely to let him in, where he watches from front row center. There is too much to see in one night, too many wonders to digest.

He is growing tired, and he yawns into his fist as he approaches the only niche he hasn't yet investigated. Another automaton takes center stage, a beautiful woman in a silk dress sketching on paper with a pencil. The crowd is so hushed Max can hear the scratch of the graphite, and he slips to the front, studying the machine's smooth wooden face painted the creamy white of porcelain. Her movements are somehow both jerky and smooth, and when she stops sketching, her head cants up as if proudly acknowledging the crowd. Her eyes are bright blue, her eyebrows slender arches.

No one moves, so Max steps forward and takes the paper from the tilted wooden board. The drawing is beautiful, accomplished if imperfect. It shows a girl—or maybe a young woman—several years older than he is, perhaps sixteen. Her hair is long and dark and straight, her smile more along the lines of a smirk, as if they're sharing an inside joke. She doesn't look like anyone else he's ever seen, and he likes that.

"Who is she?" he asks the man putting a new sheet of paper on the automaton's drawing board.

The man doesn't answer; he merely steps back as if to give the automaton her space. Her head tilts back down, and her hand moves, sketching. Max walks around to her side and notes that she is drawing a man from the crowd. A spark of hope lights in Max's chest—maybe she draws people at the ball, which means the girl in the drawing might actually be here. She's older than him, sure, but he still wants to look at her with his own eyes, to see if the drawing has captured her accurately.

He doesn't find her in the crowd, nor in the ballroom.

Maybe her image is merely something programmed, one of many possibilities chosen at random.

Slightly disappointed, Max exits with the sketch. He likes the girl in the picture. He wonders who she is, how she was selected, who drew the original that the machine re-created. He touches her lips with his finger, accidentally smearing a little chocolate across the creamy paper, and is instantly annoyed with himself.

No matter—he can come back to the ballroom anytime he pleases.

He hopes.

A little deflated, he gathers a handful of ice-cold cherries from the buffet and heads out, dropping his mask on the floor by the door. He treads up the hallway to the elevator, gets inside, and turns his key—but isn't sure where to go next.

This picture—it's his. He doesn't want to share it, doesn't want to answer any questions about it. He needs to take it somewhere secret, somewhere he knows it will be safe. Rather than going to his room, he goes to the sixth floor, carefully rolling the paper and tucking it inside his tuxedo jacket. He doesn't encounter a soul, but he enters the library quietly, just in case.

As usual, no one is there.

No one ever goes to the library.

Once inside, Max closes the door and locks it, then heads to the crowded bookshelves and presses a tiny catch in an out-of-the-way corner. The shelf swings inward, and he slides into the shadows and pushes the door shut behind him. A little farther down the cramped, black hallway, he opens a cupboard-sized door and crawls through on hands and knees.

Of all the secret places he's found so far, this one is his favorite. It's a small room painted a delicate eggshell blue, and in the center is a carved wooden pedestal that holds a skeletal tree in a large blue-and-white pot. There's another door—a door of the proper size—but behind it is only a sloppily built brick wall. The smaller door from the secret passage to the blue room goes through a china cabinet, the delicate plates and sculptures on its shelves glued down so they can't fall and break when he bumbles through.

The first time he ended up here, he thought it was very silly—a whole room, if a small one, reserved for a fake cabinet and a potted tree. There isn't enough sunlight to sustain a living plant, though—no windows means no sunlight—which led him to further examination of the room's contents.

As soon as he touched the tree, it bloomed.

And not just—oh, look, a flower.

The tall, spindly thing burst into a riot of blooms and fat oranges, filling the room with a heavenly fragrance, citrus and white flowers that spoke of secrets and far-off breezes.

Max stumbled back from the tree then, and the blooms and oranges disappeared as if reabsorbed by the little brown branches.

Over the years, this place has become his private sanctuary, the only space where he feels truly alone and like someone won't bust in accidentally or wander past. He's stored special belongings in the cabinet, squirreled away behind the boring platters and inside the tureens, and now he knows what to do with the drawing of the girl. He scrambles back to the library for a jar of pushpins and returns, choosing exactly the right place in the center of the blue wall. He hangs up the drawing with a single pin, careful to make sure it's straight. It seems to belong here, with the orange tree and its occasionally bursting blossoms. He imagines the girl smells like flowers.

Max exits the room and closes the bookshelf that is a door, leaving no sign of his passage. This secret must remain a secret; he's determined to have something for himself. Back in the library, he searches for books with information on automata and how they work, how a drawing might be created or re-created so faithfully by a machine.

But once he has a stack of books ready, he can't bring himself to open even one.

He feels the same way about the orange tree.

He knows the answers are out there, knows they are probably cunning tricks, but he believes in magic nevertheless.

For Max, belief is enough.

3.

Anna Alonso, now sixteen, looks out upon her work and smiles. Fairy lights wink in the trees outside the picture windows as the evening sky melts from lavender to sapphire blue, spangled with stars. Little girls chase circles around the dance floor in pastel dresses, their glittery wings fluttering behind them. The most stylish of Las Vegas investors stand around in their tailored suits holding flutes of champagne, waiting for the bride and groom to appear.

Satisfied that the party is going according to plan, Anna leaves the reception hall and heads down the hallway toward the lounge, clutching her planner and a large but simple silk bag. She's been to dozens of Vegas weddings, but nothing like this—nothing like her sister's. Emily may glow with love for her new husband and the happiest day of her life, but Anna glows with pride. She planned the entire event herself.

This venue, with its secret garden framed by the Vegas skyline—

Anna found it by snooping on Reddit. That dress, the perfect expression of Emily's brand of cottage chic—Anna marched past the outraged saleswoman and into the warehouse and picked it out herself. She even selected the cheeses being exclaimed over on the buffet. Emily is five years older, and she's popular, caring, and sweet, but she's also a ditz and very, very disorganized. If Emily is the family's sweetheart, Anna has become its backbone. And, today, its wedding planner.

Emily might be content to just go with the flow, but Anna is ruled by preparation, logic, research, and choosing the best course of action. After that terrible princess party when she was ten, she swore she would never again walk into a situation wide-eyed and bedazzled, that she wouldn't allow herself to be humiliated or caught out or let someone else make important choices on her behalf. And she hasn't. When everything is just so, nothing can go wrong.

She hears a soft laugh and spots Emily and JJ rounding the corner, finally heading for the door to the reception hall. She hurries toward them, opening her bag.

"You guys are five minutes late."

Emily laughs. "It's my wedding day."

"Lipstick? Deodorant? Aspirin? Mints?" Anna holds out the bag. "I've got it all."

Emily, radiant and glowing, turns to JJ. "I've got everything I need."

When Anna continues pawing through the bag, Emily puts a hand on her arm. "You did a great job. Everything is perfect. Now go relax."

"Not until everything has gone according to plan." Anna points at her thick binder. "We're already behind schedule."

Emily and JJ share a gentle smile. "The caterer you found is so good I'm sure they don't mind waiting. But I appreciate your need for order. It's clearly paid off. I could never have done this without you." It's the sort of thing only Emily can say without sounding cheesy or patronizing, and Anna feels an answering glow in her chest, knowing that she's helped make her sister so happy.

"Then go on in. I set aside a cooler of food for you guys since you won't have time to eat. It's already in the limo." Emily leans in for a hug, and Anna hugs her back, gently, so she won't crush her hair or dress.

"Thank you for making tonight perfect," Emily whispers. "It's magical."

"It's not magic—it's careful planning—but you're welcome."

Anna opens the door, and Emily and JJ step forward. Everyone in the reception hall breaks into applause and wolf whistles. Anna gives a signal, and the lights turn down as the DJ plays the song Anna helped Emily pick for the first dance—an ancient favorite that oozes class. "It Had to Be You" floats out of the speakers like velvet, but the father of the bride isn't waiting near the dance floor like he should be, like he was firmly told to be because the second dance is his. He's not in the reception hall at all. Emily looks around, expectant and concerned, but Anna shoos her down the aisle.

"Forget Dad—I'll find him before the first dance is over. Old songs are always long," she whispers.

Emily and JJ swoop onto the dance floor, Emily's dress swirling like a cloud, JJ's eyes glowing with love. Anna will have to go through the photos later to see how the dance went—she has to find out what happened to their dad and ask him why he almost ruined the reception in the three minutes and fifty-five seconds before it's his turn to dance. She heads down a hallway, and just outside the bathrooms, she hears familiar voices. What she sees makes her teeth grind and her shoulders slump.

Her parents are fighting again.

They always do this, which is why her father spends so much time away from home, managing his many properties and investments, while her mother manages her migraines and mismanages her credit cards. It's happened more and more often the older the girls have gotten—or possibly the more money their dad has made. Their parents don't even seem to like each other anymore, and it makes Emily cry and Anna start Googling marriage counselors they'll never visit. And now they're about to ruin Emily's wedding.

Not on Anna's watch.

Spring-green bridesmaid dress swishing around her knees and spindly heels clicking, she marches directly toward them.

"I'm going home," Mom mutters, her voice acidic. "You can handle the fallout yourself."

Throwing a sympathetic glance at Anna and gesturing at her permanently aching head, her mother flounces toward the parking lot, the beading on her tight taupe dress shaking. Anna pressured her to choose something more sedate, less Vegas showgirl, but much to her ongoing mortification, her mom loves glitz. At least the dress is beige and not white or hot pink.

"Mom, stop!" she calls softly.

But her mother never stops, not until she wants to.

The door slams shut, and Anna feels it in her chest, a tight lump. Her eyes are hot, but she knows that if she starts crying, it'll upset her sister, so she wills herself not to sniffle and refocuses on the problem at hand. Emily is used to their mother making abrupt, overdramatic exits from important functions, but she's a daddy's girl, so Anna has to make sure that their father, at least, doesn't disappoint.

"What did you do this time?" Anna asks her dad.

She's torn, forever torn. Her dad is always angry, always busy, always concerned with making money. But her mother is always upset with him, always a hypochondriac, always either hiding in her room or out spending money.

Although Anna loves them, and they love her, they're both kind of idiots, and she's spent her entire life standing between them with Emily by her side. Tough, logical Anna makes her parents stop shouting, and sweet, gentle Emily gets them to smile again.

With Emily occupied with her first dance, now it's up to Anna.

Her dad shakes his head and marches toward the reception hall, which is at least the right direction. Anna follows him through the door and over to the bar and watches him snatch a glass of champagne and down it before he turns back to her.

"What did I do?" he growls, but softly so he won't make a scene. "I did what I thought was the right thing. I keep forgetting: you and your mother hate surprises."

A prickle of unease skitters down Anna's neck, and she clutches her planner more tightly. "Surprise? What surprise?"

Instead of responding, her dad grabs another flute of champagne and strides powerfully past the dance floor to the DJ. When he takes the microphone and the music stops abruptly, Anna almost throws up.

None of this is part of her plan.

With the room gone quiet, everyone looks to the DJ with curiosity, whispering among themselves. Emily holds JJ's hand but looks to Anna, her blond hair shining like a halo above eyes filled with confusion and concern. Anna can only shrug helplessly—she has no idea what's going on, and whatever it is, it's too late to stop it.

Their father clears his throat into the microphone and holds up his glass of champagne.

"Friends and family, thank you for joining us today to see Emily and JJ tie the knot. They're young, but my little girl gets what she wants."

"Thank you, Daddy!" Emily calls as the crowd of five hundred claps politely.

"And that's why it's time to unveil my wedding gift. Emily, you've been telling me since you were three years old that you want to be a designer in New York City. Well, as my wedding gift to you, I bought you a condo in Manhattan. It's only two bedrooms, but that'll get you through one kid, right?" He laughs, and the crowd claps and whistles raucously.

Anna is watching Emily and sees wonder suffuse her delicate

features, sees her release JJ's hand to scurry across the room and throw herself into her father's arms. She's crying, but her mascara and lipstick are waterproof—Anna made sure of that. From what Anna can see, Emily has never been happier in her entire life, not even when JJ proposed in front of the castle at Disneyland.

But Anna?

Anna is devastated.

Anna is crying now, too, but for the opposite reason.

This is not the plan. This is not how things are supposed to go.

Emily is supposed to pick a house in a neighborhood near Vegas—Anna has several bookmarked—and use her brand-new design degree to work in one of the big casinos or do marketing for shows. JJ is in his second year as a real estate agent and doing well. They're set up. They're supposed to live five minutes away. For the next two years, Anna is supposed to babysit whatever perfect, adorable baby they have, then go to USC and fly home every weekend to coo over the next baby, then become the CEO of a *Fortune* 500 company. She's had everything planned out for years, ever since Emily met JJ at school when they were sixteen and told Anna that he was the perfect guy.

But. . . . New York? It's so far away. A world away.

Sure, Anna could fly there some weekends—her dad has plenty of cash. But she's been counting on having Emily *here*, with her through the rest of high school and then as close as possible during college. She doesn't know how to get through life with Mom and Dad without Emily. Mom doesn't understand Anna at all, and Dad doesn't have time for her and sometimes forgets she's not ten.

Emily is like her interpreter, helping Anna coax their mother into being reasonable and sweet and their father into actually coming home once in a while.

Anna needs Emily here, needs to be more than a text left on read. Phone calls aren't enough. They need their movie-and-popcorn parties, their PMS pizza parties, their Eat Your Feelings ice cream parties when something bad happens to one of them. When Anna doesn't know what to wear, she needs Emily to pick just the right outfit. When Emily doesn't know which Waterpik to buy, she needs Anna to make a spreadsheet. They're more than sisters—they're best friends. Emily has always taken care of Anna, and Anna is proud any time she can help her big sister.

But their dad. He just ruined everything.

He makes decisions without considering every side, always trusts his gut and pulls the trigger. It's worked well for him in business—he's definitely got a knack—but that doesn't mean he gets to decide what's best for Emily. What's best for them all. Anna knows him, and she knows that the Manhattan condo will be perfect, beautiful and in a decent neighborhood on the cusp of becoming great and tripling the property's value. But it's not just a real estate investment to Anna, not just a flashy gift to impress his friends and colleagues—it's a catastrophe. He's tearing the family apart.

Anna has been in some sort of panic fugue long enough for Emily and Dad to dance to "You Are the Sunshine of My Life." Everyone claps, and the party music kicks back up. Dad walks back toward Anna, grinning, as the room spins around her, the floor uncertain under her feet. Finding this sensation entirely un-welcome, Anna stiffens her backbone, sticks out her chin, and steps forward to meet him.

"Is this why Mom was so mad?" She pulls her dad into a cor-ner so they won't attract undue attention. "Because you did this without telling anyone? Because you're willing to break up our family? Did you even ask Emily if this is what she wants?"

"It was supposed to be a surprise," he replies, his smugness giv-ing way to annoyance.

And then a heavy arm lands around Anna's shoulders, envelop-ing her in the scent of expensive cologne and even more expensive cigars.

"Did you see her face?" Uncle Tony shouts, because everything he says is a shout. Uncle Tony isn't really Anna's uncle—thank God—but that's what her family calls him because he and Dad have been friends and business partners since they were little boys, hustling powdered lemonade from behind a sign promising it was fresh-squeezed. Anna disengages from Uncle Tony's big, hairy arm and steps back.

"Wait until Emily sees it. Those new floors. That view!" This from Dad's other friend, Uncle Sebastian, who's the third partner in their investment firm. If Dad is the medium bear and Uncle Tony is the big daddy bear, Sebastian is the baby bear—short, bald, and dapper. When he joined the lemonade stand, he brought a bowl of wax lemons to place on the card table to class up the joint.

"Did you even think about the taxes?" Anna mutters, knowing it's a weak argument and that her dad will probably pay those, too.

"Well, check out the jealous little sourpuss. Y'know, if you smiled more, you might get a boyfriend of your own." Uncle Tony claps her dad on the back and slides a cigar into the inside pocket of his tux as Anna seethes. "C'mon. Let's go wish these kids good luck with a stogie." The men rumble out a side door and into the garden, where they stand directly under a No Smoking sign and puff away like only stupidly rich men can.

Tony and Sebastian have muscled Anna's dad away from her like they always do. It still stings just like it did when she was little, the way they would swoop down in the weekends to take him fishing or interrupt a nice family meal for poker night. Her dad always swore they were spontaneous and liked to have fun, but Anna was pretty sure he texted them under the table whenever he got bored or needed an escape from Mom's complaints.

It doesn't matter. She can't tell her dad how she really feels now, in the middle of Emily's wedding. She loves Emily too much to ruin it for her, even if everything is ruined for Anna.

She skulks into a shadowy alcove by a wide window. Lightning flashes outside, and a few raindrops spatter against the glass. Anna wipes away her tears, feeling just like the weather, which has also taken an unexpectedly dark turn. Stormy, tearful, full of sound and fury signifying nothing. She thumps her purse and planner down on the table; it's too late to hope that things will run smoothly. The magic she worked so hard to create has fizzled away. At least her dad and his stupid friends are about to get soaked.

The rest of the wedding is like watching a silent movie, like she's a stranger watching something beautiful happening elsewhere. Dancing, cake, champagne she is offered but refuses to so much as sip because, knowing her luck, her first taste of alcohol would get her sister's wedding busted for underage drinking. Everyone lines up to blow bubbles as Emily and JJ run down the long sidewalk to their waiting limo, the guests hiding under big white umbrellas provided by the venue. The rain cascades down in waves, and the burgeoning storm seems to pause for one long moment to let the bride and groom pass before it resumes in earnest and thunder booms close enough to make the air vibrate in warning.

Anna is more of a stage manager than an actress, but she is determined to fool her sister. She smiles and laughs and hugs Emily under an umbrella by the limo, wishing her well on her honeymoon in Bali and making her promise to text daily.

The limo drives off, the rain falls like buckets of quarters, and everyone scurries inside in a tangle of ghostly white umbrellas. Anna can't contain her sobs any longer, so she stands there under the awning, alone in the dark, watching the limo's taillights disappear as tears course down her cheeks. In the heavy bag full of wedding day necessities Emily never even needed, Anna's phone screeches and vibrates against an Altoids tin.

A tornado watch. Fabulous. Their house is on the other side of the Vegas Strip. Somehow, the day got worse.

When her father texts Anna that their car is ready, she wipes her face with a tissue and prepares to give him hell.

4.

Their usual car is a black Tesla with those weird doors that open up instead of out, but this time, there's a white stretch limo waiting. Anna is not the only kid at her school with rich parents, but she is well aware that most kids don't have a family driver and is always slightly mortified by such ostentatious exhibits of wealth. It feels tacky to her. It's Emily's wedding, and all the guests are already gone; do they really need something this fancy?

When she collapses her umbrella and climbs inside, she sees why they needed a bigger car. It won't just be her and her dad heading home as she gives him a piece of her mind. Tony and Sebastian are already inside, dividing a bottle of champagne between glass flutes. Her dad's longtime driver, Steve, is in the front seat, his gleaming bald head sticking up on the other side of the partition.

The thunder booms so hard that Anna can feel it through the

leather seat, and each lightning strike penetrates the black-tinted windows, leaving red fireworks across Anna's vision. As Steve navigates the flooded roads, wind pushes and pulls the car around like an angry kid playing with toys. Steve is a good driver, careful and confident, but the weather is getting intense. Anna's father and his friends ignore her as they congratulate him on marrying off his older daughter like it's some big accomplishment, and Anna silently fumes.

When Tony says, "Only one more to sell off, am I right?" Anna can't take it any longer.

"Yes, because women are annoying chattel instead of real people. How many successful relationships have you had, Uncle Tony? I seem to remember a girl you brought over for Christmas one year who I thought was your niece—"

"Oh, Grouchy Gertie can talk," Tony shoots back. "You know, you'll never catch a man with an attitude like that."

"Catch a man? Is that like catching fish? Do I use hot dogs, or worms?"

"You use a flashy lure, honey," Sebastian adds. "The more bling, the better."

Anna snorts. "You guys have been in Vegas too long. Not everything is about money."

"It is in Vegas." Sebastian holds his champagne up as if toasting her and drinks.

"Look, Anna. I know you're upset, but you've got to let your sister grow up," her dad says tiredly. "Emily's five years older than you. It's part of life, getting married and moving on."

"I'm not angry because she got married," Anna fumes. "I'm

angry because you bought her a condo across the country and I'll barely see her! We had plans, and you didn't even ask her about them!"

Her dad looks sympathetic, which makes her heart sink.

"I did talk to her about it. She picked out the building."

It's as if the floor has dropped out from beneath Anna's feet.

Emily tells her everything, always. But Emily didn't tell her this.

"You're lying."

Her dad shakes his head. "I don't invest that kind of money unless it's a sure thing."

"But—"

"Don't know everything, do you, kid?" Uncle Tony cackles like a hyena. "That must be a first for you. Little Miss Type A just got a F."

In the stunned, painful, embarrassing silence that follows, every phone in the limo grinds out a klaxon.

"It's a tornado watch now," Sebastian says quietly, face lit red by his phone's screen. "A funnel's been spotted. It's headed directly toward us."

They all look outside, squinting through the black glass. The curious skyline of the Strip is barely visible, a jagged black silhouette under roiling clouds so thick they look solid. The Alonsos' house is on the other side of it, thirty minutes from here on a good day.

Anna's dad pushes the intercom. "Steve, just get us to the Strip. We'll crash in one of our hotels."

"Which one, boss?" Steve's voice crackles back.

"The first one we can get to. I'll tell you when to turn."

It's like a race has started, and the attitude in the limo changes completely. The men put the champagne away and scroll through their phones and stare nervously out the windows. It would be funny if it wasn't so telling, that the only thing rich men like them fear is uncertainty, a threat they can't pay to disappear. Anna continues feeling terrible, but in a different way. She's worried about her sister heading to her own hotel before taking off for the honeymoon tomorrow morning. She's worried about her fragile mother at home alone, probably suffering another one of her debilitating migraines with no one to care for her. And she's more worried than she'd like to admit about weathering a storm in a tall building surrounded by glass. She knows she's lucky, though—plenty of people have nowhere to go when tornadoes come, but wherever the limo ends up, they'll be in the safest possible position with plenty of supplies and emergency generators. She sends texts to her mother and sister and stares at her phone, willing them to respond.

They don't.

The car skids across the road in a major gust, and even with the partition up, they can hear Steve talking to the car like it's a nervous horse. There aren't many other cars around—everyone else has already taken cover.

"Try the Vesper. Turn right at the next light," her dad says through the intercom, and Steve takes the next turn through a blinking yellow light that's jerking on its wire like a fish bobber.

Lightning envelopes the world in white, thunder rattles the entire car, and all the streetlights around them go out. A trash can rolls in front of the car, and Steve stomps the brakes and swerves, sending an unbuckled Tony smashing into the door.

"Daniel, tell the driver to stay in his lane," Uncle Tony says to Anna's father, but he's interrupted by the lowering partition.

"I don't know if we can make it to the Vesper!" Steve shouts. "It's getting pretty rough out here."

"You know where we should go," Sebastian begins softly. "The closest of our hotels is—"

"No!" Uncle Tony barks. "I'm not going there."

In the charged, rain-buffeted silence, Sebastian says simply, "The Houdini."

As if in agreement, a bolt of lightning strikes so close that the car jumps.

"If our other choice is dying in this limo, I'm fine with it," Anna's dad says with something like defeat. He sits up straighter, his chest puffed out and his jaw set—his Take Charge mood. "Steve, we're going to the Houdini."

Uncle Tony deflates a little and waves his hand, giving way. "Fine, then. But it's a dump."

"The marketing team suggests we think of it as a bargain option for price-conscious consumers looking for an old-world experience with a kitschy twist." Sebastian rolls his eyes. "Whatever that means."

Even terrified out of her mind, Anna is curious. Her father and his friends own multiple hotels, most of them smaller boutique places, a couple of them huge and sprawling. But the words "bargain" and "old-world" and "kitschy" are pretty much the opposite of her dad's tastes. He likes high roller, contemporary, and sleek things, places that are all shiny surfaces and mirrors. He hates carpet, calls it a disease factory. So where is this mysterious hotel that Tony hates? And why are any of them involved in a business venture they consider a dump?

Steve isn't even trying to stay between the lines anymore as he follows her dad's directions. There are barely any cars out, and he's jerking the wheel and dodging rolling trash cans and— holy crap—tumbling benches. There are no pedestrians, no taxis. Under every hotel entrance they pass, cars are jammed in, nearly touching, as people bolt for the front doors, soaked and dragging their suitcases through ankle-deep puddles. The thunder and lightning overlap, the world a furious cacophony of light and sound. Anna is afraid to touch anything metal in case they take a direct lightning hit. Steve turns a corner, and they're off the main Strip and among the lesser hotels, the kinds of places her dad usually scoffs at. The one they're driving toward is the opposite of her dad's style. It's a squat, old-fashioned brick building, not even ten stories, the neon sign gone dark.

"Almost there," her dad says.

Tony leans forward. "I take it back. I can't do it. Maybe we can try the—"

Lightning strikes in a shower of fireworks, and a telephone pole falls in what feels like slow motion but isn't. It lands on the roof of the car, and everyone screams and ducks. The roof buckles with a meaty crunch, and rain pours in as the sunroof shatters. Anna shoves on her door, but it's warped from the accident and won't budge.

Steve jumps out of the front seat and tugs on the back door, his suit immediately soaked. "It won't open!" he shouts.

Uncle Tony slams a beefy shoulder into one door and then the other. They're both dented and won't open more than a few inches. "We're stuck, boys," he says to Anna's dad and Sebastian.

"Anna can squeeze out through the partition." Her dad grabs her by her upper arms, looks into her face. She's numb, shaking, already soaked by the rain pouring in the broken sunroof, can't feel her feet in the spindly heels.

"Look, honey. Climb through there. Go to the front desk. Ask for the manager. Tell 'em you're my kid." Anna just blinks dumbly at her dad, water sheeting down her face and drenching her flimsy dress. She's never seen him look scared before. "Go! You can do it. You can do anything. I need to know you're safe. Take care of yourself, no matter what. Don't wait for me. Promise?"

"Dad, I can't—"

"Promise me, Anna. I need to hear it."

"I—I promise."

He kisses her gently on the forehead and pushes her toward the front seats.

Thunder booms a warning, and Anna hitches her purse up over her shoulder and clambers through the narrow divider. Steve is still outside, and he reaches in to help her while she slithers into the driver's seat. The door is open, and Steve helps her out.

"Run, honey. Hurry," he says. It's the first time in five years of service that he's sounded nervous.

And she runs. There's an old-timey awning, striped burgundy and cream, flapping violently over the revolving doors, and she scrambles across the asphalt, lunging through rivers of pouring water, losing a shoe in the process. She doesn't look back to see if her dad and his friends are behind her. When she slips again, she kicks off her remaining shoe and books it barefoot for the front door, heaving the heavy glass with all her power until it revolves with painful slowness.

Finally she's inside, but the Houdini—

It's not what she expected at all.

5.

Anna lands on a deep, plush carpet in a lobby that's the opposite of every hotel her dad has ever brought her along to see—smaller, elegant, with wallpaper and gold leaf and rich, dark wood everywhere. It looks better than it did on the outside and smells like leather and furniture polish with a hint of lemon, warm and welcoming, like it's been waiting politely just for her. On her way to the front desk, she catches sight of herself in a mirror. She looks like a bedraggled Muppet, her long dark hair fallen loose and stringy from its updo and her tasteful dress drooping and dripping green dye. At least her mascara and lipstick, like Emily's, are still firmly in place, and at least she's still got her big purse of supplies, for all that it's completely waterlogged.

The single front desk is tall and elegant, the wood lovingly cared for and luminous. Swag curtains the color of fir needles hide what must be the employee area beyond it. Just above and behind the desk is an enticing wall of wooden cubbies for mail. Each has a golden key hanging from a nail on the wall in back, their tags unreadable. With a cursory glance, Anna counts all but three keys—too many vacancies for a working hotel, so this must be part of the kitsch. Sitting on top of the cubbies is an ornate old clock under a bell jar, the brass casing immaculately shined. Its hands read exactly 12:01, and Anna can't believe it's that late—except that her feet hurt and she's exhausted, so maybe she can.

The lobby is completely empty, and her pulse skyrockets. Where is everyone? Why is no one manning the front desk if the door is unlocked? She's spent the past eight years in and out of dozens of hotels, and there's always someone around—valets, bellboys, janitors, front desk managers. But here? Not a soul.

This is a big, big deal.

Something is deeply wrong.

She waits for a moment, always hoping to be polite. When no one appears, she gingerly taps the little brass bell, then glances back at the revolving door, waiting for her dad and his crew to barrel in. She can't see anything outside, just swirling, pounding, dizzying darkness beyond the glass.

They should be here by now. Unless something's happened—

Anna abandons the bell and runs back to the revolving door. The darkness outside is all-consuming. Rain pounds against the glass door, and all the millions of lights that make the Strip the Strip are out. She pushes on the door, pulls on it, yanks on it desperately, but it won't budge. She beats her fist against the glass before sliding to her knees on the thick carpet feeling boneless and empty. She wants to sink into the floor and cry until there are no tears left. Doors are supposed to open. Hotel doors should never be locked. Why is everything suddenly wrong?

For a single moment, she allows herself to fall apart, to consider every horrible thing that has happened—and that might still happen.

What if her dad is still trapped in the car? Or worse—what if he made it out of the car . . . but couldn't make it to the hotel? What if he's hurt? What if lightning strikes again? What if—

No. She can't think that way. One foot in front of the other, making the best possible decisions—that's the logical way forward. He made her promise she would take care of herself. She agreed. And her dad is a stickler for contracts.

Anna carefully crosses the slick checkered floor and taps the bell again, harder than she'd like. Her father has owned hotels since before she was born, but he always treats the staff well and has taught his daughters to do the same. After what she experienced at the birthday party—and then later with those same girls at private school—she's determined to never make anyone feel lesser. She's somewhat embarrassed of her dad's money—and how her mom spends it—but for now, she'll take any help the Alonso name will offer that involves a towel and a fluffy hotel robe.

As she waits, barefoot, soaked, cold, and shivering, Anna focuses on the moment. The worst is over, it has to be. She's out of the elements. Hotels feel safe and comfortable, and there's probably a basement where she can find refuge. She forces herself to take a full breath, her dress clinging as tightly as frog skin, and exhales in relief, willing her heart to stop its erratic thumping. This storm—she's lived in Vegas her whole life and never seen anything like it. The moment her hands are dry, she needs to text Emily and their mom again, make sure everyone she cares about is as safe as they can be. She keeps glancing at the door.

Her dad should definitely be inside by now.

Anna returns to the glass door, puts her face against it and curls her hands around her eyes to see better. It doesn't help; nothing can. The storm rages on, the night is too dark to see anything, and no matter what she does, the door is now, somehow, impossibly, firmly locked.

If no one appears soon she's going to go look for a back door. She has to find her dad.

"Hello?" she shouts, wincing at the echo of her voice in the silent lobby.

There is no answer. Time to go behind the desk, even if it feels wrong.

It's a bulky wooden thing, and there is no computer—odd, but perhaps they use laptops and have them locked up somewhere safe while no one is around. The staff must be sheltering from the storm with their guests. With another look around the lobby, Anna steps fully behind the desk and moves the green curtain, hoping to find someone hiding in the back room, but her hands land on a wall papered with images of old-fashioned magicians pulling rabbits from hats and sawing women in half and dramatically holding up hoops for small poodles to leap through. All of her father's other hotels are big, slick behemoths with calming, hip, subtle themes—water, wind, Zen, lavender—but this one seems to have a magic theme, which is not at all her dad's sort of thing.

Anna is fascinated by the thought that her father could possibly be involved in a strange little place like this. If Uncle Tony hates it and Sebastian looks down on it, why haven't they sold it?

Finding no answers, she inspects the beautifully carved desk, looking for a phone, but it's utterly devoid of tech. Devoid of anything, really. No pens or stapler, no calendar or jar of lollipops for the rare but unhappy children dragged to casinos. The floor is black-and-white checkered tile with red carpets down the middle, and there are cozy vignettes here and there, formed by artfully grouped chairs in crimson, indigo, goldenrod, and emerald. Something about the scattered colors strikes her as familiar, but her brain is too rattled to remember why. The air is frigid, and she is drenched and shivering in her knee-length dress, her teeth chattering and her arms crossed over her chest. The thin material, already dripping dye, is beginning to fall apart.

From this angle, Anna sees a shop across the lobby that she didn't notice on her way in—the Magician's Trunk, according to the elaborate black and gold letters painted on the glass. She sags in relief to see that the door is open.

There's no Back in Fifteen Minutes sign, but there's also no one running the register.

"Hello?" she calls again, stepping into the silent, empty shop.

She checks every inch of the ceiling for the cameras every such business has to deter shoplifters but can't spot a single one. Still, they must be hidden somewhere, and she doesn't want to get anyone in trouble, including herself.

The small shop has a single rack of clothes, and its walls are covered with old-timey toys, puppets, and boxed collections of magic tricks. Even though she tells herself she's free to take anything, it still feels wrong, so she walks around the shop first, looking for any sign of what's happening. In the corner by the register, she sees a white rabbit in a cage and checks that it has plenty of water and food and is in good condition.

"Wish I had a carrot to offer you," she says, sticking her fingers through the cage. The rabbit hops over and nibbles her fingers gently, and she strokes its soft fur. "Tonight is such a mess," she tells the rabbit. "But since you're the only living creature I've seen, I guess I'd better tell you. I'm Anna Alonso. My dad owns this hotel. I'm going to get some dry clothes and leave the tags on the register. I hope that's okay."

It all feels completely ridiculous, but the rabbit wiggles its nose, and that seems like a reasonable response, so she walks over to the rack of clothes and tries to figure out how the organization system works. Usually these little hotel shops exist to sell overpriced bland clothes to people who forgot to pack something important. But the circular rack isn't in order by size or even divided up by the clothing's type, purpose, or color. And it's all . . . hideous. Maybe that's uncharitable, but the styles definitely lean toward the elderly and out of fashion, all paisley muumuus and polyester nightgowns and T-shirts that are too weird to be normcore. Without many choices, Anna grabs a capacious muumuu decorated with playing cards before realizing there's no fitting room.

The only thing that looks even vaguely promising is a door she didn't notice before, back behind the counter. A slightly ratty red velvet curtain stretches across it, with a paper sign pinned to it that reads, THIS WAY TO THE EGRESS.

"Ha ha. Very magical," Anna grumbles to herself, knowing full well "egress" means exit.

Still, an exit is better than being stuck here.

She does not want to go into an employees-only area and use her dad's name to get what she needs, but so far, being polite hasn't worked. All she wants is to be safe and alone in a clean white hotel room, to wrap herself in a cozy hotel robe, take a soak in a big tub, and go to sleep on a heavenly bed. But before that, she needs to make sure Emily and Mom are okay and then have a big cry at how her father ruined the wedding—and her future. She needs him to get inside with his friends so she can stop worrying about him and go back to being furious with him. And then she needs to start making plans for Emily's move to New York.

"Hello?" she calls as she moves the curtain aside, revealing a lightless room without any of the comforts she so desperately needs. "I just need a place to change—well, actually, I need a lot of things—"

She steps through the curtain . . .

And falls straight through the floor.

6.

In the penthouse suite of the Houdini hotel, a lone figure walks to a window, a beautiful woman nearing fifty. She's stately and sharp-featured, draped in the shimmering emerald, fur-trimmed robe of a silent film star, her bleached-blond hair pulled back into an elegant chignon. She moves the heavy damask curtains aside and waves a hand, and the rain beyond the glass breaks long enough to show her a scene that makes her ruby-red lips curl up in satisfaction.

Outside, far below, lit only by near-constant lightning strikes, a bald man in a black suit fruitlessly tugs at the doors of a limousine. Shouting what must be a colorful curse indeed, he leaps into the front seat right as an impressive spear of lightning strikes exactly where he was just standing. The limo might as well be a lightning rod, and it's delicious, thinking about how those trapped inside it must feel right now.

Thunder rumbles threateningly, and a man pops out of the

limo's sunroof like a cartoon prairie dog and hops to the flooding concrete. Once he's safely out of the car, two more men clamber out of the sunroof, with differing levels of success. The smaller man has no problem and slides nimbly down the windshield, but the biggest man has to pry himself out like a difficult cork in an indifferent wine bottle. The three men, urged on by another aggressively close lightning strike, run for the front door of the hotel. The bald man, like the captain of a sinking ship, stays behind.

Down below, the revolving door opens, and the men tumble into the lobby.

"Excellent," the woman murmurs.

The door opens, and a second figure appears in the suite and walks over to join the woman at her window. This young man is somewhere in his teens, old enough to have stubble but young enough to know that he's not yet capable of growing a decent beard without lots of useless itching. His longish black hair curls over his ears, and he's dressed in corduroy pants, a crisp white button-down with carefully rolled sleeves, and a green tweed waistcoat. While the woman is smiling like the Cheshire cat her young companion is cocking his head like a worried dog.

"What are you looking at?" the boy asks.

The woman snatches the curtains closed before he reaches her side. "Nothing. You know there's nothing to see."

"Then why are you at the window?"

She sighs. "Old habits, I suppose."

"I wish we could go out," the boy says, more wistful than whining. "I wish there was somewhere to go out to."

"Honestly, we've been over this a thousand times at least. We mustn't complain about things we can't change. Que será, será."

He snorts and looks away, hands in his pockets. "Not here. Not always."

The woman peeks out the window once more and waves a hand, and the tornado's funnel veers away. Darkness descends, and the limo is lost to view.

"Sit down, Maximillian. Let me tell you a fairy tale." The woman points at a swooping couch of sumptuous red velvet.

"Didn't you once say I'm too old for fairy tales?"

She snaps her fingers, and the boy walks to the couch as if sleepwalking and plunks down, waiting. A toy poodle, dyed flamingo pink, briefly glares at him from a nearby tuffet.

"Once upon a time, there was a princess who dreamed of ruling her own kingdom. But on coronation day—"

"You haven't told me a story in a decade. Why now? Why were you at the window? This is all very strange."

"Life is strange, and maybe I don't tell you stories anymore because you're always interrupting."

"I'm fairly certain I've read every fairy tale in the library," the boy says curtly. "But I haven't heard this one. Girls never inherit anything in fairy tales. And honestly, without the relevant details and context, a story can never make much sense."

"Stories make as much sense as you bring to them," the woman chides. "You read too many pulp novels."

"What else is there?"

"The whole world, if you're willing to do the work."

He gestures with one hand at the room, at the window. "It's not much of a world."

With a weary sigh that suggests this argument is not new, the woman snaps her fingers in front of the boy's face, and his eyelids fall like a vaudeville curtain. His head slips sideways, and then he rolls over and curls up on the couch with his head pillowed on the arm. He's already sleeping heavily, cheeks pink and lips parted. He looks so young, like this.

"Not much of a world? Ha. Neither is the other one," the woman croons, brushing his hair back and smiling at him, now that he can't see her tenderness.

After straightening up with a determined sigh, she marches across the room to a brass button on the wall. It makes a warbling buzz when she pushes it and speaks into the grill. "Arielle?"

"Yes, Miss Phoebe?"

The answering voice is young, female, bubbly, as eager to please as a bright-eyed starlet ready for her audition.

"How is the plan coming along?"

The woman—Phoebe—presses the button each time she speaks into the grill and releases it to listen for Arielle's answer.

"Just great, boss. The storm is a doozy, and the three fellas you wanted are inside. Didn't harm a hair on a single head. So it's all eggs in coffee, boss. Arielle's done it again."

"And you have my appreciation. But our work isn't over—"

"Hey, boss?"

Phoebe's cat-in-cream smile curdles into a frown. "Yes?"

"Not to be a pill, but since things are going so swell—"

"Get to the point, Arielle."

Arielle clears her throat, her voice now soft and deferential through the tinny system. "Remember how you promised to let me skiddoo?"

"We have a contract."

A sorrowful sigh. "But I've done everything you ever asked, and you promised. Shouldn't promises count as much as contracts?"

Phoebe runs a fingertip over a place where the flocked wallpaper has worn thin, and at her touch, it seems to bloom back to its original beauty, the change rippling along the wall until it looks brand-new. "No. That's why contracts require a signature. Do you require a reminder of how I found you? The state you were in, thanks to that awful Celeste? She was going to give you to that nasty son of hers, but I intervened. And I have been benevolent. When I could be . . ." A meaningful pause. "A lot worse."

"I know, boss." For a moment, there is silence, and then Phoebe huffs dramatically and clears her throat, waiting for Arielle to continue. "Sorry, boss. Glad to serve. What's on the docket?"

Phoebe smiles, a treacherous thing. "Keep those men occupied. Don't let them near Max."

"Aye-aye, captain."

The grill goes silent, and Phoebe nods at it, pleased, before returning to the couch where the boy sleeps.

"Time to wake up," she says in a sweet, innocent voice.

He blinks and sits up. "Did I fall asleep? That's odd."

"You're a growing boy. You need your rest. Now, come along. We need to go see Colin."

The young man grimaces. "Do we have to? I find him very creepy."

"If you're to run this place after me, you must learn to deal with your employees. Come along, Maximilian." She strides toward the door, and the boy sits up, his head in his hands.

"This place is insane," he murmurs to himself.

"It's what you make it," Phoebe snaps. "Like any place. Come on."

He shakes his head and follows, slouching, hands in his pockets. It's a long journey, involving multiple halls and an elevator, which they ride down to the basement after Phoebe has inserted a key she keeps on a silver chain around her neck. The elevator doors open on a nightmare of a hallway, concrete with the dead scent of cold metal interrupted by the lonely, far-off drip of pipes. Phoebe holds up her skirts with one hand as she disappears into the long, secretive shadows that yawn between the twitchy orange gaslights.

Finally, they hear a low, sonorous voice singing along with the scratchy tones of a record so well-worn it's barely audible.

"Colin!" Phoebe barks.

Max flinches and subtly moves behind her.

"Yes, Phoebe?"

The man who looks up from his mopping could be anywhere from thirty to sixty, his skin the waxy white-pink of a cave fish and the top of his balding head shining moistly. His eyebrows and eyelashes are see-through, and he's shaped like a rotting pear, his shoulders sunken in his stained janitor's uniform. He holds an ancient mop, swishing it around on the dirty floor.

"I think you mean *Yes, miss.*"

Colin bares his teeth; they are not good teeth. "I said what I meant. Would you prefer I say 'Yes, thief'?"

Phoebe draws herself up coldly and glares down at him.

"You can't steal what you can't possess, Colin."

"This place belonged to my mother, and when she died, it should've passed on to me—" he begins, the words clipped and firm as if he's practiced them in his head a thousand times every day of his life. His eyes have the focused rage of an oft-kicked dog biding its time.

"Show me a deed, then," Phoebe hisses. "Any legal document. Call a lawyer."

This last bit is cruel and mocking, and Max turns away, feigning interest in a spot on the floor as Phoebe and Colin sneer at each other, their rage adding a new layer of frost to the already icy hallway.

Colin, of course, breaks first, his steel withering to rusted desperation. "You could at least show a little kindness. You make me sleep down here when there are plenty of rooms—"

Phoebe tsks. "I gave you a room in the hotel proper, once. A nice one. And you destroyed it."

"Because of you! You know what I was looking for—"

"I don't have time for your delusions, Colin. When you were done with your pretty room, the walls were reduced to timbers. The sofa was unstuffed. The carpet was torn up. You rooted through the place like a pig. The cost of such damages—"

"What cost? What money? This place—"

"This place is entirely under my jurisdiction, no matter what you may believe. And since I'm your boss, you're to keep out of view and do your job." She puts a hand on one hip, inspects the floor. "God, you can't even mop. Go polish the floors somewhere else. Be useful. And, Colin . . ."

He looks at her, eyes blazing hatred, and she leans in close and whispers, "There are three men in the hotel. You're to stay away from them."

Colin slops his mop into the dirty bucket and slams it on the ground, splashing gray, filthy water over Phoebe's emerald-green slippers. "You don't control me."

Phoebe dances back, gasping her outrage, and glares at him. "Order whatever you wish for dinner tonight. It won't sit well, whatever it is."

Colin finally has the grace to look sorry.

"Please, miss. No. The last time I had chowder, it had already turned. . . . The old plumbing in the basement can't handle . . ."

Phoebe smiles again. "And to think, you'd have to mop that up, too. Do a good job with your polishing, follow my orders, and we'll see what the kitchen thinks you deserve."

Colin nods, bobbing his head in a sort of bow. "Yes, miss. Sorry, miss. Thank you, miss." He picks up the bucket and mop and shuffles off looking six inches shorter.

With an aggrieved sigh, Phoebe flicks her fingers at her robe as if banishing filth. "I need to change," she murmurs.

"I don't like Colin, but I don't understand why you torture him. He's right about the rooms. And it's not like we're going to run out of food." Max keeps his voice calm and careful as he follows Phoebe back to the elevator, walking so fast to escape the dank hallway that he accidentally treads on her robe and gets a glare of his own. "Maybe if you were nicer, he wouldn't be so horrid."

"He tried to kill me once. And clumsily. Let that be a lesson."

"Why'd he do it?"

Phoebe taps one foot as the elevator takes its sweet time. "Because he didn't like to see me in charge. The fool thought he could take over the Houdini. He was wrong."

Max snorts and rocks back on his heels. "Colin? Tried to kill you? I can't imagine that. Are you sure it wasn't some kind of misunderstanding? Or a mistake?"

"Murder is considerably more than a mistake, Max. If you're going to commit one, you'd best be ready to finish it."

Phoebe steps into the waiting elevator and considers Max coolly. "Furthermore, there are mistakes, and then there are acts of war. I may be a lady, and I may be the boss, but I am also a simmering cauldron of rage, hell-bent on revenge."

"I'll put that on your birthday card," he murmurs, stepping in beside her.

Her hand lands on the back of his neck, a gesture both tender and controlling.

"Revenge is a dish best served cold with a cherry on top. Never forget that."

Raised by a woman like her, how could he?

7.

Anna is falling.

The floor of the dressing room disappeared, and so did she.

She does not plummet like a bird, nor does she gently float down like Alice in Wonderland, her skirt forming a perfect, polite parachute. She does not plunge or swoon or flutter. She shrieks and flails and awkwardly lands on her butt in what feels like an ocean of someone else's dirty clothes.

Wherever she is, it's pitch-black and smells like her dead grandmother's attic. She struggles to stand, feet tangled in fabric, hands out and finding nothing. Looking up, she shouts, "Hello?"

But there is no square of light from the room above, no laughing face looking down at her, the latest casualty of a very bad joke. Just more smooth darkness. It's puzzling—the ground was beneath her, and then it wasn't.

But—oh.

The Houdini is obviously a themed hotel, and that theme is

magic. Everything she saw in the gift shop was covered in top hats and rabbits and playing card suits. The curtain Anna passed through was even based on an old trick by P. T. Barnum that she remembers reading about somewhere. The floor was rigged to dump her. This must be some part of the game, like the volcano at the Mirage or the Eiffel Tower at the Paris. She'll have to tell her dad that it needs some work—there should be one of those thick pads they use for stunt falls, not a pile of what feel like ancient, moth-eaten theater curtains. If she'd fallen wrong, she could have broken something, including her skull. It's a liability nightmare.

After freeing her bare feet from the tangle of cloth, Anna shuffles forward, hands out in front of her, feeling for anything of substance. All her senses are on high alert, and her ears tell her the room is small, and that she's alone. There is no whoosh of a breeze, no hum of air conditioners, no murmur of far-off voices, no echo, no cadence of unfamiliar breathing. She bumps her shins against what feels like a wooden box, finds it with her fingers, and feels her way around it with a muttered, "Ouch."

When she stubs her toes on the next box, she grumbles, "A little light wouldn't hurt."

As if in answer, a light flares to life, warm and flickering. It's a glass lamp, attached to the wall, and the flame looks like a real one—surely another code violation, kitsch or no. When her eyes adjust, her assumption is confirmed; she's in some sort of storage room, every surface painted black. It looks like the one where her school drama club keeps all their old props. That room drives her insane, but they'll never let her unleash her organizing skills on it. She argued up and down when she was prop manager for *Our*

Town, but Mrs. Carroway just flapped a wrinkled hand and said she knew where everything was. Anna was the one who had to search and poke and flounder in the dark.

She's at the door now. She turns the knob—cold and speckled brass—and pushes it open.

8.

Max sits on the floor, his back against the eggshell-blue wall. He stares up at the orange tree, unchanged all these years. Same size, same pot. He's never yet figured out a way to make it bloom when he's not directly touching it, never been able to enjoy the full view. As such, it's currently just spindly wood in a pretty pot, but he can feel its potential hanging in the air, smell the ghosts of the fruit and flowers waiting within.

He once used a pushpin to attach a pencil drawing of a pretty girl to the wall directly across from where he currently sits. There are now one hundred eleven such portraits.

They spiral out from the original like a huge white flower, forever in bloom.

He has searched every inch of the hotel, found dozens of secret passages, sat by every fountain, wistful, coin in hand, wish waiting to be made. He has never found her.

Still, he comes to this room whenever he feels like he's starting to lose it, when the loneliness drives him to tears or screams. The room grounds him, gives him hope. He knows there's something more somewhere; he's seen *I Love Lucy* and *The Sound of Music*, he's read Charles Dickens and Shakespeare and Jane Austen. Somewhere else, there is a world filled with people and friends and family and laughter and danger.

Maybe that's where this girl is.

Somewhere else.

Somewhere else he just hasn't found yet.

9.

Anna opens the first of many doors.

"Hello?" she calls, her echoing voice the only reply.

It feels like she's trespassing, like maybe she's accidentally ended up backstage at one of the theaters every big Vegas hotel has for its shows. She's terrified she'll end up intruding on a chorus or in a green room with some angsty comedian with no sense of humor, provided that the rest of the hotel is, miraculously, up and running. But no—the door leads to a long hallway, dark and dank, that feels like it's deep underground. At least she's safe from the tornado. But she doesn't know about her dad and his friends. Sure, she's still mad at him—furious, even—but she prefers being mad at people who are safe and dry and can properly experience her rage. Her hand flies to her purse, and she yanks out her phone.

Which is dead.

Which makes no sense, because it's waterproof. Her whole purse is sopping, everything in it pretty much ruined. After a moment's consideration, Anna goes back into the room she just left and quickly changes out of the disintegrating bridesmaid dress and into the muumuu that fell down with her. She shoves her phone and wallet into the muumuu's baggy pocket, abandons the rest of the sodden bag, and closes the door behind her when she leaves. If she's in the bowels of the hotel, she should soon see a glowing green Exit sign that will lead her outside, and then she can run around to the limo and make sure her dad is safe—while looking like an absolute fool. At least the muumuu is comfortable and dry.

Yes, maybe going back outside is going against her promise, but when there are tornadoes involved, all bets are off. Anna is unaccustomed to breaking promises or forgoing rules, but she doesn't know what else to do. She usually feels very adult, but right now she is painfully aware that she is a child, and she still needs her father.

The hallway is like something out of a horror movie, endlessly long with distressingly blind corners. The walls are dark-gray cement, marked with water and rust stains. The glass lamps are placed at long intervals that leave far too much of the hallway in shadow. The floor is a darker, wetter gray, crumbly and cold against Anna's bare feet as she splashes through puddles she'd rather not see too well. Pipes of all sizes run along the ceiling, dripping erratically. There are several doors, but none marked Exit. They are all locked. Anna knows this because she tries every doorknob.

The lights are burning low. She can barely see what's ten feet ahead of her. It feels like she's walked for miles and taken all the wrong turns, and she begins to wish she had some sort of weapon, but there's not even a fire extinguisher hanging on the wall. That's another code violation to add to her mental tally; her dad is going to be furious.

"Hello?" she calls. "Anybody?"

"Hello?" a voice replies—a male voice she doesn't recognize. Footsteps splash toward her, first tentatively and then more swiftly. "Who's there? Stop!"

Something deep in Anna's heart, some animal sense, tells her to run, and she does. Her heart is beating frantically, and she realizes she's being chased. The hallway is endless, and she runs on and on and on until her feet hurt, skidding around the first corner that appears, then another and another. She begins to think she must have gone far beyond the limits of the Houdini. She's heard there are tunnels under the Vegas Strip, and that they're dangerous. She hopes that's not where she's inexplicably landed.

"Help," she murmurs to herself, low and experimental, since she's not the sort of person who usually needs any help, and because she doesn't want help from the man who's chasing her. At least his footsteps have stopped. Maybe she lost him.

There's a flash of something bright up ahead, and Anna stops and squints, hunting for movement.

There.

On the ground.

Not a person.

Something white.

A . . . rabbit?

Surely not.

She takes a few steps forward and can clearly see the shape of it now, a soft white rabbit about the size of a football, surprisingly clean for anything on the floor of this disgusting hallway. The rabbit reminds Anna of the one she saw upstairs, in the gift shop, but there's no way it could be the same one. Some hotels have a rat problem. Could a magic-themed hotel possibly have a rabbit problem?

"Hey, buddy," she calls.

In response, the rabbit turns and hops away down the hall.

She follows, reasoning that if this creature is alive and healthy down here, it must know what's safe and what's not. The rabbit isn't running, more gently lolloping down the hall and around corners, occasionally looking back as if to make sure Anna is still following and hasn't missed a turn. It doesn't seem scared of her, but then again, she's not trying to touch it. Rabbits, she knows, are easily frightened.

The rabbit disappears around the next corner, and Anna exhales with relief when she rounds the bend to find something familiar: an elevator. It's a small elevator, and there is only one button—the Up button—but up is exactly where she wants to go. When she pushes it, it sticks a little, but then the elevator makes a cheerful if old-fashioned *ding!*, and the door rattles open.

Only then does she think to wonder where the rabbit has gone, but when she looks around, it's disappeared. She softly calls, "Thanks!" to the empty hallway before stepping into the waiting elevator.

"You! Stop!"

Anna sees a shape lumbering toward her down the dark hall—a man in a janitor's uniform? She frantically pushes the Door Close button, even though she's heard they never work.

This one, thankfully, does. The elevator starts rumbling upward, and Anna sighs in relief. Something was off about that guy.

The inside of the elevator is a marvel compared to the outside, a tarnished brass geode knocked open to reveal gleaming gold, shining wood, and the gentlemanly flicker of a gas lamp, although how a gas line could run through a moving elevator Anna can't even begin to comprehend. It must be fake, something Sebastian chose to enhance the old-world charm. Tinkly music plays softly, crackling and far away, from an overhead speaker. It sounds like something from the '30s or '40s, a jaunty song about a pocketful of dreams.

The panel on the wall has brass buttons in a neat row over the *B* for basement and *L* for lobby, with numbers 1 through 6 and then an *R,* probably for roof. Number 6 is lit up with a golden glow, but Anna knows where she wants to go, which is right back to the lobby to have a little talk with her father about the trapdoor in the shop and how his code-ignoring basement is going to get the whole building shut down, if not condemned, and also how the janitor scared her.

But when she presses the *L* button to go to the lobby, it doesn't light up. Neither does 1 or 2. None of the other numbers do. Just that stubborn, glowing 6.

Ah. There's a keyhole, but no key. This elevator must be ancient, from a time when elevator operators were paid to spend their days pressing buttons to ferry folks up and down.

Anna has a brief moment of wild discomfort, like she always feels right before a roller coaster takes off. She is not in control, and she doesn't know who is, and she doesn't trust them, but she knows she's trapped. Also, the elevator has no building code certificate. And no emergency call button.

She can feel the elevator rising slowly, feel the shining black marble shake under the soles of her bare feet, and she tells herself that whatever is on the sixth floor is certainly better than what's in the basement. At the very least, she should be able to find a pair of septuagenarian card sharks to direct her back to the lobby, and if not, there will surely be stairs. It's the slowest elevator she's ever been on, but Anna is a logical person, so she takes a few deep, relaxing breaths to slow her heart rate and calm her mind. The song croons on about luxury and dreams, which fit well with the elevator but not with the basement. Her eyes stray to the walls, which are not mirrors like those in the elevators she's used to, but glowing diamonds of cut wood.

To think—her dad called this place a dump. This elevator is obviously an old-world masterpiece, the sort of thing they just don't make anymore. After a while, all the identical white marble and bluish glass he loves start to blur together, whereas nowhere and nothing else on earth could be mistaken for this elevator. There's a level of realness and authenticity to it that's sorely lacking in the Vegas Anna knows. Someone's hands made this with pride.

After an eternity of upward groaning, the elevator shudders to a halt. Anna tucks her ruined hair behind her ears and puts on the smile she's perfected for when she needs to charm adults. The door laboriously slides open, and she's facing another hallway. This one is nothing like the basement, thank goodness. The carpet, patterned in shades of burgundy and amber, is rich and deep, and her toes sink in when she steps onto it. The walls are more polished wood with wainscoting, glowing in the warm orange flicker of the strange lights that are everywhere. Doors march neatly down the hallway, each with a small brass plaque and a number beginning with a six. At first, it seems like there are hundreds of doors, but it must be some kind of illusion, maybe something cleverly done with mirrors. Anna saw this hotel from the outside, and there's no way it can be that big. When she counts, there are only fourteen doors, seven down each side. Ahead, on her left, one of the doors is partially open, and she hears a soft thump and someone mutter, "Ah, hell."

Anna stops. Looks up and down the hall. Looks back at the elevator, which is slowly rattling shut. That voice sounded nothing like the angry man downstairs. She tiptoes to the open door, the carpet swallowing the sound of her footsteps. The door's small brass plaque, polished to a shine, says, simply, Library. The hallway smells of comfortable age, lemon polish, rose perfume, and, faintly, old cigars. But here, right in front of the door, Anna smells one of her very favorite things.

Books.

She peeks in but can't see much through the barely open door. Just the tiniest sliver of a bookshelf—a good bookshelf. A tall bookshelf. A *Beauty and the Beast* bookshelf. She puts a hand on the door and pushes it, calling, for what feels like the hundredth time, "Hello?"

She expected the door to catch on the thick carpet, to be as balky and recalcitrant as the elevator, but this one swings open like it was freshly oiled. Anna's senses are dominated by the bookshelf, which stretches nearly twice as high as the ceiling in the hallway. The shelves are yet more polished wood, and the books nestled along them range from esoteric leather tomes with gold-stamped spines to cozy families of encyclopedias to yellowed paperbacks with audaciously pulpy titles. A tall ladder leans against the shelves, its black wheels clinging to an iron railing so it can zoom back and forth. A record player with a speaker shaped like a golden lily plays a song dominated by slinky, sleepy, bluesy saxophone. The smell of old books and leather is overpowering, as if the word "tome" had been turned into a Yankee Candle and someone lit a thousand of them, and it is glorious.

When she was little, Anna loved libraries. She dreamed of having one like this when she was grown. But around age ten, she put that sort of silly dream behind her and started focusing on reality, on forging her path instead of daydreaming. Her private school library was a sleek, modern place, with not even one wooden card catalog. She'd almost forgotten that such places existed. As she smells the room and relishes the glint of lamplight on gilt, she feels that old love stir like a cat that's been asleep too long.

"Hello?" she says again, and only then does she notice the figure.

It's a boy—a guy her age, or maybe a little older. He's high up on another ladder, ostensibly making his way down to collect the fallen novel that lies open on the carpet below. He looks like he's stepped out of another time, with baggy corduroys, a white button-down rolled perfectly at the elbows, and a tweed vest with two chains hooked on a buttonhole and disappearing into a pocket. His hair curls down to his collar and is exactly the color of a well-pulled espresso under the crema. Her eyes are drawn to his two-toned oxfords as he hops lightly to the floor, smoothly kneeling for the book and gracefully swooping to stand, already opening it and running a finger along the opening paragraph, oblivious to her entrance.

"Hello?"

Anna hates saying it again, hates repeating herself three times, but he hasn't yet looked at her, and she's beginning to feel like a creeper, standing here as he grins at the book.

The boy's eyes flick up to hers and fly open wide, as if he's seen a ghost. His mouth falls open, but no sound comes out. The book tumbles out of his hands to land on the floor with a soft thump.

"Okay," Anna says, feeling unusually self-conscious. "Sorry to interrupt, but could you please tell me how the elevator works so I can leave you and that book alone for some private time?"

The boy's attitude changes so fast it's comical. It's like he's rebooting. His mouth snaps shut, he shakes his head, and his eyes focus on her, fierce and unblinking, blue as a rooftop pool.

"What did you just say?"

Anna shoves her hands in her pockets and feels deeply awkward being stared at this aggressively while wearing something as ridiculous as an ancient casino gift shop muumuu.

"I said something about being sorry to interrupt you but needing help with the elevator? Or maybe the emergency stairs? My dad should be waiting for me in the lobby by now, but this place has a steep learning curve. Part of the fun, I guess." He's still staring, so she does jazz hands and shrugs and mutters, "Magic! All that."

The boy is across the room in a heartbeat, close enough to touch. She can see the stubble on his jaw, the little flecks in his blue eyes.

"Holy mackerel, are you real?" he asks.

Anna steps back; he's really intense for some rando in a hotel. A little too close, a little too earnest. And deeply weird.

"Of course I'm real. You're the one dressed like a newsie."

His eyebrows go up, and he grins and sputters. "A newsie? Like, the kids who sell papers?"

"Yeah. I mean, *sold* papers. In the musical *Newsies.* You just need a little cap and a bad accent."

He looks at her like a baby seeing a Christmas tree for the first time. Eyes wide and dancing, teeth flashing, dimples out. There's an open, childlike wonder to him that feels utterly foreign and new. He holds out a hand like he's about to touch her face, and Anna steps back, wary, muttering, "Um, personal space."

"You're real," the boy says, his voice soft and deep, the words heavy with meaning that she can't quite parse. "Where'd you come from? How'd you get here?"

Anna glances at the open door, wondering if maybe he's drunk or recently hit his head.

"Of course I'm real. We're all real. I came in the revolving door like anyone else." She looks around the room, which is empty. "Although I haven't seen a single other person since then. Just some rabbits and you. And a creepy guy who chased me in the basement. It's freaking me out, honestly." She pauses, having just remembered why she's here. There are no windows in the room, so she can't see how close the storm is, and she hasn't heard thunder since she landed in the lobby. Worry thrums down her spine, the urge to run somewhere, anywhere, to safety. "Wait. Is everyone else sheltering from the tornado? We should get to the basement. I could see the funnel when I ran inside, and that was like twenty minutes ago."

The boy steps forward, brazen yet also shy. If he heard the word "tornado," it doesn't seem to be affecting him.

"You look just like . . ." He smiles crookedly and looks down for a moment. "Well . . . someone I saw once."

"Okay, but did you hear me say *tornado*?"

He shrugs, as if the word means nothing to him. "Don't worry about that. You're inside."

"Yeah, but tornadoes can tear down buildings."

"Not the Houdini."

All the while, the record has been playing in the background, the saxophone shuffling softly as the boy watches her like she's a wild animal that might bolt if he moves too quickly. His hands are in his pockets, and he closes his eyes and slowly opens them again, breaking out in another huge grin.

"Well, hotsy-totsy. You didn't disappear."

This boy . . . is definitely not normal.

"Dude, are you okay? Why would I disappear?" Anna asks him.

"Dude? Me?" He holds out his arms and looks down. "You can't exactly call me a city slicker. And I'm more than okay. I'm rapt." He steps closer, and she catches a whiff of cologne, woody and warm and dry like the inside of a guitar.

Anna steps back again, several steps this time; they're doing a very odd dance. "Listen, we need to get underground. Somewhere safe."

"I'm sorry. I'm doing this all wrong." He sweeps a bow. "I'm Max." He looks up, eyes dancing. "And you are?"

"Anna." She doesn't tell him her last name. He omitted his, and she knows that when she says her father's name in hotels, everyone acts differently around her. The boy's behavior is odd, and yet she doesn't want him to act differently because of who her father is.

"Anna." He says it like he's tasting his favorite flavor of ice cream. "Welcome to the Houdini, Anna. I'm sorry if I'm acting strange, it's just . . ."

He looks into her eyes, puzzled and breathless.

"You shouldn't be here."

10.

On the wall across from the bookshelves, there is a very nice painting of a sad but frosty-looking queen clutching an ermine. Although Anna and Max don't notice it, the queen's eyes blink more often than a painting's eyes should.

Phoebe is furious but unsurprised by the current course of events. She's spent years learning just the right way to give Arielle commands that can't be misinterpreted, but that means Arielle has become very good at finding loopholes. Phoebe told Arielle to let her know when the men entered the hotel, but she wasn't expecting Daniel Alonso's daughter, and thus she hadn't mentioned her. The men must've sent her in first. Now she's here, and it's too late.

There's not much that can be done. Max is already besotted with the girl, but at least Anna seems wary. Fine, then. Let the children do what lonely children always do. Let them distract each other. Now that Phoebe thinks about it, that suits her scheming quite well. As long as they're kept away from the men, they can't really do any harm.

Satisfied that her plan is not in jeopardy, Phoebe withdraws from her post and silently slides the painting's real eyes back into place, giving the queen a far less lively mien. Barefoot, she pads across the sound-swallowing carpet of the dark, narrow hall between the rooms, her way lit by lamps at knee-level turned down low.

Max has had the run of the Houdini since he learned how to open a door, but Phoebe made sure he never found her own secret warren of tunnels. She didn't even know about this particular one herself until Arielle was in hot water and needed to buy some goodwill. Sometimes Phoebe gets the feeling that the hotel doesn't like her. The place has become strange over the years, as if it has a mind of its own.

Contemplating her next move, she navigates back to her private suite in the penthouse on the secret seventh floor and fixes herself a Bee's Knees at her bar. Her mind is going a mile a minute, but she knows what needs to be done.

Abandoning her empty glass on a side table with a Tiffany lamp shaped like a peacock, she pushes the intercom button.

"Yeah, boss?"

There's an annoyed tone to Arielle's usual perky greeting.

"The men in the hotel—I need you to make sure they're kept away from Anna. I want Daniel Alonso to feel the terror that comes with a missing child. Don't let the men explore beyond the second floor."

"For how long, boss?"

Phoebe taps her long nails on the wall. "The foreseeable future. I'll let you know."

"Anything else?"

A curling smile. "Offer them some refreshments. Cigars, perhaps. You know what to do."

There's a miffed little sigh like that of an annoyed kitten. "You got it, boss."

The speaker goes quiet.

Filled with a sudden energy, that odd zing when things are happening but not nearly fast enough to satisfy, Phoebe heads to her closet and changes into another robe, this one silk and bright with fighting peacocks flashing the red under their wings. She cleans her feet with a perfumed cloth, shuddering at the thought of that awful Colin's filthy mop water slopping onto her skin. She touches up her lipstick and walks through a cloud of perfume sprayed from an elegant glass bottle with a gold mesh bulb.

The gin sings in Phoebe's blood, and she turns up her favorite record and dances and paces and tries, and fails, to read books from pedantic to sordid. She opens the curtains to see that the storm has settled down, giving way to a glimmering indigo sky peppered with stars that can only be seen when half the city's electricity has been gutted—and from this particular suite. She checks the clock, counting down the hours.

She wants to walk down the main drag of the Strip, feel the breeze on her skin.

She can't, of course. A long time ago, she chose captivity because she knew it would one day lead to revenge against those who'd wronged her.

Today is that day.

Or, more accurately, tonight is that night.

11.

Three men stand in the hotel lobby, dripping on an emerald-green carpet.

"Where the hell is my daughter?" Daniel Alonso growls, struggling with his bow tie until it dangles limply down either side of his white shirt.

"Forget your daughter. Where's the manager?" Tony steps forward, already shrugging out of his waterlogged suit jacket and throttling it like he wishes it was someone's neck. "No doorman with an umbrella, no space heater by the door. I swear, this old dump needs to go. Somebody's getting fired."

"The Houdini is not our most profitable hotel, but it is an institution," Sebastian reminds him.

"Nobody cares," Tony grumbles dangerously. "As soon as this storm's over, we're finally gonna demolish this place. I know we've been trying for years, but this time, I'll make it happen if I have to swing a crowbar myself." He's a big man, and right now he looks like a half-drowned bear as he lumbers to the front desk. Finding no one, he slams his big hand on the brass bell five times in quick succession. "Hello? Anybody?"

"Perhaps they're sheltering from the storm," Sebastian offers, wiping off his forehead with a handkerchief. As the handkerchief is already soaked, it doesn't do him much good. He wanders to the closed gift shop and tries the locked door. "That would make the most sense. The basement, perhaps?"

"I don't care if there's a tornado. If the front door is open, there should be somebody up here. People could steal anything!" Tony picks up the little brass bell he's been ringing continuously and throws it at the nearest wall. It hits with a disappointing *donk* and falls to the floor with a more disappointing *bong*.

"Okay, so we'll make a note to talk with management about that," Daniel says, ever the level-headed diplomat. "But for now, we need to find Anna and get somewhere safe. The tornado's still coming. She's got to be in the basement already. Anybody see the stairs?"

"I see the elevator." Tony lumbers over and presses the Down button, but the elevator appears to be out of order, so he rears back and punches the button, which also does nothing.

Daniel whips out his phone, but its buttons are likewise useless. "Dead! It was at sixty percent before we left the wedding. Newest model, my ass!" He stares at the phone like he wants to throw it at the same wall as the bell, but then he shoves it back in his pocket. "You know, I told Emily to get married in the winter.

Better rates, and you can count on the weather. But no. It had to be spring. Anna put her up to this, I bet. Emily always did what I said until Anna got so pushy—"

"Let it go." Sebastian claps him on the back with a squelching noise. "We'll find your girl. Everything'll be fine."

"Nothing can be fine as long as we're in this depressing money pit. A buncha bull—" Tony stops abruptly, perking up. "Hey, you guys hear that?"

Over the soft, old-fashioned music pumping in through the speakers in the ceiling, there's a distant tapping noise that grows louder with each tap.

"Cigars! Mints! Candy for your best girl!" a woman's voice calls, high and perky.

"Finally!" Tony barks. He takes off down the hall, following the click of high heels.

"Sugar Babies for your baby! Red Hots for your red-hot dame!" the voice calls from farther on as Daniel and Sebastian follow Tony.

The empty hallway stretches out before them, the endless black-and-white chessboard tiles throwing illusions like an Escher. The men half jog to catch up to the voice, slipping in their leather-soled shoes as they turn the next corner.

"I saw a cigarette girl up ahead, I swear. Fishnets and red heels," Tony says, huffing and puffing. "Honey, stop! We're the hotel owners!"

"Hot Lips! Smarties! Dum-Dums! How's about a nice cheroot? It's La Palina hour somewhere!"

The men hurry down the next hallway, out of breath, leaving a trail of wet footprints behind them.

"She should definitely stop if she wants to keep her job," Sebastian mutters.

"Since when do we still have cigarette girls?" Daniel asks before calling, "Please stop, miss! We need your help."

"There's a big tip in it for you," Tony adds, but they all know that's a lie. If the girl does stop, her tip will be to respond faster the next time Anthony Pappas tells her to do something.

Up ahead, the heels stop clicking, and the men breathe a sigh of relief as they round the next corner and find themselves in a cozy lobby filled with furniture. On a low coffee table sits a cigarette girl's tray, red lacquer with black straps. Within it nestle all sorts of old-fashioned candies and wrapped cigars.

"Where'd she go?" Sebastian asks, peering down the nearest hallway. "I don't see any doors."

Tony selects a cigar. "Probably got scared when she heard us shouting," he says. "At least she left her loot behind. Of course, we'll have to dock her for that when we find the manager. Nothing's complimentary here." He grabs another cigar and hands it to Sebastian, who eyes it appreciatively, while Daniel waves them away. "You got a light?"

Sebastian reaches into the box for a chased silver lighter and cigar cutter, which he hands to Tony. Tony cuts the cigar, sticks it in his mouth, and murmurs around it, "Vegas. Only place in America you can still smoke to your heart's content. Gotta love it."

Thick gray smoke billows through the lobby, swirling up to

the ceiling as Tony and Sebastian get their stogies going. Daniel wrinkles his nose; he promised his daughters he wouldn't smoke anymore, after their grandpa died of lung cancer, but it's hard to avoid breathing the smoke in just now. He picks up a pack of candy, inspecting the logo.

"I've never heard of this one before. Is it something local, or do we ship it in special for the Houdini?"

Sebastian puffs a series of smoke rings. "That's below my pay grade, thank goodness. If you want to put something called Lucky Elephant in your body, be my guest." When he yawns, smoke billows out of his mouth like a small, fastidious dragon.

Daniel yawns, too, rubbing at his smoke-reddened eyes. He woke up early this morning to work out, and then he had to stop in at a few of his hotels, and then there was the whole wedding thing, and then the storm, and he can't find Anna, and—

Suddenly, he realizes he's lost in the haze and leaning against a wall. His head is floating, spinning, fading in and out. It's almost like being drunk, but his mind can't quite grasp what that might mean. Everything is dull and muffled, obscured by the swirling gray. Somewhere, on the other side of the thick, heavy smoke, the woman's shoes start tapping again, but they're moving farther and farther away. Tony calls for her, his voice slurring angrily. How can he be drunk when there's no alcohol? Were they drugged? Is this some kind of—

Some kind of something.

What was he just thinking about?

Daniel looks down, and there's an inviting burgundy chair, deep and soft, just waiting for him. He sinks into it gratefully, his eyes fluttering shut. He's so tired. There's something wrong—it feels like he's falling off a cliff into some dark, jagged place—but he can't stop it, he can't stop anything, he can't even open his eyes.

The speakers crackle as a new record starts up, playing a lullaby.

12.

Max stares at Anna, and Anna stares at Max. They are only a few feet apart, but the gulf between them is as wide as the Grand Canyon. He's distractingly cute and interesting and just . . . different from anyone Anna has ever met.

But what he just said?

Was pretty rude.

"I shouldn't be here?" Anna asks, incredulous. "I have every right to be here! It's a hotel, not the Oscars. Sure, these aren't my regular clothes—obviously—and I look like a drowned rat, and I'm barefoot, and this is clearly not how I generally check in to a hotel. Do you think I'm too poor to be here or too low-class? You don't know who I am, what my family has been through to get here. I belong here just as much as you do."

The look that passes over Max's face is as dark as the clouds outside. "You don't understand. No one ever does. Not until it's too late."

"Too late for what? God, you are seriously cryptic." Anna wants to stay mad at him, but he suddenly looks so lost that she feels she must be missing something very important.

"Cryptic. Yeah, that's me." Max gives a sad chuckle and shoves his hands in his pockets. "But we might as well enjoy ourselves while we can. Are you hungry? Thirsty? Do you need shoes?"

"Shoes?"

He does a little shuffle, shows her his shoe. "Like you said, you're barefoot."

"Like I said, I know."

"So do you want shoes, or don't you?"

Anna is suddenly very aware of how little her clothes cover her compared to his. The chill of the storm is still with her, still soaked into her hair and her bones. She doesn't like how vulnerable she feels, how off-kilter everything has been since she landed in the lobby of the Houdini. She prefers control and familiarity.

She prefers to know where her dad is.

"Shoes would be good, but the lobby shop didn't have any."

A secretive grin. "It usually doesn't. There are other places, if you know where to look."

Anna pats the pocket that contains her wallet. She can pay for shoes, at least. Her father always makes her keep a folded hundred with her at all times, just in case.

"Shoes and then food. Do you like Italian?" Max picks up the book he dropped like it's a bird's egg and reverently places it on a table beside a big, squashy chair and a reading lamp. Without a hint of pageantry, he pats the book like he's promising not to leave it alone too long. At the door, he turns back to Anna, eyes on fire, hand out like he thinks she's just going to . . . take it.

She stares at his hand until he sheepishly withdraws it.

But he recovers quickly.

"Well? Italian? Or there's—"

"Italian's fine. But I really need to find my dad first."

His grin is electric. "If he's here, we'll cross paths eventually. Come on. I'll show you around." He gallantly holds the door open as she walks out, then closes it softly behind them. "You don't need a key for this one, if you ever want to come back. Do you like to read?"

Anna's memory flashes to a childhood spent wrapped in books, voraciously devouring her favorite series about magic school and warrior cats and shape-shifting aliens, and rereading everything as soon as she finished each tearful finale. But since she started private school, she's been running a race—against her fellow high achievers, against time. She has a plan, her entire future mapped out, and being valedictorian is her current entrée, with side dishes of AP classes and good SAT scores. She hasn't read for pleasure since the summer before sixth grade, and she misses it—and resents how dull most of the books she has to dissect for her honors English classes are. Still, she's determined to achieve on her own merits, not coast by on her father's fortune, so she keeps pushing herself.

"I love to read," she tells Max, because it's true, even if she's speaking about a different version of herself in a different life, a version of Anna she can barely remember sometimes.

He leads her down the hall, back toward the elevator, and she realizes that she's drifting off course, just following along—but she's too tired to care. It's not a large hotel, after all; they have a good chance of finding her dad and his annoying friends, especially since Uncle Tony goes crazy for Italian food and wants to believe he's the Tony Soprano of Vegas. Max's fingers dip into his vest pocket and remove a golden key, which he twirls on its chain as he walks. In another boy, this action might read as showing off or trying to be cool, but in Max, it seems more like a thoughtless, practiced fidget, like the only thing he knows to do with his hands.

"I also love to read," he says. "Probably a little too much pulp, if I'm honest, but I've studied the classics, too. What's your favorite book?"

Anna's tongue sticks to the roof of her mouth. Her favorite book. Should she tell him it's one of the deep, heavy, tragic ones she's read for school? Or should she bring up a classic she used to love, something with retro cred? Or dig deep into her youthful obsessions? Or . . .

"Probably *The Night Circus*."

It feels right in her heart and in the context of the library they've just left. Anna found it in an indie bookstore when she was nine and inspecting the Staff Favorites shelf and she had to argue with her mom to let her buy it. It was the first book that made her feel like she might one day actually be an adult in a bigger world. She hasn't thought about it in years. The whole thing, after all, is predicated on magic, and she lost the taste for magic long ago.

As the elevator doors grind open, Max holds out his arm, inviting her to go first. "I haven't heard of that one. Who's the author?"

"Erin Morgenstern."

Anna steps into the elevator and doesn't recall until Max is right beside her that it is not, in fact, a large elevator. It could hold four people uncomfortably, maybe, and she feels like if she leans too much, they'll bump shoulders. Which wouldn't necessarily be a tragedy, but the thing is, Anna has spent so much time planning her future and keeping her family's calendar and making sure her mom goes to her doctor appointments and her sister has the perfect wedding that she oftentimes forgets that boys exist, and when she does remember them, she looks around her school and finds them deeply wanting. The chances of finding an intellectual equal with any sort of aesthetic sense is pretty much impossible, which is why she can't wait to get to college. In short, she has very little experience with boys of any sort.

Max pulls out a small notebook and a stub of a pencil and starts scribbling. Anna peeks over his shoulder.

"Erin with an *E*. Female Erin," she corrects.

"A lady author? Interesting."

Anna's hackles rise. "Excuse you? *A lady author?*"

Max grimaces, steps to the side, puts his key in the elevator, and presses the 5 button, clutching his notebook like he's hoping Anna will forget it exists. "I just . . . outside of the classics, female authors are far outnumbered by male authors. I want to read it. I hope the library has it. Or can get it. The title alone is enticing." He glances at her, swallows hard when he sees her death glare. "I'm a huge fan of Austen. And the Brontës. And Agatha Christie. And Mary Shelley. And Shirley Jackson. Please don't kill me."

The elevator continues its slow descent, the air within thick with mingled annoyance and mortification. Max whips out a pocket watch, opens it, closes it, tucks it away with his notebook, stuffs his hands in his trouser pockets. The overhead speaker plays a jaunty, old-fashioned dance number like a dare. When the doors open, Anna steps off, still glaring, and Max follows.

"Look, I can tell you're angry. But I . . . there's context. Let me start again."

The elevator doors close. They're alone in a hall identical to the one upstairs: glowing wood walls, thick burgundy and gold carpet, sputtering flames in blown glass domes.

Anna raises her eyebrows.

"What year did you come from?" Max asks.

That is not what Anna expected him to say. She was expecting the usual misogynistic arguments about sexual dimorphism and statistics and whatever other incel bullcrap Chad Huckabee was going to use in Debate to get the other guys to vote him captain instead of her.

"What year did I come from?"

Max nods, earnest. "Yeah. Are we still in the nineteen hundreds, at least?"

Anna shakes her head sadly. He's nuts. Cute, but completely cuckoo bugnuts crazy.

"Two thousand twenty-three."

"Ah, hell." It comes out soft. He's looking down, hands still in his pockets. "The oldest book in the library is from the nineteen sixties." Now he looks up impishly, a little grin starting. "But it sounds like things have gotten a lot better for women in your time, so hats off to that." When Anna doesn't respond, he shakes his head and murmurs softly to himself, "Okay, that didn't work. But I can get you shoes. If nothing else, shoes. And food."

"Why doesn't your library have any books that are under sixty years old?" Anna asks.

"Because . . ." His mouth stays open, but nothing comes out. "I'll explain at the restaurant."

He nods decisively and walks down the hallway. For a moment, she doesn't follow, but . . . well, what else is she going to do? At least he can work the elevator. And there's something about him—about Max. He looks weird, he talks weird, he acts weird, and yet outside of what he actually says, he seems completely sane and himself, which is more than Anna can say of most people. The phrase "in your time" flutters around in her head, but so many strange things are fluttering around like confused butterflies that it doesn't quite land. She remembers briefly that they're supposed to be in the middle of a tornado, but there is no evidence, no booms or shakes or sirens, and she can't stop being so aware of Max. When he stops at another door, key in hand, and waits for her, she joins him.

"What about the tornado?" she asks, knowing it sounds like she's giving in.

His look is wry but sad. "It can't hurt the Houdini."

"How do you know?"

"I just do. There are windows where we're going, if you need to see for yourself."

"I definitely do. Tornadoes don't just stop."

He raises an eyebrow. "If they didn't stop, they would go on interminably. Just, tornadoes forever and ever."

"That's not what I mean! They don't stop after ten minutes!"

"We've been talking for more than ten minutes."

"You're infuriating!"

A sheepish grin. "I hear that a lot. Come and see for yourself, though, whether the tornado is currently a problem."

What choice does she have?

"Okay, then, but for the record, none of this makes sense, and I don't like it."

"Doesn't matter whether you like it or not; it refuses to change. Que será, será, right? All you can do is go with it. So, we call this the Wardrobe." He unlocks the door with his key and pushes it open.

"Whoa," Anna murmurs.

She was expecting a regular hotel room, maybe a lost and found with some old lady's worn-out sandals. But this place is . . .

"Unreal."

The room is lined with metal clothing racks like the ones backstage at a play, and each rack is bursting with clothing in all sorts of colors and textures. There's no rhyme or reason to it, no marked sizes or collections of tops or bottoms. Nubby brown slacks hang beside spangled cocktail dresses and fluffy ballet skirts. A bellhop's uniform sticks out from between a satiny clown suit and a plaid dress. Ties and cummerbunds and flowing scarves dangle like pennants. And on the floor, between and around the racks, shoes cluster in pairs like crowds at a concert pushing up against the stage. Boots, slippers, brogues, kitten heels, sharp two-toned pumps.

"Unreal. Ha." Max rocks back on his heels. "Very astute. Please, take whatever you like." He looks down, blushes a bit. "I know we just agreed to shoes, but I saw you shivering. If you'd like to change, you're welcome to anything. Parts of the hotel can get drafty."

It's true—her hair is still wet, and the billowy muumuu isn't keeping her warm. Anna feels vulnerable in it, and awkward and ugly, which . . . well, she'd rather not feel awkward and ugly just now. Tentative, she approaches a rack and sifts through it. It's the strangest lost and found she's ever seen, and everything looks and feels brand-new and clean. There are no terrible odors of mothballs or armpits.

And yet . . .

"Are there any normal clothes?" she asks.

Another impish grin. "Define normal."

"Jeans, tees, hoodies, sneakers? Bras that don't look like rocket launchers? I didn't have much luck in the shop in the lobby, either, but everything here just feels very costumey." Anna holds up a gorgeous chartreuse satin gown.

"An excellent choice. But you'd probably feel overdressed for the restaurant. Let's see." Max approaches another rack, digs around, and comes up with a soft pink dress with a circle skirt and embroidered collar, very 1950s. "Is this normal enough?"

Anna snorts and shakes her head. "I'm not going to a sock hop."

"Okay. How about this one?" The next dress he digs out looks even older, with pastel flowers and a bow at the neck. The hem would fall halfway between her knees and her ankles. It looks like the dress her grandmother was buried in.

Anna doesn't know whether to laugh or cry. "I had a bad night and then I almost died in a tornado and I fell through a hole in the floor and I could really go for some comfort, you know?"

Max looks at her critically, dives back into a rack, and comes up with a pair of men's striped pajamas with an embroidered *A* on the chest pocket. "I think this might be as comfortable as we've got, but it's not quite dressing for dinner." He shrugs. "Not that there's anyone to complain. I'll wait outside, and you can change—or not, as you wish—and freshen up. Please, help yourself to anything you find here."

He nods at her encouragingly, hangs the pajamas back on the rack, and leaves, shutting the door softly behind him. As soon as he's gone, Anna hurries to the nearest window and pulls back the curtains, bracing herself for the return of all her worries and fears.

What she sees outside scrambles her brain.

She can't see Vegas, or the parking lot, or even raindrops. Definitely no tornado.

Just solid gray.

13.

What Anna sees outside the window is not the sort of gray that comes with the center of a storm, when details swirl with the streaming water and lashing trees, and objects blink in and out of sight as the wind changes direction. No, this gray is like when a plane flies through a storm cloud, a thick, fuzzy, opaque gray, unnaturally still. Nothing moving, no hint of anything beyond. Just looking at it makes her dizzy. She hurries to the other window and finds the same thing. She's done two circuits of the room like a hamster looking for a way out of a cage before it occurs to her that she's not alone.

"Max?" she calls through the closed door.

"Yes?"

"I looked outside."

A pause.

"Ah."

Silence.

"That's not . . . You see, the storm clouds . . . ," he tries. And fails. A soft thump against the wood is probably his forehead. "I'll explain as best I can. Please do get dressed however you like and use the vanity as you wish and join me. It'll be easier face to face. With food. Food will help."

Without the distracting visual and utter strangeness Max presents, Anna can't help but notice the antiquated way he speaks, how his accent is off and he overenunciates everything. Another puzzle in a world of puzzles. She looks back toward the pajamas on the end of the rack. Something tells her not to put them on, that whatever she has to face tonight will require the sort of emotional armor only proper clothes can provide.

She runs her hand over the nearest fabrics. Sumptuous velvet, rich satin, slubby silk, rough tweed, crisp cotton. None of the amorphous softness of her own closet—no athleisure here.

Anna considers dozens of options before selecting a short-sleeved dress in rich indigo that reminds her of *Downton Abbey*, loose and flowy with a swooping neckline and drop waist with embroidered roses. She also finds a lace-trimmed camisole—those bullet bras are just too much—and decides to keep on her underpants rather than trade them for random ones of uncertain origin. There is no fitting room, but there is a door that in a hotel room would lead to a bathroom, and it does here, too. The pink-tiled counter is covered in bottles and tubes and cosmetics and a single, beautiful brush that she dearly hopes isn't made of real tortoiseshell.

Soon Anna is dressed, glad she's found an outfit that isn't too uncomfortable but still seems presentable and has pockets for her phone and wallet. She tosses the muumuu in a bin, brushes her hair until it crackles, splashes water on her face, and takes a moment to appreciate that even after all she's been through, her waterproof mascara and lipstick are still going strong.

God—the wedding. How many hours ago was it she stood beside her sister as maid of honor, holding her bouquet as Emily exchanged rings with JJ? It feels like days ago, a lifetime ago. Before their father's announcement, everything was going so well. Her sister, her best friend, was happy, constantly grabbing Anna's arm to tell her how beautiful everything was. Anna remembers now, much later, saying something about how she couldn't wait until Emily and JJ were back from their honeymoon and could start looking for their first house, and Emily just looked away and smiled a faraway smile. Back then, Anna thought her sister was dreaming of the same future she envisioned. Now she knows Emily already had a home picked out, but far away, in New York.

And Emily never told her.

It stings, realizing that perhaps she doesn't know Emily as well as she thought she did.

Anna shakes her head.

She has to put that thought away, lock it up on a shelf in her memory. There's too much to worry about now before she can have a real discussion with Emily and try to talk her into staying.

Everything is wrong and nothing makes sense, but Anna is too tired and confused to be angry. She has to keep moving forward, and that means leaving this powder room and rejoining Max.

When she's satisfied that she's fit to be seen in one of her dad's hotel restaurants, she finds a pair of flats that match the dress and miraculously fit, which is just too strange a coincidence. Picking one up, she sees that there's no size printed on it, not even a company name. Her eyes narrow, and she picks up the next pair of shoes that catch her eye, heeled pumps that look like they were made for ballroom dancing. They likewise have no markings, and they also fit perfectly. As does the dress.

The thought crosses her mind that she might be dead or in a coma or otherwise seriously messed up, but Anna Alonso is not the sort of person to freak out about seemingly impossible possibilities, and it's not like screaming herself hoarse would change anything. For now, this is reality, and Anna is nothing if not realistic. Even when everything defies logic, she will take the next logical step.

This is her plan: keep going.

She opens the door a little harder than necessary, feeling more out of control than she'd like to admit. "What the hell is going on?" she asks Max in a tone she learned from her father, one that cannot be ignored.

He's leaning against the hallway wall, staring at her, his eyes wide and soft. "Wow," he murmurs.

"Don't 'wow' me. I want to know what's going on. This hotel, that gray stuff outside the windows, this room of new old clothes and shoes that inexplicably fit. Something is really messed up, and you're not telling me what it is."

Max looks down, gathering his thoughts, then looks up with a smile that's half-pitying, half-wry. He seems to have a smile for every unlikely scenario.

"Dinner," he says, "and I'll do my best. Hot bread makes

everything easier." He holds out his arm like he's an usher at a wedding, and Anna stares at him until he lowers it. "This way."

Max leads her back into the elevator and uses his key to go down to the fourth floor. Anna has decided not to speak until he answers her questions and explains everything, and he has apparently decided not to do that until they're at dinner. That's fine. She can work the silent treatment—one of her dad's power moves involves forcing the other person to speak first, putting them at a disadvantage. When the elevator opens on the fourth floor, Anna finally sees something worthy of one of her dad's hotels.

Instead of opening onto another hallway, whether poorly lit concrete or plush carpet, the elevator doors reveal a grand foyer with a soaring, domed ceiling painted a deep peacock blue and peppered with astrological signs picked out in twinkling gold stars. The floor is black-and-white checks, perfectly clean, and the walls are white-and-gray marble that seems to glow from within. A grand chandelier hangs from the center of the dome, its thousand glimmering crystals dancing in what appears to be sunlight, although there are no windows. Max's heels click as he steps onto the tile floor, and Anna joins him. Under the chandelier sits a polished wood table with an enormous vase of flowers in shades of white, indigo, and mauve—perfectly matching Anna's dress—and their light, white scent dances across Anna's senses.

"That's a nice touch," Max says, as if pleased. "Almost there."

He leads her toward an open door with the words HARRY'S HIDEAWAY hand-painted in swooping, curling gold across the glass. The music in the foyer is a light waltz, piped in through hidden speakers, and it follows them into the restaurant. It's an intimate space, deep-burgundy walls and dark wood floors, the tables draped in pristine white tablecloths. Couples and small groups sit at the tables, each of which is lit with a candle in an old green wine bottle. Elegant waiters in black tuxes flit to and fro. The scent of flowers fades, overpowered by the warm, heady aromas of garlic and baking bread. The murmur of voices and the clink of silverware and glasses are a comfort after all the emptiness and silence, although Anna desperately wants to ask why no one is sheltering from the storm.

But as Max leads her to a table, bypassing the host's lectern, little details come to the fore. Strange details.

Everyone is dressed in old-fashioned costumes, dresses like the ones she passed up on the racks and timeless menswear like what Max wears. Anna can hear murmurs but can't pick out actual words.

Most troubling of all, when she really focuses, the people are partially see-through and blurry.

"Are we in hell?" she asks, voice trembling as she numbly sits in the chair Max has pulled out for her.

"I don't think so."

The fact that he's taken the question so seriously is slightly terrifying.

Anna stares at him, her entire body gone stiff and frozen with existential dread, but Max doesn't seem at all perturbed.

"Purgatory or limbo, maybe," he continues, his tone almost breezy. "Possibly an alternate dimension or some sort of pocket world. Perhaps some odd corner of Narnia. I've read everything I can on the topic, but I haven't yet found the answer, nor any helpful fauns." He sits, drapes a white cloth napkin across his lap, and looks up at her, utterly earnest. "I was born here, and I've never left. Almost everyone else in the hotel, as you can see, is . . . pretty much a ghost."

"So . . . what's going on?"

Max picks up a wineglass, inspects it as if for smudges.

"It's magic," he says, plain as day.

14.

Anna stares at Max, her entire world narrowed down to one word.

"Did you just say it . . . this hotel . . . this restaurant . . . it's magic?"

"Magic."

"Magic magic?"

He shrugs. "Magic."

Her instinct is to look around the room at the impossibly blurry people and confirm what he's just said, but some frightened lizard part of her brain wants very much to believe that everything is just fine and logical, thank you, and she's in total control of the situation, so she locks eyes with him, which might actually be a mistake, because dang.

She swallows hard and tries to remember how to word. "I mean, yeah, I know it's supposed to be a magic hotel. Like, magicians and rabbits in top hats and card tricks. I get the gimmick, the decor, the themed shows, and all that. I was born in Vegas. But I don't see how that's—"

"Anna." The word falls like a feather, soft and delicate. "Look around you. If this isn't magic, then what is it?"

She forces her head to turn and her eyes to take it all in. The people at the nearest table are partially transparent and hazy, like they're the work of a projector on an invisible screen; she can barely see the wall behind them. They're a man and a woman in their fifties, probably, a bit thick around the middle and jolly. The woman wears a dress like Anna's but with more coverage, and a matching cloche hat, the colors a muddy gold with geometric embroidery in copper. The man is in baggy pants and a white button-down with suspenders. Two half-eaten plates of spaghetti sit in front of them, but they only have eyes for each other, their soft murmurs as far away and indecipherable as a radio behind a closed door.

"Can they see us?" Anna asks, voice low.

"Some can, some can't. I can usually talk to the single ones, especially the ones doing jobs, but the couples are harder to reach, like they're in their own little completed loop. I don't know if they're memories or ghosts or what. When I was small, I could play with the children, but then I got bigger, and it's like they can't see me anymore."

Anna looks at Max closely, at his particulars. He's as solid as she is, and he has little flaws here and there that reveal him to be a real person—one tooth a bit crooked, a few freckles, an ink stain on one sleeve. She looks down at her own hands, which are twisting the napkin in her lap to a rag. There are her bitten cuticles, which Emily's manicurist couldn't quite smooth out, although the coat of mint-green polish on her short, round nails is still mostly intact. She is imperfect, too, which is a comfort. It seems like a ghost would lose those little touches, that flaws would fade away until all details were lost. None of these people have freckles or stains or wrinkles.

Even still, she can't help asking Max, "So how do you know we're real?"

He looks at his hands, like he's asked himself this question so many times that it's not threatening anymore. "I guess we don't. I mean, didn't you have moments in your other world where you stopped and stared at your hand or in the mirror and felt like a stranger who had just arrived, like, 'Oh, I'm a person'? I don't think they"—he inclines his head toward a passing waiter—"do that. They don't seem self-aware or philosophical. But I eat, and when I eat, the food is gone. I sleep, and when I wake up, I've had dreams." He smiles at Anna, and she is quite certain he smiles more than anyone she knows, and that he has a thousand smiles, one for every possible situation. "And then you showed up, and you are not only corporeal but very different from the only people I know. So you have to be real. Right?"

Anna is certain that she's about to say something very deep when her stomach grumbles loudly. At least no one else in the restaurant looks over, impudently or with curiosity. Max picks up the menu on the table, a piece of creamy paper with two columns of print in an elegant font.

"Get whatever you like. It's all good. I've tried everything."

Anna raises an eyebrow. "So the people aren't real, but the food is?"

Max shrugs. "I haven't starved yet. But don't ask me where the food comes from—I've been trying to catch it all my life, and I've never yet succeeded."

"Catch it?"

"The mechanism. If I order room service, it's placed outside the door. I've never seen by whom. The tray disappears when I place it back in the hall. In the restaurants, I tell a waiter my order, and the food appears in the window. There's no one in the kitchen. I leave my plates on the table, and when I'm gone, they get bused. I have absolutely no clue how, and as long as I'm watching, nothing happens. I'll show you."

Max raises a hand and smiles, and a waiter hurries over. He's an older man, tall and olive-skinned with slicked-back white hair and an expectant air. Like Max said, he's more corporeal than the diners, barely see-through at all.

"Welcome to Harry's Hideaway, sir, miss. What can I bring you?"

"We'd like to start with— Do you drink?" Max asks, turning to Anna.

A dead stare. "I'm sixteen."

"Me too. Whatever this place is, trust me, they don't care."

"I do. It's illegal. I'll have a Shirley Temple." Even if she was the sort of person to experiment with illegal substances, especially under extraordinary circumstances with strange boys, she can't help remembering that her dad is a part owner of this hotel, and he's drilled into Anna from a very young age that when she's in one of his hotels, she is required to behave faultlessly.

"Two Shirley Temples, please," Max tells the waiter.

The waiter nods and bustles off to the kitchen, where he disappears through the swinging door like any regular person would.

"Ah, there we are."

Anna was so busy staring at the swinging door that she didn't notice any movement at the half-moon window in the wall between the kitchen and the dining room. Two tall glasses of fizzing pink liquid sit there, filled with ice and topped with cherries. Max fetches them and puts one in front of her. She can smell it, the sweetness of the syrup and the fizz of the mineral water. But she's not ready to drink yet. There's a very *Alice in Wonderland* feel to—whatever this is. This could be Hades or Faerie or Wonderland, or someplace else, without a name, and she's all too aware that there historically are consequences when you eat or drink in a magical place with rules. Max has no such compunction. He pulls the red-and-white-striped paper straw toward him and takes a long drink.

"It's good. I mean, I don't have much to compare it to, but I like it. And I haven't died yet." He gets a faraway look that Anna doesn't quite understand. "I . . . think about this a lot."

Anna stares at her drink and realizes a Shirley Temple has perhaps never been so important. It's a line of demarcation, the Rubicon waiting to be crossed. If she drinks it, she commits to . . . whatever this is, a version of existence that isn't normal, rational, or familiar. From then on, she's all in. She'll eat what she's served and start to act as if this might be a new normal. If she doesn't drink it, she rejects the entire concept—and starts either a short trip to Dehydrationville or a long understanding of purgatory. For a deeply logical person, the entire question is ridiculous. She's utterly out of her depth. She loves making decisions in general, but that's because she carries a supercomputer in her pocket and can find all the answers and evidence she needs with a few quick searches and then choose the safest path.

The only time she's dealt with something like this before was at that one awful party she went to when she was ten, when the magician found her in the gazebo and gave her back Emily's gold hoop earring. Over the years, Anna has almost convinced herself that was a dream, because she could never come up with a feasible explanation for it.

She can't come up with a feasible explanation for this place, either. But she knows one thing that will get her one step closer to okay.

"So, can you help me find my dad?"

Max looks around, frowning. "Only if the Houdini wants us to find him. That's another thing. Sometimes it wants to help you, and sometimes it seems to actively work against you. I've found all sorts of wonderful things, but I've also had things I liked taken from me and never returned. I've found places once and never again. Things shift. Like a poltergeist? But a thoughtful one. I think of it like a playful and mischievous child. I try not to get on its bad side."

"And by 'it,' you mean—the hotel?"

He puts a hand on the wall, almost fondly. "I had to come up with some way to understand it. I've read up on magic, science, religion, and philosophy, trying to make sense of it all, and this one quote really hit home for me. Something about how we think we know what's possible, but the magician proves otherwise."

Max's words reach deep into Anna's memory, back to a half-lit gazebo at a party and a magician who did the impossible—and said something quite similar. She had forgotten that part of the conversation . . . until now.

"So in this particular case, who's the magician?"

Max ignores that. "You know, I had to learn that my world was the odd one by reading books from yours. My life begins and ends at the revolving door." He looks horribly sad as he sips his Shirley Temple, and Anna wants to comfort him, despite the fact that she's the one who was recently transported to another world and who is unsure whether her father is alive.

At least she knows what's real. At least she knows what's out there. If what Max says is true, he's never set foot outside this hotel. And it's a beautiful hotel, but that's an awfully small life to live.

"Books are probably better," she tells him. "My world is a total mess. Politics, climate change, violence." Anna wants to pat his hand or his arm, and the thought is slightly terrifying and also scandalous, and she worries it will be awkward, but then her hand does it anyway, just lands on his forearm like a bird alighting, and he smiles again, and she's certain it was the right decision.

"Shall we simply accept our fate, then, and order some spaghetti before we go hunting for your father?" Max holds up a finger to summon the waiter, and Anna likes it, his confidence.

The chivalry she's read about in books is not something she's ever seen in her world, and she appreciates that Max behaves like a gentleman. He's not even sure if these people are real, but he still speaks to the waiter with respect and kindness. A person could easily turn into a monster in a place like this.

But Max didn't.

"What would you like to eat?" he asks. "Everything is good. Except the olives. I despise olives."

"I also despise olives." Anna looks over the menu, marveling at the thick, typed letters, but she's already read it a dozen times. The prices are in pennies. And she's a little startled by some of what she sees, like mayonnaise being treated as a legitimate sauce and turkey jelly salad with all three words squished together. The waiter is waiting, polite and partially see-through. "I'll have the chicken Milanese, please."

"And I'll have the pigeon," Max says. "Thank you." The waiter nods and glides off to his door.

"Pigeon?" Anna asks, incredulous.

Max looks mortified. "Is that bad? Is there something wrong with pigeon?"

"We mostly think of them as flying rats in my time."

He grimaces. "It's just a smaller, tastier chicken here. But I've never seen one alive—just in books. And the museum."

Anna perks up. "There's a museum?"

He nods eagerly, matching her energy. "The Museum of Magic, on the third floor. It's full of old posters, art, and artifacts. I like it because it changes every so often. Some pieces are always there, but there are also curated exhibits. I particularly liked the one on spirit photographs. Ah. One moment."

Max gets up to fetch the plates, steaming slightly as they sit on the sill. Anna can smell the food, and her mouth waters. His back is turned for only a moment, but she sips her Shirley Temple quickly, secretively, needing this chasm to be crossed on her own terms, without an audience. It tastes of bubbles and cherry and nothing more, no additional magic or strangeness, no puff of glitter or laughing fairy voices to mark any sort of sealed pact. The sensation is utterly normal and anticlimactic. Max puts her plate down first, then his, before fetching a basket of napkin-wrapped bread.

"So you have two parents?" he asks, a little wistful.

"Yes, but they don't like each other very much."

Realizing she's been lured into saying something personal, Anna takes a moment to chew. She's never articulated this before. The only person she confides in is Emily, and Emily already understands.

"I mean, they love each other, but when they met, my mom was a waitress working two jobs and my dad was a salesman. Once my dad made a bunch of money, they weren't any happier. All she does is shop and pretend to have migraines when she doesn't get enough attention, and all he does is work. So I have to be the adult, pretty much."

"Do you like that? Or would you prefer it the other way around? Because I have the opposite problem. I'm never really allowed to grow up."

Anna dabs at her lips with her napkin. "I don't think it really matters if I like it. Someone has to be responsible. If I don't do it, who will?"

Max sits back and cocks his head. "Fair enough. But what do you do for fun?"

"Fun . . ." This is not a question Anna Alonso asks herself. "Well, I tutor in the mornings. Then school. Then Debate Club,

Academic Bowl, NHS, Beta Club. And theater, but I mainly do stage management. And then there's homework."

His brows draw together. "It sounds like your hobbies mostly involve doing more work."

Flustered, Anna looks down. "I mean, it's all for the future, right? If I want to get into the right school and get the right degree and become a CEO, I have to put in the work."

"Why?"

No one has ever asked her this before. She hasn't really asked herself. It's just been her goal since she was a kid—to be in charge—and back home, everyone applauds it.

"Because I want to make a difference."

"A difference to what?"

"The world!" She gestures with her hands, and her napkin goes flying. "I want to matter. I want to do great things. What about you? What do you want to do?"

Max shrugs, amused and not rising to the bait. "What work is there? I've tried cooking a bit, but there's no one to share a meal with. I do calisthenics, I paint—badly. I play instruments. There are movies and books, of course. I like learning."

"So do I."

"Then we have that in common." He retrieves her napkin and two more Shirley Temples that have magically appeared in the window. "So how did you end up here?" he asks between bites. "I didn't see you come in."

Anna tells him about the wedding and how it went wrong and then describes the storm, but instead of focusing on the whole nearly-died-in-a-tornado thing, like most people would, Max rumples his forehead and says, "So it was a bad thing, your father giving your sister an apartment?"

She looks down at her plate, picks at her peas. Uncanny, that he would zero in on that part. "I mean, wedding gifts are expected. But he didn't even ask—" Anna breaks off. According to what she heard in the limo afterward, her dad did ask. Emily knew about it all along. "She was supposed to stay here, in Vegas. And instead, my dad's torn the family apart."

Max chews and thinks, but the silence isn't awkward. "But you said it's Emily's dream. Aren't you happy for her?"

"Of course, but . . . we had plans. We made plans."

Max blinks at her, holding back a smile. "But plans change."

Anna looks away. "Sometimes they shouldn't."

"And yet changed plans brought you here."

When she looks back, Max's eyes are shining softly with the sort of vulnerability she's only ever seen from men in the *Lord of the Rings* movies and maybe Ryan Gosling.

"It wasn't so much changed plans as a tornado that brought me here."

"Well, the tornado changed your plans."

Anna is annoyed with him and possibly a little annoyed with herself, but she's also, finally, smiling. If this is flirting, she needs to do it more often. She sips her drink so she won't look like a dang loon. It's odd, how she generally hates being challenged and yet somehow appreciates that Max is willing to challenge her.

He changes the subject, asking her about her favorite movies. She doesn't feel talked over or manipulated or awkward with him, which is like a miracle, as she almost always feels one of those things during social interactions. Everyone wants something from her—her meticulous notes, access to her father, to find out if her older sister is single. But Max seems to revel in her mere existence, which is a welcome change. He really listens. Anna is beginning to realize that she rarely feels truly heard.

She is also very glad she didn't go with the spaghetti, as she's fairly certain she would have either dropped a meatball into her lap or slurped tomato sauce all over her face. Max flusters her, and she's always thought herself unflusterable.

Then again, so is he—in an entirely different way. Anna thrives on organization, schedules, and managing her family's joint calendar. But from what she can tell, Max does the exact opposite. There are no calendars here. He doesn't know what day it is; he has no curfew. His life is entirely unstructured, and Anna is uniquely horrified. And fascinated.

"How are you not a complete mess?" she finally asks, because it's been bothering her all night—

Day? What is time?

Max puts down his knife and fork just so and dabs self-consciously at his mouth with his napkin. "A complete mess?"

"I mean, if you've never left this building, how are you not an absolute weirdo?"

Max looks away, a little shyly. "I was kind of worried that I was."

"You're not."

"Then I'll reveal that I take a three-pronged approach." He holds up a finger. "First, as previously discussed, I read voraciously and watch tons of old movies. Books tell you who the good guys and bad guys are. I try to be half Mr. Darcy, half Charles Bingley." He holds up a second finger. "Second, I looked at the only two people I do know and decided to be the opposite. And third"—he holds up a third finger and grins—"I've spent years practicing conversations with people who may or may not be real. What's one more?"

Anna's eyebrows climb into her hair. "You're still not sure if I'm real? Even after talking to me all this time?"

His eyes go far away.

"No. But that's okay. I'll take what I can get in the time we have left."

Anna puts down her knife and fork and looks him dead in the eye. "Okay, what's that supposed to mean?"

"It's just that . . ." Max puts his elbows on the table, his chin on his hands. "Do you have to ask so many questions? Can't you just enjoy the ride?"

Anna firmly shakes her head. "No. What do you mean by 'the time we have left'? Because that was ominous."

He stands suddenly, and his chair falls backward, bouncing off the tiles. "It was ominous for a reason, okay? Don't you get it? People just show up and never leave! I'm the only one who stays the same."

"People don't just show up at hotels and live there forever."

"I do, Anna! And these people, or ghosts, or memories, or whatever they are—they do, too. Even if what they do isn't actually living. No one ever, ever leaves. Ever."

Anna rights his chair and puts it back where it belongs. "I'm trying my hardest to understand, okay? None of this makes sense.

I'm in a hotel. This is what's real. I'm going to find my dad, and we're going to leave. It's that simple."

Max's laugh edges on madness. "I wish that were true, I really do. But that's not how this place—this magic—works. People occasionally stumble in, people from different times and different places, and they're here for a day, and I get my hopes up, and then I wake up and they're ghosts, and I'm alone again."

"I'm not going to become a ghost, Max."

He points to a cat clock on the wall, its tail swishing. It reads 1:30 a.m. Anna is quite certain it wasn't there when they walked in.

"Anna, if you believe nothing else I tell you, believe this: when that clock reaches the next midnight, you're going to be stuck here forever, just like the rest of them."

15.

Tony wakes up from the strangest dream and panics the moment he smells smoke. He flails and falls off a chair, landing hard on his rump on the black-and-white-tiled floor.

"Fire!" he shouts. "Smoke!"

"It's just cigars, you big baby," Sebastian mutters. He's curled up on a tufted ottoman, drooling onto the velvet.

Tony blinks and looks around. There's his cigar, lying on the floor, a last, sad plume of smoke rising before it goes out. Thick gray clouds wreath the ceiling, drifting lazily, but it does smell more like tobacco than a lawsuit. It's just him and Sebastian—no Daniel, no cute cigarette girl in sky-high heels.

"Honey, where'd you run off to?" he calls, his voice sharp. He'd been talking to Sebastian about baseball and his bookie, and then he must've fallen asleep, and now the red lacquer box of goodies has disappeared, right when he could use a mint.

"She appears to be gone." Sebastian sits up, rubbing his eyes, which are always wet and leaky, like those of the tiny dog one of Tony's girlfriends carries in her purse.

"I swear, this place deserves to burn to the ground," Tony growls.

"No. This place is a quiet gold mine. It just needs a complete overhaul." Sebastian fiddles with his glasses, cleaning them off on the ottoman. "Too many nooks and crannies, not enough signage."

"Then we should just sell it and good riddance," Tony says, scanning the hallway with annoyance. "And where'd Daniel go? This place is a maze."

Sebastian turns this way and that and when the smoke shifts, he spots Daniel at the other end of the long hallway, a sodden lump curled up in an old chair that must be hell to keep clean and deodorized. "Ah. There he is. Still asleep. How much champagne did the father of the bride drink tonight, anyway?"

Tony tosses the rest of his cigar in a nearby brass ashtray shaped like a palm tree. He squelches down the hallway and stands over Daniel, lips twitching and then curling into a slow, dark smile.

"You know, Sebastian, seems to me we've been in a situation like this before. Alone in this hotel with somebody who's more trouble than they're worth. This place belonged to my family, and I know all of us pitched in way back when, but maybe it's time to stop splitting things three ways."

Sebastian steps up beside him and rubs out his cigar on the bottom of his shoe. "You make an excellent point. Daniel definitely has a talent for getting properties off the ground, but this one is already past that point and therefore beyond his skill set. It does seem that we could simply split our continuing profits *two* ways. Not only the Houdini but all our holdings from now on, actually."

The haze of cigar smoke is nearly gone now, and the two men silently separate to investigate the hallway, pushing back curtains and trying every visible door to make sure they're alone. The song echoing from the overhead speaker is garbled and mumbly, something maudlin about deals with the devil and crossroads.

"Hey, Daniel!" Tony's voice is half whisper, half shout. "Let's get you to a bed, buddy."

When Daniel doesn't stir, the two other men give one another a decisive nod, and then Tony eases Daniel out of the chair and onto the floor, cradling his head so it won't slam on the tile. They take one more look around to make sure they're still alone before each grabbing an ankle and dragging Daniel down the hallway.

For two men who say they're unfamiliar with the Houdini, Tony and Sebastian don't falter. They know exactly where they're going. The only sounds are the fatalistic music from the speaker and the long, slow squelch of Daniel's jacket leaving a slug trail down the hall, plus Sebastian's occasional grunts of exertion and Tony's murmured "This is what you get for doing cardio instead of weights, Seb." The hallway is longer than it should be, and then Tony opens an unmarked door that leads to a narrower, dingier hall with a high ceiling and old wallpaper of a kind no longer made, deep emerald green with black illustrations that look like squiggles but are actually snakes, branches, and apples.

"Almost there, pal," Tony says, and he and Sebastian share a chuckle as Tony holds the door open with his foot.

Together alone, they understand each other perfectly.

Before they can drag Daniel into the hall, there's a loud screech from the overhead speaker, followed by the thump and scratch of a record being changed. A trumpet blares so loudly that it makes Tony and Sebastian wince and drop Daniel's feet.

"Hey, what?" Daniel sits up, rubbing his eyes in confusion.

Overhead, the trumpet leads into "Boogie Woogie Bugle Boy," and the volume mercifully fades.

Daniel, awake and alert now, stands and squints down the short, dark hallway, rubbing his forehead. "What are you doing? Were you carrying me?"

"You conked out," Tony says, his voice high and hard. "Just fell asleep in the lobby. We saw . . . there were . . ." He looks at Sebastian, desperate. Tony has never been the creative one.

"There were rats," Sebastian declares. "Big ones. You wouldn't wake up, so we had to drag you away." He glances at Tony, whose relief at the lie is palpable. "This place should be condemned. Or at least redecorated."

"Well, where are we? Did you find the cigarette girl? Have you seen any staff yet?" Daniel asks.

Tony looks around the hallway as if this is the first time he's been here, as if he hasn't stood right here with Sebastian before.

"These look like staff offices," he offers. "Admin, billing, whatever. We should just start knocking."

Daniel rubs his temples, blinks at the warm-orange lamps. "God, my head is killing me. This night could not possibly get any worse." He steps to the first door in the short hall, painted shiny black, and knocks firmly. "Hello? Anyone? Anna?"

Behind him, Tony and Sebastian exchange a very specific nod, a nod that says, *Daniel's night is definitely going to get a lot worse.*

16.

Anna sits in her chair at Harry's Hideaway staring at the cat clock, its eyes mischievously flicking left and right as its tail swings.

A cat clock can't control her destiny.

No clock can.

At midnight, nothing will happen, and then it will be 12:01, and life will go on as it always has. She's not going to—what, become a ghost?

That's ridiculous.

Max must be a lot more messed up than she assumed, because he's clearly delusional.

Maybe what's happening here is very odd, but Anna is still very much herself, very real. She puts a hand to her face and touches her cheek to make sure she still has substance. The same scene continues around her, the ghostly people laughing and chatting to the phantasmal clink of glasses that aren't quite there. They don't seem unhappy, these people. But that doesn't mean she wants to join them.

"I'm real, and I don't plan on disappearing, Max."

She says it firmly, as if giving reality itself an order.

"I'm glad, Anna."

But he doesn't look like he believes it.

He looks like he's already given up.

"So how can we stop it?"

He fiddles with his watch chain. "How can you stop air from being air? How do you stop gravity? You can't stop it. There is no obvious mechanism. I know every inch of this hotel, and it's not like there's a mysterious door labeled 'The Room That Makes Ghosts.' All I can tell you is that all the clocks show the exact same time, and they're all counting down the minutes you have left."

"I don't accept that."

"Accept it or not, it is what it is."

It's maddening and nonsensical, everything Anna Alonso hates.

And . . . well, she doesn't know how to go about stopping it.

Time is the only thing that can't be controlled, which is not a great realization for a control freak.

Max looks down at Anna's plate, which is littered with bread crusts and a few rogue pea skins. When he speaks, his voice is soft. "Well then. You can shake your fist at time all you like, but I say we enjoy the hours we have left. Are you ready for dessert?"

Glad for the chance to take decisive action, Anna runs a finger down the menu but doesn't see a single dessert. "Do they have it?"

Max stands, leaving his napkin on his chair. "Oh, they definitely do. Come along. I think you'll like this." There's a certain melancholy about him now, and Anna wonders how many girls he's brought to dinner, knowing they'll fade away by breakfast.

No. Absolutely not.

She won't think that way.

This is just another puzzle to solve.

"Can we look for my dad first?"

A shrug. "Since we have no idea where he is, the dessert room is as good a place to start as any. He might be anywhere."

Anna can't argue with that logic. She dabs at her mouth and stands. Since they entered the restaurant, the people seem . . . more corporeal, somehow. She can pick out words in their murmurs, hear their laughter. The waiter is asking the older couple if they enjoyed their meal. The clank and clatter of plates is audible from the kitchen, and the soft patter of music from the speaker has never stopped, she's just gotten used to it. Everything feels more solid, more certain. Which scares her.

She looks down at her plate. Has she made the ultimate noob move? Did she eat food in Faerie, slip pomegranate seeds between her lips while telling herself she wasn't in Hades? The food was good, but it wasn't good enough to trade her regular life for, wasn't good enough to die for. Was the food some kind of . . . ghost poison?

The thought is too ridiculous for someone as logical as Anna, but what's done is done. She can't untaste her meal. She can only take the next logical step. When you don't know where to look, any place is a good starting point.

Max waits, hands in his pockets, smiling sadly at her. His pants are hiked up stupidly high, like he's from some old movie about fast-talking detectives, but somehow it works, probably because he's utterly unaware of how dorky he would look in Anna's world. He is what he is, and there's something to that. But Anna is also Anna, and so now her worries tumble through. What is this place really, and where is her dad, and is Emily okay, and what about her mom, and how can she get home? If she ignores the ludicrous threat of midnight and allows all her other anxieties to rush in, she's all too aware that a tornado just rocked Vegas to its heart, and her mother and sister are fragile and will require her support. Max says she can't leave, but even if she's starting to believe in some kind of magic, she can't grasp the concept of a building that can't be escaped.

If Max doesn't believe she'll find a way, he doesn't understand her at all.

This is a building, and buildings have doors. And windows. And exterior walls that can be hit with sledgehammers. She won't just sit around drinking Shirley Temples until some random clock decides her time is up. Unless the limo was actually in an accident, and she's in a coma, and . . .

Her brain offers her a sad flash: her mother opening the mailbox to find her SAT scores, and breaking into tears, and—

Well, the scores arrive digitally, but still.

"Are you ready?"

Anna has been standing here like an absolute coward, so she places her napkin on the chair, wondering who or what will clean up after them. She thinks Max is going to walk out the front door of the restaurant and into the domed foyer, but he leads her deeper into Harry's Hideaway, beyond the kitchen and down a narrow hall painted green, past two doors labeled UOMINI and DONNE, past old black-and-white photos of Italian cathedrals, and around a corner.

The hallway gets darker, blocked up ahead with heavy curtains, and in her own world, with someone else, Anna would start to hear the small voice in her gut that reminds her this is probably an employees-only area and they might get in trouble. She's also very aware that she's in a small, dark space with a strange boy. But Max doesn't slow down and doesn't seem in any way predatory, and even if he was, it's not like he needs to go to this much trouble. If he wanted to hurt her, he could have just attacked her at the beginning, or at any moment thereafter. He could've chased her like the mysterious, threatening figure in the basement. When Max holds open a pair of molten-chocolate curtains, she realizes she's made the decision to follow him down what feels more and more like Alice's rabbit hole.

Soft velvet brushes Anna's cheek and she's plunged into darkness. Her hands instinctively search for something to hold on to. They find Max's vest, the tweed comfortably nubby under her fingertips, his body warm and his chest rising and falling with a terribly personal sort of relief.

She stumbles back, mumbling, "Sorry."

"Whoa there. I should've mentioned—it gets a little dark. All part of the fun."

He takes one of Anna's hands from his chest and leads her forward, into the darkness. As Anna doesn't know the way and doesn't want to fall and break her leg, this touch is acceptable. Up ahead, she can see votives set into niches in the walls, but that's it. Other than those tiny flickers of light, there is nothing, simply a void. The tinny music has changed to something about stardust and kisses, and smells dancing along on the still air begin to tempt her, coffee and cinnamon and chocolate vying for her attention. She speeds up, curious now, drawn forward by the gumdrop path of candles and the scent of good things. It's easier to let wonder take the wheel when the entire world is reduced to a single dark, seductive path with no exits.

"There are some steps here. You can go first," Max murmurs, his voice soft.

Back home, no business could be run this way, without plenty of light, without reflective tape on the stairs, without legal warnings, without emergency exit signs glowing at reasonable intervals. It's exciting, not knowing what's next. This, as much as anything, convinces Anna she is someplace new and strange where the impossible, as Max has said, might just happen. In a world overrun with lawsuits, there is no such childlike exploration of the dark without signing a release form. She realizes she has forgotten the list of code violations from earlier. There is no code to violate here. Reality has taken a rain check.

Anna shuffles forward until her toes find the steps. The first one is awkward, but her body quickly adjusts. It's narrow, this stairwell, and she can see a single line of warm light at the top, the bottom of a door. Max's bulk behind her is a comfort; without him here, she would be lost and anxious. But he's calm and knows the way, and she realizes that she trusts him. She has to. Everything he's told her so far has seemed so illogical as to be impossible, and yet it has all unfolded exactly as he said it would, which suggests an inner logic and consistency that Anna's brain craves, even if the overall framework is so alien and strange that when she thinks about it too much, she starts to worry about having a panic attack.

"The door is unlocked," Max says.

As Anna nears that glowing line of light, she holds her hands out in front of her, waiting for the welcome touch of wood and the cool kiss of a crystal doorknob.

There. She turns the knob, squinting as the door opens, unsure of what she'll find.

The light isn't blinding, though—the same orange lights from elsewhere illuminate a hallway that's a study in red. The walls are red-on-red wallpaper, the carpet is deep, plush, blood-red, all reflected on shining brown wood molding. The effect is cozy but deeply sensual, and Anna can only imagine what she would think if a boy back home brought her to a place like this on a first date.

"Just pick a barrel and have a seat," Max says from behind her, still down a step, at a respectful distance.

The instruction makes no sense until Anna realizes that the doorways jutting off the hall don't go into more hallways or rooms.

Each doorway opens into . . . a giant barrel.

And each barrel is huge, at least six feet in diameter, with a slice cut out to allow access to the booth inside. Anna selects the second barrel, because she never goes with the first one, and slides into the booth. The scent of warm wood washes over her, along with the faint tang of old, mellow wine. Two menus wait on the table, and at the end of the booth, against the curving barrel wall, there's a small silver machine similar to a jukebox. It has a row of buttons, each with a style of music printed on a card that's slipped into a slot—waltz, polka, jazz, swing, rock 'n' roll, boogie-woogie. REQUESTS WELCOME, a nicely lettered sign reads, with an arrow pointing at yet another button.

"Requests?" she asks as Max sits across from her.

The orange lights make his eyes shine. "Push the button and ask."

It sounds like a dare, but a simple one. Anna pushes the button, and the speaker crackles, expectant.

"Could you please play . . . uh . . ." Anna doesn't actually know much about music. She listens to podcasts and NPR. She takes her finger off the button, hoping the low lights hide her blush, as she's unaccustomed to not having the answer. "What do you like?"

"You pick something first."

Frustrated, she pushes the button and says, "Something from my time."

The speaker flares with the chorus of "About Damn Time" by Lizzo, loud as a jet plane, and Max slams his hands over his ears like there's a velociraptor screaming in his face.

"This is music from your time?" he shouts. The volume is definitely louder than anything Anna has heard in the hotel so far.

"Yeah, Lizzo's great, when your eardrums aren't bursting. They played it at Emily's wedding!" she shouts back.

Max nods, his face pained. "I don't mean any criticism of the songstress, but it's just . . ." His eyes roll upward, toward the speaker. "It's very loud."

"I don't listen to a ton of music," Anna confesses. "Why don't you change it to something you like?"

He pushes the button, eyes crinkling, and shouts, "Could you please play Max's set list?"

The music stops with the scritch of a record being changed, and the soft tones of piano take over, something Anna thinks she might recognize but could never name, something that feels soft and secret. She relaxes, her shoulders slumping down from around her ears.

"Sorry about that. I should've been more specific," she says.

"That's all right." Max pats the silver box affectionately. "I told you—the hotel has a sense of humor."

The song that's playing now has a delicate timelessness that Anna likes. It's soothing.

"So you have a playlist?" she asks.

Max fiddles with his key, twirling it on its chain, suddenly shy. "I suppose so—like musicians have for their concerts. I wrote it out and left it on the table one time, just to see what would happen, and the next time I came, I requested it, and here it is. I don't know who plays the piano, but it's lovely."

When Anna realizes it's live, her experience of the music changes. She can tell the difference between prerecorded music and fingers on ivory even through the janky speaker system. There's an intimacy to it. There is no one else here, but somewhere, someone knows exactly where they're sitting and has agreed to play this song just for them in this moment. How, then, did it choose Lizzo? she wonders. And why at such an impractical volume? And how can a hotel be mischievous?

Max nudges a menu toward her. "Again, everything here is

good. The coffee especially." He chuckles. "Not that I have much with which to compare it."

Everything about this place is enchanting, tempting all of Anna's senses, but it's impossible for her to give in completely. "This is wonderful—it is—but I really need to find my dad, and he's obviously not here, and it seems like dessert might take a while. Is there an intercom? Maybe whoever plays the piano might know?" She moves to push the button and ask, but Max covers it with his hand.

"Do you think I've never asked? Do you think I haven't pressed every button in this hotel, asked and then begged and then screamed my questions? No one ever answers. The music changes sometimes, almost like it's apologizing, but there is no voice. There is no manager, no switchboard operator, no omniscient god who condescends to offer any solace. It doesn't work like that."

"Then how does it work? Because everything has a system." Anna is getting annoyed with this place—with Max. It feels like he's not telling her something.

But Max just takes his hand off the button and looks down, his eyes shining wetly. "You accept what the Houdini offers, and if something is supposed to happen, it will. If your dad made it inside, he's in the same situation we are. Safe but stuck. He's probably found a restaurant or a bed—whatever the hotel wanted him to find."

"He's probably looking for me."

"And if the Houdini wants him to find you, believe me, he will."

This answer is not one Anna can accept. When something needs to be done, she finds a way to get it done. As much as she generally likes coffee and dessert, she's not willing to pretend that you get what you want by sitting around and waiting for some mercurial magic to make things happen. She slides out of the booth and stands.

"I've got to go look for him."

Max looks up at her, defeated. "Sure. I understand the necessity you feel. I'll be waiting right here."

Anna cocks her head. "You're not coming with? You won't help me?"

"I just think this is something you need to experience for yourself. Try to go where the Houdini doesn't want you. Try to leave a situation it created just for you. The dessert room doesn't always appear. Sometimes, instead of a curtain, there's a wall. As I said, this place . . ." Max looks around, runs a hand along the curved wall of the barrel. "Just go on. You'll see. If I'm right, maybe it will convince you to stop fighting what you can't best. If I'm wrong, I hope you find what you're looking for. I'll be here."

Confused and, yes, a little disappointed in his response, Anna stalks back down the red hall the way they came. It's not far to the door they entered through, but when she tugs on the knob, the door is locked. Or, more accurately, it feels like it's glued to the jamb, as it doesn't even rattle and the knob doesn't turn.

"Just open, please, will you? I'm getting desperate," she says . . . to the door. Or maybe the hotel.

When she turns the knob again, the door obligingly opens.

But on the other side, she doesn't find the dark stairway lit with candles.

She finds a red hall. She thinks it might be a new one until she comes upon Max waiting in the second-to-last booth. She spins around, certain that he was sitting in the second booth from the door when she left him.

"Confusing, isn't it?" he says.

"This makes no sense."

"Darling, don't I know it." Anna huffs a sigh, and Max adds, "Go on. Try it again. Whatever it will take to convince you."

"Fine!"

Anna storms up the hallway in one direction, then another, tries the door again, pleads with it, shouts at it, stomps her feet. But no matter what she does, there is only a long red hallway and a door.

No way out.

She slumps back into the booth, her mind as fragile as a cracked teacup.

"This is insane."

"Only until you accept it." Max points to the menu. "Sugar will help."

Anna stares at him, a terrifying thought scratching at the back of her brain. "Are you doing this? Are you . . ." A god? The devil? The one in control? She doesn't know how to finish the sentence.

He puts his head in his hands, an ancient sorrow dragging him down. "Believe me, I'm not in charge. I can't control any of this. If I had my way, we'd both find a way out. And you would've gotten here years ago. I'm as trapped as you are."

Anna can't figure out if this is purgatory or if she's going insane, but she's exhausted and tired of trying to make it all make sense, and it's not like she can leave right now anyway. Sugar does sound good. She turns her attention to the extravagant menu, which has dozens of desserts listed, many that she's never even heard of. The long list of coffee drinks grabs her attention; she has to stay alert if she's going to find her dad and plan an escape. Maybe if she does what Max suggests, the hotel—or Max, or whatever—will let her leave. She will give in, or at least pretend to. But she'll be alert. Because someone is messing with her, and she hates that.

Anna looks outside, into the hallway, but there are no half-real waiters, no fellow diners. "Where is everyone?" she asks.

"I've never seen anyone else here. I can only get to the dessert room after I've eaten dinner at Harry's—and only sometimes. I went to the restroom once and saw the velvet curtains for the first time. I've never told anyone about it before." Max runs a finger up and down the polished whorls on the wood table. "I honestly wasn't sure if it would show itself to you. This place has always felt . . . a little shy." He shakes his head like he knows how silly that sounds. "Are you ready to order?"

Anna nods, and he pushes the Requests button.

"An affogato and a tiramisu, please. And?" He looks at Anna, his finger still on the button.

"Affogato and a banana split, please."

Max's lips quirk up just a little as he takes his finger off the button and fiddles with his key. Now that Anna knows no one else is here, not even see-through waiters and dining ghosts, she feels the cloak of intimacy descend, the sudden shyness infecting her, too. Max looks up, and his eyes are just a little too shiny, a little too hopeful. . . .

"Anna, I—"

"Restroom?" she asks, because she feels like he's about to say something she's not ready to hear. It's just too much, too soon, and she needs to see herself in the mirror, slap herself or splash water on her face or find something stuck in her teeth.

She needs proof, on her own, that this is real, and that she really is here.

She needs proof that she, too, is still real.

The more time she spends around Max, the less *real* everything feels.

Maybe the hotel won't let her leave, but surely it'll let her pee.

"Go down the hall and through the door. You can't miss it. When it's behaving, the whole place is a circle."

"But it was just the hallway and the door, before."

"Perhaps it will be something different now."

Now that you're not trying to defy it, he means.

Anna glances back over her shoulder as she heads down the hall, feeling Max's presence like an anchor. He is a riddle to her. Despite the insanity they currently inhabit, he's so at ease, so genuine. So intense. He has no worries, no phone to glance at. She's never met anyone like that. And yet . . . there's something about him she doesn't quite trust. She gives a little nod and follows his directions.

He's right. This time, it's different. The door opens easily and whispers shut behind her. The hallway on the other side—so many hallways!—is brief. There are three doors, two of them purple and marked with gold rabbits, one wearing a top hat and one a dainty tiara. Anna reaches for the doorknob to the lady rabbit's room, but a heavy hand lands on her shoulder, its nails digging in like knives.

"Stop right there."

Anna spins around, flinches, backs away from that hand, those claws.

A new kind of fear thrums in her blood.

A woman stands there, tall and imperious in a suit from the '50s, maybe: a tight, straight skirt and sharply cut jacket with high heels and a pillbox hat. She has bleached-blond hair and looks like Cruella de Vil's younger sister.

Anna steps back, knowing there's no safe place for her here, wondering if she should call out for Max. He said he knew only two people, and he didn't want to be like either of them. Anna wouldn't want to be like this woman, either.

"I'm with Max," Anna says, hands up, as the woman looks like she might try to slash out her eyes with her pointy nails.

"You're not a paying guest of the Houdini."

Anna feels her shoulders go back, her chin jut out. She doesn't like to call attention to her position, but she's not about to roll belly-up for some petty tyrant of a hotel middle manager. "My father is one of the owners of this hotel. Daniel Alonso. He's around here somewhere, and I don't think he'll want to hear that I'm being threatened."

The woman strains to rearrange her face into something like a smile. "Threatened?" She gestures airily, looking around the cave-like room as if hunting for a hidden guillotine. "No one is threatening you. But I will need to confirm your identity, whether you are Mr. Alonso's daughter. That, of course, would be a different situation entirely."

Anna goes for her pockets, but her wallet isn't there. Neither is her phone. She is certain she put them both in the same pocket when she changed, and she's even certain she touched her wallet before dining with Max downstairs, but now they are simply gone. Instead, she finds a deck of cards, which she can't help staring at in the low light. It's like she went for a life jacket and was handed a stone.

"My wallet is gone—"

"I see. Well then. We can't have trespassers in the Houdini, can we? *Mr. Alonso*"—the name comes out mockingly—"would never allow that."

Anna is about to get assertive, but the woman grabs her by the upper arm and yanks her through the wooden door that leads away from where Max waits. They're in a new hallway identical to Max's hall, with a long row of open barrels, each one utterly empty.

"Max!" Anna gulps, right before the woman shoves her into the nearest barrel.

Anna lands hard on the wooden bench and flails to clamber back out of the booth. No one has ever put hands on her before, and her heart is going crazy, her whole body numb, and she wants to kick and lash out and run away, she has to get to safety, but the woman puts her hands on the barrel and spins it with an evil grin. Anna spins with it, and it reminds her of those sickening playground merry-go-rounds that fling children out onto the dirt, but the booth rotates into darkness and stops. The force slams her into the table, knocking the wind out of her. The light is gone. The red hallway is gone. Anna's mouth is open, her body desperate for air, but it only comes in little gasps. The woman has somehow spun the barrel to trap Anna against the wall.

Anna's heart stutters, her blood freezes, she's going to die here, alone, suffocated against a wall—

Except . . . when she extends her arms, there is no wall. Just air. She feels her way out of the booth in complete, consuming, echoing darkness and steps down onto what feels like dusty wood. She's panting now, each breath a desperate gasp.

"Dad?" she yelps. "Max? Somebody, please help."

She turns back to the booth, kneels on the wooden bench, pounds a fist on the back of the barrel, which must be facing the hallway. "Max!" she screams, again and again, hard, feeling that shred in the back of her throat, but there is no answer from the other side, no fist's thumping in response to her own. "Help! Anyone! Please, help!" She calls Max's name again, one last time, a question, but there is no reply.

He's not coming.

No one is.

Anna steps back out into the silent, empty space beyond the booth and flounders along until her fingertips find something smooth. A wall. Shoes shuffling in the dust, fingertips searching along sanded wood boards, tears burning down her cheeks, Anna begins to follow it.

Max said there were hidden places, secret tunnels throughout the Houdini.

It looks like Anna has been abandoned to die in one of them.

17.

Phoebe leaves the barrel turned away and stalks down the hall and out the door before Max comes running and catches her here. The boy has always been full of questions, but she is determined to preserve his ignorance tonight. The girl will disappear, as they always do, and that will be that.

Of all the Houdini's restaurants, this one has never appealed to her—kitschy, the thought of dining in an old wine cask, gorging on gooey sweets and syrupy coffee drinks. She sometimes wonders if the hotel shifts to accommodate those within, if Max brought this place into existence just by wishing it so. It's exactly the thing a darling little mooncalf like him would crave—odd, intimate, mysterious. She loves her boy, would do anything for him, but teenage hormones have made him distant and resentful, as if it's her fault they're trapped here. When he was a baby, he was her entire world, and they explored the hotel together, hand in hand, delighting at each new surprise. But the older he gets, the less there is to discover, and the less he wants to spend time with her, which breaks her heart. He's lonely and depressed, but there's not much she can do about it here. It's not like there's a psychologist on call in this particular magical hotel.

At least whoever brought the dessert room into existence, whether with hands or mind or magic, gave it a shape that allows Phoebe to enter when she wills it, take care of her business, and exit without being forced to explain herself to anyone. The Houdini sometimes resists her. Oddly, this time, it does not.

She doesn't generally think herself cruel, but she needs to separate these children. She is very aware that Max is too malleable, too open, too desperate to taste infatuation. He'd probably fall for a mop wearing a dress, if it agreed to dance to his favorite song, as they used to when he was young. They would put on the gramophone and do the foxtrot, the waltz, East Coast swing. He hasn't asked her to dance in a long time.

It's a bit strange for her, watching her chubby little baby become a man. It was men who landed her in the Houdini, after all. And then there was Colin, with his foolish schemes against her. Not to mention Max's father, who abandoned her once he found out she was pregnant. Her record with men is not good.

So, yes, the would-be lovers must be ripped asunder. Anna is revealing far too much about the other world, which Phoebe has taken such pains to hide from Max. And what's more, the girl is barely putting up a fight against Max's batted eyelashes—how did she possibly come from Daniel Alonso, that heartless, aggressive shark?—and Max is altogether too worshipful already. He stares at Anna like she's the most perfect creature ever put on earth, which is offensive on multiple levels. Phoebe knows that Alonso and the other men need their own time in the hotel to marinate, that her plan has yet to come to fruition. The timing has to be just right. Now that Anna is involved, Phoebe wants Daniel to be desperate to find his daughter; he needs to be confused and lost and frantic, just like Phoebe herself was when she first came here. As for Tony and Sebastian, they need to get past the relief of escaping the storm and start to steep in the unpleasant recognition of what they did the last time they were here. Like Daniel, they need to suffer.

But Anna . . . well, fine. Phoebe is uncomfortable with the way she's influencing Max.

He shouldn't be so attached. He knows what's going to happen to the girl, after all.

And besides, it's perfectly safe. This secret passageway trundles along for a bit and then simply opens up on the fifth-floor hall as if it's any other room. The hotel will keep Anna safe—at least until the clock strikes midnight. Probably.

That's part of the magic for Phoebe and her son—it may be lonely and strange and quiet, but Phoebe never worried that baby Max would topple out a window or tumble down the stairs or stick a sterling silver fork into an ancient electrical outlet. The hotel loves Max, and Arielle has been given firm orders to keep him safe without ever allowing herself to be in the same room with him—not that she can, technically, be in any of the rooms. Even Phoebe doesn't know how Arielle does it, whether it's a projection or a mirage or what. The magic governing her is as peculiar as that which controls the Houdini, but Phoebe has learned enough to ensure her bidding is done.

Although Anna has no such protections, she's most likely safe enough. If there's any danger in the Houdini, it's that one can wander for so long, enamored of discovery and charmed by magic, with neither ambition nor direction. One can lose one's way— almost as if the hotel wished it so. In a place without beginnings and ends, it's possible to go more than a bit mad.

But not Phoebe. She's focused. She's certain. She's been waiting for this day for a very long time. She knows what needs to happen, and she knows how things will turn out. Let the children be lost for a while. Let the men wander.

Everything will go her way, in the end. Her little pet Arielle will make sure of it.

18.

Anna feels like she's underground in some ancient catacomb, not in a secret hallway in a hotel. The tunnel behind the barrel goes on far longer than it has any right to. She should have asked Max more about his secret passageways, but then again, she has so many questions for Max that it can feel a little overwhelming.

Time has no meaning as she struggles through the darkness. With no way to see where she is and where she's been, there's no telling how far she's walked, how many minutes have ticked past on the clock.

There's no way to know how close it is to midnight, or even if the midnight deadline is real. Logic and reason suggest that people don't just turn into ghosts because a clock hand moves. But the look on Max's face, the desolation there—

Anna walks faster.

The passage goes on forever, far past the physical bounds of the building itself. The darkness never changes. There are no openings, no corners, no doors or windows. She even switches sides a few times to see if perhaps she's just been on the wrong side of the hallway, but both sides are equally infuriating, equally dark. She knocks on the walls, feels along the seam between the floor and the footboard. But as far as she can tell, there are no openings, no secret triggers. She feels like Sarah in *Labyrinth* but is far too self-conscious, even in this state, to have a similar temper tantrum.

"A little light might help?" she tentatively asks.

"Help help help," the hallway echoes back at her, but no helpful string of lights drives the darkness away.

Her progress is painfully slow, as going too fast could end with her tumbling into a hole or tripping and falling hard on the floor. This secret cavern is no place to be hurt. She shuffles forward, senses reaching, mind begging for some kind of change, something to signal that she's near the end, whatever the end may be.

Finally, exhausted, her feet aching and dusty, Anna puts her back against the wall—which turned from wood to stone somewhere along the way—and slides down to sit, her legs out in front of her. The dress, once elegant and light, now feels like a filthy potato sack, stuck to her lower back with sweat. The shoes, although well fitting, were not made for this much walking. Cobwebs halo her head, and her fingertips are coated with grime.

"Hello?" she calls down the hallway.

"Hello?" the echo returns.

"Are you there?"

"Are you there?"

"I think so."

"I think so."

It's only an echo, but it reminds her that she is real, that whatever this is must be the middle of her journey, not the end. Discomfort, after all, is what happens in the middle of things. Despite her racing heart, Anna won't lose hope, won't give up, won't dare let herself fall asleep here. The thought of waking up in the unforgiving dark, alone, is terrifying.

The thought of waking up here and discovering she's not alone is even worse.

"A little help would be wonderful," she calls. "I'm getting scared."

This time, the echo doesn't return, but there is a sound, somewhere up ahead, a light, nervous scrabbling in the scree. Anna pulls herself to standing, her legs aching.

"Hello?" she calls again, nervous now.

When she squints, she can just make out a smudge of white against the darkness, down on the ground. Surely it's not . . . another rabbit?

Anna hurries after it, sending out her senses, watching the shifting shape, keeping one hand running along the wall. The manner of movement certainly suggests that it's a rabbit, alternately sprinting and pausing and lolloping. It doesn't make sense that it's the same rabbit she saw in the basement, because this is obviously not the basement and rabbits aren't known for being good at stairs or elevators, but it *is* her third instance of seeing a rabbit in the Houdini, and that supports the idea that the hotel is somehow overrun with them. Perhaps, long ago, some magician's pet rabbits got loose and did what rabbits do, and now here she is, blundering after one of their great-grandchildren in the dark. It appears and disappears and reappears up ahead, flashing like a shooting star, and Anna follows as best she can.

Finally, her shoe strikes something—but gently at least, as she's been prepared for this eventuality. She stops, feels around with her foot, decides that it's maybe the size of a cinder block. Up ahead, there's a flickering orange light. She can't see the rabbit anywhere. Slowly, carefully, she steps over the stone and feels for the next one amid a tumble of gravel. The floor has gone from dusty wood boards to ragged stone littered with . . .

Anna stoops down, feels around. Chunks of rock, rough but with some cut edges, like rejects from a quarry. She leaves the safety of the wall, uses both her hands to crawl along toward the light, squatting and climbing, sitting and hopping down as the rocks get bigger. There's a rip, and she grimaces, thinking about the damage the beautiful old dress must be suffering. The light is closer now, revealing more stones and one bigger structure, upright and so familiar.

Is it . . . a vault?

Like in a cemetery?

It's a smallish building with columns and two lights, one on either side of a door, throwing grotesque shadows over gargoyles that leer down from a sloping roof. In front of the door is a statue, a woman slumped over in a tall chair.

But wait—the statue isn't striated gray marble like the rest of the structure. It's painted in white and peach, and—

Anna does not like horror movies or books, and the thought of a dead body fills her with dread. Yes, it's quite logical, dying, but she doesn't want to do it anytime soon, nor does she consider it a good idea to mess with the dead. She doesn't want to be alone in . . . here. With . . . that.

The shape sighs, and Anna just about collapses in relief.

"Hello?" she all but whispers, her voice loud in the silent crypt.

The shape looks up and rises from its slump, and it's a beautiful girl in a long white nightdress, her white-blond hair to her hips and loose with ripples. She looks like she walked out of the moors in an Emily Brontë novel and sat down in the first chair she found, and her eyes, such a light blue they might be white, are wet with tears.

"Are you all right?" Anna asks.

"All right?" the girl echoes, considering it. "No way, kid. Things have been wrong for a long time."

The girl stands with an odd clanking sound, cocks her head, and looks Anna up and down. Now that Anna's eyes have adjusted to the low light, she can see more details. It would indeed appear that they're in an underground cavern with nothing but this strange, lonely, out-of-place crypt, and there are more lights beyond the structure, angling up a set of stone steps. Anna desperately wants to rush to those well-lit stairs like a moth to flame, but she's not about to leave someone crying in a crypt, all alone, even if that someone is really, really strange.

Everything here, as it turns out, is really, really strange.

The girl shuffles her feet, and metal scrapes on stone.

There—a chain, its metal cuff tight around the girl's ankle.

Someone *chained this girl to a crypt.*

Adrenaline pumps into Anna's system. She searches the shadows for some waiting monster, her ears straining for the footsteps of the girl's returning captor like she's been air-dropped into a serial killer movie. "Are we in danger? Do I need to find help?" She reaches down and picks up a rock.

At that, the girl smiles and puts up her hands with a calm gentleness that does not match the current situation. "We're not in danger. At least, you're not. I've been chained here for years. But there is a way you can help me."

The girl is maybe Emily's age, in her early twenties. She looks young and innocent but also tired and sad. Anna wonders if Max knows about her—but surely not. He's not the kind of person who could happily live his life with some girl chained up in the hotel.

Is he?

No, not Max.

But the creeper in the basement or the cruel woman who pushed Anna into the tunnel?

Maybe.

Which makes Anna wonder: Max said he knew two other people, but Anna has now met three other people. So does that mean Max is unaware of the cruel woman, the aggressive janitor, or the captive girl?

Hopefully the captive girl. That makes the most sense.

That makes Max someone she can trust.

Then again, from what Anna understands so far, not everything here is what it seems and can be trusted. The girl's form, at least, is solid, not like the diners in the restaurant. You can't chain someone to a rock if they don't have form. This girl seems . . . more real. And yet that's not comforting. Whatever the girl is, she's definitely not normal, and she shouldn't be here. Anna's practical side notes that there's no food tray, no jug of water, no bucket for bodily functions, no way to wash the long, silken hair that doesn't appear neglected. She said she's been here for years, but she looks like she just arrived. It makes no sense.

"What do you need?" Anna asks, willing her heart to calm before its pounding fills the cavern.

The girl steps forward, eager, her chain dragging and pulling taut. She lifts up her leg to show a heavy lock holding the manacle. "All I need is the key."

Anna looks around the cavern, her suspicions in no way lessened. Is this . . . some kind of dungeon? The ceiling is higher here, the scent of cold rock and old dust hangs heavy. It doesn't seem like part of a hotel. "Can we just bash it in? I have this rock—"

"It won't work. Believe me—I've tried. I need the key."

"Where is it?"

The girl shakes her head. "I don't know exactly. Somewhere in the Houdini."

Anna's brain requires more information than this to function. Her mind is spinning like she's short-circuiting, her breath coming fast like she's possibly having her first non-schoolwork-related panic attack. "So you were kidnapped, but you're not currently in danger, and someone chained you to a rock, and now I need to find the key, but you can't tell me where it is? Can't we just call the police?"

The girl sits back down on the chair looking sad and exhausted beyond her years. "Surely you've been here long enough to know the police can't help."

Anna shrugs, considers what she knows of the Houdini so far and what Max has told her. "I've been here long enough to know that if the key was easy to find, and if the Houdini wanted you to have it, then you would already have it. None of this makes any sense. There's no logic."

"There used to be logic. Perfectly good logic. But then things went all topsy-turvy." The girl's eyes are piercing, fierce and sad. "I've been trapped here so long that I think I might be going a bit mad."

"Okay" is all Anna can say. "But why—"

The girl interrupts, speaking in a rush. "Aw, applesauce, honey. Look, it's easy. I landed in the wrong spot and got stuck here a long time ago, and I was naive and stupid and trusted the wrong person, and I got betrayed. I should've been free to go, but Phoebe chained me up again so I couldn't leave." Her voice is high and quick, like the women in those old musicals Emily loves, the ones where everyone breaks out into song and choreographed dances. It sounds out of place, here in a crypt, as if Anna expected her to sound like a consumptive English girl in a Poe story.

"Is Phoebe the mean blond lady with the fingernails?" The girl nods. "And she did this to you?"

"Phoebe didn't catch me, but she didn't let me go," the girl corrects unhelpfully. "And all I need's the key. So will you help me?"

Anna glances at the wall of the crypt, right over the girl's head.

It has only one word, she sees now: CELESTE. There are no dates. "But who's Celeste? Is that you?"

The girl wrinkles her nose. "Heavens no. She's the one who was in charge before Phoebe. They're both bad apples. All I want's to be free. Surely you can understand that." She gives a wink and points to a grandfather clock that has suddenly appeared out of nowhere, sprouting from the rock like an awkward sunflower.

Three-fifteen.

A shiver ripples down Anna's back.

This is madness. This is something out of a movie. This is a hallucination.

Crypts don't belong in hotels in Las Vegas.

Girls are not chained to rocks.

Clocks do not appear from the ether.

"I don't understand—" she starts, voice quavering.

"Just say you'll find it. Please. You're my only hope."

Anna feels the weight of everything she needs to do bearing down on her shoulders—escape the tunnel, find Max, find her dad, find some mysterious key, check on Emily and her mom, get out of the hotel and back to her regular life—by midnight—or she'll get turned into a ghost. But what is she going to say? No?

No, sorry, I'll be abandoning you in your torture dungeon next to a grave.

"I'll try. What does this key look like? Where should it be?" And before the girl can tell her, Anna adds, "I just got here, so I don't know my way around. Which is how I ended up down here, I guess."

The girl exhales and refocuses with a hopeful smile. "Look, kid, I don't know what the key looks like. I can't see it. I've been forbidden to look for it. Phoebe's hidden it from me." She leans forward. "But you can find it, because Phoebe underestimates you. If you get me that key, I can get you out, too. Once I'm free, I can get all of us out. But you have to find it by midnight. That's checkout time."

"But I got here at midnight. . . ."

The girl smiles softly like she's talking to a silly child. "The next midnight, of course."

Anna's dad owns several hotels, and she knows full well that a midnight checkout is complete nonsense, but she doesn't want to argue. "Okay, but . . . even if you haven't seen the key, you've got to tell me what to look for. Do you think it would be the same metal as the lock?"

The girl cocks her head. "I got no idea. It's just a key. But it's different. Special. Magical. Might have a kind of glow about it. And Phoebe will do anything to keep it."

"Where is it?"

The girl's eyes are fathomlessly mournful. "Ya know that ol' joke about whether God could make a rock so big God himself couldn't lift it? Let's just say that if I knew where it was, I'd already be gone."

Anna looks down. It's so dark here that she can't see her feet, they just disappear under the hem of her dress. Her hands shake; she has that homesick feeling she got her first time skiing, like she was so far from home and comfort and everything familiar that she wanted to lie down and cry in the snow. "This place is huge and weird, and I keep getting lost, and the elevator won't do what I want it to. What hope do I have?"

The girl grabs her by the shoulders and shakes her once, decisively. "I have faith in you, kid. You're the first good thing that's happened here in sixteen years."

"What happened sixteen years ago?"

The girl sits back down on the stone chair, pulling her knees up to her chin. Her hair shimmers in the flickering light.

"Max was born," she says softly. "He's a sweet boy, but . . ."

Anna goes on alert. "But?"

The girl leans her head back against the stone wall, closes her eyes, and sighs. "But he can't help me. He can't see me. He doesn't even know I'm here."

"Why not?"

The girl puts her feet down on the ground, lines her arms up on the chair's arms. Her eyes go distant, like she's looking past Anna, past time itself. "Because his mother forbade it. So many rules about little Maximillian. So many rules *for* him. He has wants of his own, you know. We could all be free, but Phoebe made her own cage. . . ."

Understanding falls like a stone. Anna can't believe she didn't see it before—

The resemblance. If Phoebe's hair wasn't dyed—

"Wait, are you saying . . . Phoebe is Max's mom?"

The girl nods. "Come on, kid. You're a sharp cookie. Did you think they were strangers?" She tilts her head. "He didn't tell you, then. . . ."

"No, he didn't."

One shoulder lifts. "Max has secrets of his own, I guess."

"What's that supposed to mean?"

At first, Anna thought the girl's eyes were light, but now they seem much darker, some trick of the shadow.

"I'm saying everything I'm allowed to. There are limits. You've got to do some of the work yourself, honey. Just promise me you'll find the key. And promise me you won't tell Max anything about me."

"Why not?"

"Contracts and loopholes. There are things here beyond your understanding. Just promise."

The moment is awkward and charged. "I . . . I don't know. . . ."

"No! Promise you'll help me. Promise you'll find it. Promise you won't say anything." The sound of the chain rattling is threatening in the silence, and Anna stares at the heavy links, wondering how long the manacle has been there and if the girl's ankle is rubbed raw and bloody under the hem of her nightgown, and why the woman—Phoebe—would do such a thing, and how?

"Who feeds you?" she asks the girl, the true depths of this tragedy sinking in. "Surely they bring you water?"

"Promise me!" the girl screams, and it seems to echo forever through the cavern.

It hurts, it hurts down to Anna's bones, and she covers her ears but it doesn't help, and when she can't handle it anymore, she shouts, "Fine! I promise!" just so the sound will stop.

And stop it does.

The cavern goes completely silent.

"What was that?" Anna asks hoarsely in the emptiness afterward.

The girl doesn't answer. When Anna steps closer, some strange illusion makes the girl seem like she, too, is part of the tomb, chiseled out of cold marble, forever rigid on a chair.

"Hello?" Anna says.

The girl doesn't answer, but there's an echo up ahead, where orange lights flicker promisingly.

When Anna reaches out to shake the girl's shoulder, she finds only hard rock.

The girl is a statue.

Even her shackle and chain are carved into the stone.

A chill runs up Anna's spine as she realizes she's alone.

Either it's a trick or it's magic, and either way, Anna doesn't want to be here anymore.

She turns away from the stone girl and toward the lights, and without her brain's input, her body scrambles over the rocks and toward the candles, following the little flames up a ragged set of stone stairs and down another tunnel. She's desperate to get out of this place, to be back in the hotel proper, back to carpet and gaslights and warmth and chummy, old-timey tunes, back to a place where the people might be incorporeal but at least they're not hewn into crypts, blood warm one moment and deathly cold the next.

Up ahead, there's a bright line of light shining under a door. Anna moves faster to reach it. The stones get progressively smaller, and then she's back on wood floors littered with pebbles, then dust. The walls close in, a hallway narrow enough for her to touch the sides with both hands. When she looks over her shoulder, she's not sure what she's scared of, but she can't wait to escape it.

Still, there's some lingering feeling, like she's not quite alone.

With the next heartbeat, Anna reaches the door, puts a hand firmly on warm wood and exhales. This is the feeling a child gets playing tag, when they hit home base right before they were going to be caught.

"Can I trust Max?" she asks the empty darkness behind her.

When the unmistakable voice answers, it sounds like it's coming through yet another one of those crackling speakers overhead, not echoing from the crypt in the darkness. "Honey, if I've learned anything here, it's that trusting people just puts you in their power. Maybe you think someone's a good egg, but you never know what's under that shiny shell. So don't say boo. You have until midnight to find the key."

Anna stares up at the nothingness. There are so many rules, so few answers. It goes against her grain, against who she is. She needs a framework of logic, the safety net of reason. She needs things to make sense, and they very much don't.

"What happens if I can't find the key before midnight?" Anna presses.

"Then we're all stuck here together in our gilded cage." The voice is sad now, resigned. "Phoebe and Max will go on as they are, but you'll be just like the rest of the guests, fading away to a memory. There's no vacancies here. Ever."

In the silence that follows, Anna thinks about the people in the restaurant, forever murmuring and eating, blurry and clueless and not quite there. A chill descends, and she rubs her arms, willing warmth back into her skin. What would it feel like, to be one of those people, to go from a living, breathing person to a thoughtless, insubstantial loop forever caught on replay?

It's like dying, but almost worse, somehow.

"Who are you?" Anna calls.

There's no answer.

She's more lost than she was before.

She turns the doorknob and pushes the door open.

19.

Max waits a reasonable amount of time—or what he thinks might be reasonable, because how would he know?—and then checks his pocket watch for the hundredth time and stands. Both of their affogatos have melted to soup, and still Anna hasn't come back. He would assume that following a lady to the restroom is considered rude in any time and culture, but he can't imagine what might have happened to her.

He checks his breath—coffee-tinted by now, but not horrible—and walks down the hall toward the restroom, calling her name like a besotted Shakespearean fool.

"Anna? Hello? Are you well?"

There is no answer, no shuffle of reticent shoes in the hall.

Did he offend her?

Did he frighten her?

Is he secretly as repugnant as Colin?

Max pushes past the wood door and into the hall that connects the two sides of the restaurant. Maybe there's been some sort of bathroom malfunction or she's had a feminine problem. He's always been curious, and he's read up on the female experience in both nonfiction and fiction, with a particular interest in romance novels, but the books are decidedly coy about the secret mysteries of femininity, and there's no way he could broach the topic with his mother. It occurs to him that he has never entered a women's restroom in the hotel, that he has no idea how it might differ from the men's room.

God, what awkward things to think about while he's worried he's lost Anna forever.

He knocks on the door.

"Anna? I don't want to seem uncouth, but it's been . . . a while."

There's no answer.

"I'm coming in."

Max's heart is in his throat as he pushes open the mysterious, forbidden door, whispering an apology to the lady bunny with her crown. The room within is a reflection of the men's room across the hall, except that there are lights around the mirror and a wicker cabinet by the sink. There is no sign of Anna, and both stall doors are wide open, leaving no room for anyone to hide.

"Curiouser and curiouser," he mumbles, checking both stalls thoroughly just to be sure that Anna hasn't, say, fallen into a toilet or something equally odd. In the Houdini, anything is possible. One of the ovens in the kitchen of Harry's Hideaway, for example, leads to a dollhouse in the back of the toy store.

To his great concern, and relief, Anna is not in a toilet. On his way out, he opens the wicker chest and pokes around, glad to see that despite the fact that Phoebe is the only woman in the Houdini and she detests the dessert room, a wide variety of helpful items have been provided, from hygiene products to dental floss, toothbrushes, lotion, and a single tube of lipstick that Max is too shy to open.

There is no place in the restroom where Anna could possibly hide, no hidden door in the chest, no way to conceal a panel or trapdoor amid the tile. She didn't pass by his booth, so she must have gone out through the door that leads to the other side of the restaurant—and the Houdini must have allowed it. Max's cheeks go hot—the hotel has made him a liar. He told her she wouldn't get anywhere, but she has clearly gone somewhere else.

Back in the hallway, he continues on, through the wooden door and into the empty side, the only logical place Anna could be. It usually connects back to the front lobby, and he's often wondered why it exists at all, but over the years, he's discovered many things in the hotel that have no reason to exist—stairs to nowhere, an elevator with only one floor, a room inexplicably filled with broken eyeglasses—so he's merely accepted it.

There.

One of the barrels is . . . facing the wrong way?

In every other doorway, there's a matching booth, table, and call box, but in this one, there is only the rounded back of a wine barrel pushing out into the hall. Max puts a hand flat against the curved wood.

He's never seen the dessert room do this. He didn't know any of the barrels could turn.

This must be where Anna has gone, although he can't think of a single explanation for it.

He thumps on the wood, calls her name, struggles to spin the barrel back around.

It won't budge.

Max tries to turn the next booth, and then the next, every barrel down both sides of the hallway, but none of them so much as wiggle. He runs his hands all around the doorway, looks for the buttons and levers and switches that he's come to recognize as calling cards of some mysterious new pathway to add to the map of the hotel he keeps rolled up under the library couch, started years ago in shaky pencil and continued with stronger lines once he got older and grew more confident in his drafting skills. He doesn't think there's a tunnel here, but he could be wrong. He needs to go check.

As he stands alone in the hallway, a shiver skitters up his neck. He knows this hotel. He grew up here. He trusts it. It may play tricks, but it has never harmed him. It has, in fact, gone out of its way to keep him safe, even when he didn't wish it.

So why did it help Anna leave him? He wants her back more than he's ever wanted anything in his entire life.

His mind rushes a mile a minute, his heart struggling to match it, as he considers the other people in this hotel. Phoebe and Colin. Anna's father and her father's friends, supposedly.

Anna must be with one of them.

And Max *will* get her back.

He walks the entire perimeter of the restaurant, shoes falling soft on the red carpet, calling Anna's name. At first he is tentative, then brash, then angry. He checks both restrooms again, runs his hands over the walls looking for secret tunnels he's never sought before, kicks the trash can over, denting it, punches a wall and, as always, hits a stud. The Houdini does not like being punched. He tries every barrel down the original hall, unsurprised when none of them move despite his desperate wrenching and shoving.

Back at his table, Max considers the objects at hand and picks up his spoon. He stirs Anna's neglected affogato until it's a uniform mess of gold-tinged melted ice cream and carefully, so carefully, uses the sugary liquid to spell out his message on the dark wood table. Brevity is important, so he hopes she'll understand the lack of any flourishes.

I wait where we met. —M.

He wants to say more, but they are not the only people in the hotel. And anyway, no one writes florid letters to people they just met using melted ice cream. Sure, he might've used his notebook, but paper is so easily blown away or slipped into a pocket. He also knows damn well that Anna doesn't have an elevator key, which means he has no idea how she could possibly get to the library, provided that's where she wanted to go, provided she isn't actively running away from him because he's a strange, lonely boy who grew up playing with ghosts and talking into a speaker, but . . .

Well, she found the library in the first place, didn't she? And what else is there for him to say, to do? As ever, he is at the mercy of the Houdini, and now, so is she.

This missive will have to suffice.

Satisfied, Max pushes the button on the call box and leans

in to speak. "I left her a message. Please don't clean it up until I find her."

In response, the piano picks up with a soulful rendition of Patsy Cline's "Walkin' After Midnight." Max snorts. He wonders if he's the only person in the world with his own personal soundtrack. He long ago stopped wondering how it works. It's just a part of him now.

He calls Anna's name on his way down the stairs, out through Harry's Hideaway, and into the foyer. He sees no sign of her. The table where they sat earlier is spotless again, the chairs pushed in and the menus and folded napkins waiting. The same people continue to have the same conversations they've had in the same seats for the past sixteen years. Max has watched enough movies to wonder if this is how normal people think about trees, things that are there and alive but unreachable, unknowable beings that can only serve as landmarks. He would very much like to see a real, live tree one day.

He checks every restaurant and shop on the fourth floor. Anna is nowhere to be found. There is no glass slipper left behind to mark her passage, no trail of gumdrops to follow. He twirls his key, checks his pocket watch, even though time is an imaginary construct when there's no day and night. His mother gave him the watch when he was quite young, told him that caring for fine things was a mark of maturity. He keeps it tightly wound and set to the clock in the lobby, even though there's no reason to be on time. It gives him a sense of comfort and stability, somehow.

In the elevator, he considers searching every floor, but Phoebe forbade him to interact with the men, and he knows better than to disobey her. He isn't sure how she manages it, but she knows his every rebellious move, knows any time he crosses some invisible line—and punishes him for it. The first time he tried to run away, he was six and unhappy with her thoughts on eating dessert for every meal. They quarreled, and he said some passionate but laughable things, crafted a bindle out of a handkerchief and an old, twisted wand he found in a prop room, and headed for the back door, which he'd found while exploring a few days before.

But when he emerged from the secret passageway, bindle in hand, there was Phoebe, frowning, arms crossed.

"Go on and try," she said. "Try to leave."

Max stepped forward, uncertain. Was this a game? Would she punish him for following her command?

He put his hand on the metal push bar of the door marked Exit, and he pushed with all his might, and it didn't move a single bit.

"I told you that you can never leave. Did you think it was a rule I made up?" Tall and imperious and strong as iron, Phoebe put her adult hands on the same bar and leaned into it, pushing hard enough to make herself grunt. "I can't leave either. We're trapped here together. You'll come back here and push on it some time when you think I'm not watching, my love, and you'll find it just as unmoving as I."

She was right.

Over the years, Max went back to that door, again and again. When he was older, when he was bigger, when he'd been doing a hundred push-ups a day, then five hundred. When he'd learned to pick locks and craft minor explosives, because old books are incredible things.

The door never budged.

It did have a slight smear from an explosion.

And Phoebe always knew.

"Tried again, did we?" she said over supper, back when they used to dine together. "And how did that work for you?" When he didn't answer, just kept eating his soup, she added, "You might as well accept our reality. We're fortunate. Children are starving in Africa, as your grandmother used to say."

"There is no Africa here," he muttered back.

"Exactly."

And the next day, the door was gone, just a smoothly wall-papered wall where it once stood. Max still checks the revolving door in the lobby every day. It never opens or even moves. He would try it again right now if he was willing to run into the interlopers and risk Phoebe's wrath.

Thing is—and he's thought about this a good bit—Phoebe never told him not to speak with Anna. She didn't even tell him Anna is here—hell, she might not even know. So he's in the clear to search for her, to find her, to stare at her over a candlelit table, to smell the faint, floral perfume in her hair when he's behind her on the stairs, a scent so different from anything he's ever known, lighter somehow, airier.

The elevator feels bigger without Anna beside him. The rooms feel drafty. The hallway seems dark and empty and perhaps a little shabby. Max checks that Phoebe isn't around—not that she spends much time on this floor. They've just naturally divided the hotel up into their own domains over the years, and she prefers her penthouse on the top floor and the ballroom on the second. They keep to their territories. When Max was thirteen and hit his first growth spurt, she walked in on him inspecting a very intriguing magazine he'd found, and he angrily told her he needed more privacy, and then she stopped checking in unless she had a reason. They've grown distant, since then. Even though it's not Phoebe's fault they're stuck here, he still blames her, knowing full well she seems just as miserable as he is.

Max bursts into the library, hoping against hope that Anna will be there. She's not, but he's accustomed to disappointment. He switches out records, puts on *Nina Simone at Town Hall* and pulls out his map from under the couch. There must be something behind that turned barrel in the dessert room.

But what?

20.

There is a room in the Houdini Max
has never seen—well, there are actually many rooms he's never
seen—but this one in particular is dominated by slot machines,
brightly colored behemoths that each look like a friendly robot
made babies with a nuclear-era refrigerator. This casino can only
be found if one looks in just the right place, and if one is the sort
of person who might be enticed by the opportunity to pull a lever
and hear the musical chime of pennies hitting the floor as bright
lights blink. A preternatural fug of cigarette smoke forever drifts
aimlessly about the ceiling.

"I didn't know the Houdini had a casino," Sebastian says as the
men stumble in from the endless hallway.

"I'll take anything other than doors that won't open." Tony
twists this way and that until his back cracks.

The last to emerge from the hallway, Daniel perks up and
rushes forward. "Anna? Anna!" he calls, his voice thick with worry.

"She's not in here, bud," Tony says, clapping him roughly, almost punishingly, on the shoulder. His eyes light up as he approaches a brightly blinking slot machine with a bucket of shiny pennies sitting alluringly beside it. "But maybe you should look around while we take a little break."

Tony sits on the stool and pops a penny into the machine, his eyes going glassy as he pulls the lever.

"Looks like everyone left in a hurry." Sebastian finds an open bottle of champagne and three flutes sitting on the bar. "Good tornado safety, bad business practice." He pours out the champagne and delivers drinks to his friends.

Daniel just stares at his champagne and shakes his head before setting the glass down. "Come on, guys. We wasted enough time with the cigars. My daughter is missing. We've got to find her and get somewhere safe. Put down the champagne and pennies and let's keep looking."

Tony blows a raspberry and pulls the lever again. "I keep telling you, Danny boy, the girl's fine. She ran inside, they took her to the basement, and that's all there is to it. You saw her come in. What do you think she did, run out the back door and right into the tornado?"

Daniel's face is suffused in horror. "Oh God, do you think she'd do that? Do you think she went back for us? She's always so worried about everybody else—"

"It was a joke!" Tony growls, feeding another penny into the slot machine. "Just settle down and ride out the storm."

Sebastian finds another bucket of pennies on a different slot machine and flicks out his jacket before sitting down and pulling his own lever. "She's fine. These are big jackpots, and the pennies are free. What else are we going to do?"

"Look for Anna!" Daniel roars.

"Don't be an idiot."

Daniel strides to Tony's slot machine and slaps the bucket of pennies to the ground, where they scatter and roll everywhere. "Worrying about my daughter does not make me an idiot!"

Tony stands, his hands in fists. "Nobody said it did!"

Daniel shakes his head, confused. "You just said, 'Don't be an idiot.'"

Tony sneers. "I didn't say that."

"You did. You said, 'Don't be an idiot,' clear as day. You think I don't know your voice?" Daniel looks to Sebastian. "You heard that, right?"

Sebastian nods, his eyes not leaving the blinking machine. "He did indeed say that. I heard it."

Tony's jaw drops. "I didn't say it, but you're both acting like idiots now!"

Sebastian huffs fussily. "I'm just minding my own business. This night is entirely ridiculous."

"You're ridiculous!"

Sebastian abruptly stands, sending his stool crashing to the ground. "Don't shout at me because you're annoyed with him!" he all but shrieks at Daniel.

But now Daniel looks entirely perplexed. "I didn't."

"You did!" Tony shouts. His face is red, his champagne long gone. "I heard you!" Mockingly, he says, "Think I don't know your voice?"

Daniel looks around the cavernous, hazy room. There are no other people, no windows. The air smells of cigarette smoke and desperation with a hint of spilled liquor gone sticky. Music gently flutters down from the speakers set high overhead, women singing something jaunty and German about beer. "I don't want to fight with you guys. We've got over twenty years of working together, and we can't let one crazy storm and too much liquor come between us."

Tony nods once, says, "Yeah, fine, whatever," and ducks down to scrape a few pennies off the floor, then moves to the next slot machine. He yanks the handle and comes up with a cherry, an orange, and a sideways blue grape. He hasn't won yet, and the longer he goes without a win, the angrier he gets. This is why Daniel tries to keep him away from casinos. "Sebastian, top me up?"

Sebastian reluctantly leaves his own slot machine to bring over the champagne, but before he can fill the glass, Tony grabs the bottle and swigs from it.

"Guys, you can go to the casino any time you want. We've got to find my daughter—" Daniel starts.

Across the room a bell rings—a winning slot machine. Lights blink on and off and pennies pour to the ground. Tony and Sebastian run for it and scoop the coins into their pockets.

"Are you kidding me?" Daniel follows them, incredulous. "You both make more than that in an hour while you're asleep. We've got to keep looking for Anna—"

Halfway across the room, another jackpot sounds, and Tony and Sebastian look at one another, confused, for a single heartbeat before running toward the musical sound of coins pouring forth. These are nickels, and they go through a comical dance, turning the pennies out of their pockets and shoving in nickels instead.

"There's more money in the bucket than there is on the ground!" Daniel shouts, but it's like they don't even hear him.

As soon as the bell stops ringing, yet another machine goes berserk, a higher bell, and the two men run to it as one, called to the promise of money raining onto the carpet. Dimes! They pull out nickels and pennies, stuff down dimes. They look like yokels on some game show, so overcome with bells and lights their brains are short-circuiting.

When the fourth machine sounds, they take off at a run, knowing the pattern. If it began with pennies, then nickels, then dimes, this one will surely be—quarters!

"How drunk are you guys?" Daniel asks, trailing behind. He picks up the champagne bottle—empty now, of course—and slams it back on the counter. "This isn't important—"

"You know what?" Tony says, scooping quarters into his pockets. "Maybe you're not the one who should get to decide what's important. You act so high and mighty, like you're in charge, but let me tell you, bud—you're not my boss. And maybe I'm sick of letting you call the shots."

Daniel steps forward, tosses his jacket on the ground, and unbuttons his cuffs. "Okay, you want to go there? Fine, we'll go there. What are you gonna do about it?"

Sebastian subtly picks up the empty champagne bottle, fist tightening around its neck. "Don't start a fight you can't win, Daniel."

"This has been a long time coming, old buddy," Tony says, standing and cracking his knuckles.

His sleeves rolled up and his hands in fists, Daniel squares off with his two best friends. "I'm not scared of you. Either of you."

Tony steps forward, a grin spreading under his oft-broken nose.

"Maybe you should be."

21.

Anna has no idea what she'll find when she pushes open the mysterious door—she just hopes it isn't another crypt. She squints against the light and steps into something she's never seen but has definitely heard of.

A speakeasy.

It's a small bar with the same antediluvian elegance as the rest of the hotel. The walls are a deep, luscious green with dark wood trim, and the floor is all hexagonal white tiles with, every so often, a tile painted with a birdcage or a dainty yellow canary or a golden star. Hundreds of old-fashioned Edison light bulbs hang from the tin ceiling at slightly different elevations. The bar is a great, hulking carved masterpiece of gleaming wood that holds what seems like a thousand bottles reflected in the cracked mirror behind, and the only seats are high stools along it. The short wall Anna has just come through is a black bookshelf filled with gorgeous leather tomes, their gilt stampings glowing gold in the light. The whole bar is maybe ten feet across and four times as long. It feels intimate, like a train car, like the whole room might suddenly start vibrating and roll somewhere else entirely. Knowing what she knows of the Houdini so far, the idea isn't so far-fetched.

As in the rest of the hotel, there are people here, or rather the shadows of them. Several couples, their heads close together as they whisper, and a few singletons. Everyone has a drink but no two drinks are alike, not their glasses or their colors or their garnishes. One is tall and black with a big flower of pineapple hanging off the side; one is juicy magenta and foamy; one is literally on fire, blue flame in a ceramic bowl. The drinkers are a strange mixture of there and not there, watered down but not see-through, three-dimensional but not solid. The orchestral music piped in from the overhead speakers is jaunty and galloping, no vocals.

The bartender is handsome in that old-fashioned, beard-and-a-curly-mustache way that Emily loves, with a brightly colored handkerchief in his back pocket and his crisp white sleeves rolled up to show a single tattoo of a faded snake on one arm. He's polishing a glass, utterly absorbed in his work, and Anna has the oddest instinct not to bother him.

But here's the other thing: there is no door.

She turns to look at the one she just walked through, but it somehow closed silently behind her and now blends in perfectly with the wall of books, and when she tries to tug it open, it doesn't give, nor does it have an obvious mechanism—a statue or a book poking out, just so—that invites inquiry. Anna can't even tell where the bookcase becomes a door, or if it has simply ceased to be a door. It's just her and the bar, and she has no idea what to do.

There's nothing for it; she has to ask the bartender. She walks up to him, puts a hand on the bar. He looks down at her hand, raises an eyebrow, and she hides that hand behind her back.

"Can you please tell me how to leave?" she asks, well aware that her voice is the loudest one in the space, maybe in the whole hotel.

One corner of his mouth quirks up. "You'll need the password, doll." She's almost surprised that he answered. He's the most solid person in the room, but his voice sounds once removed, like she's hearing him underwater or from the other side of a door. Still, like the waiter, he is clearly responding to her and isn't just, say, acting out a memory.

"I thought you needed a password to get into a speakeasy, not get out of one," Anna says.

"Both sides of the door have a keyhole. You just need the right key." He winks and goes back to polishing his glass. There's a clock sitting on the bar beside him, an elegant antique in green marble. Its hands suggest it's sometime around six, although there's no way to tell if that's a.m. or p.m. or if it's even accurate.

Anna looks around the room, hoping there will be an obvious clue, like the blackboards in coffee shops that alert customers to the Wi-Fi password. There is no such thing. She looks for the bar's name, for a sign or a coaster or a menu. There are no visible signs, coasters, or menus.

"Are there menus?" she asks.

The bartender shakes his head, eyes dancing. He's more solid when they're interacting, and fades a bit, like he's out of focus, when Anna's attention is elsewhere.

"So how do you order?"

"You don't. I just make something you're going to love."

"May I have a drink then, please?"

The bartender nods like a gratified teacher and reaches up, pulling down a tall, sparkling glass. Anna opens her mouth to remind him that she's underage, and then decides she's more curious about his process. *Something you're going to love.* Based on what? Does he size up a person's looks, clothing, posture, word choice? Does he make it to match their outfit? Does he watch their eyes flit to their favorite bottles behind the bar?

He doesn't look at her while he works; he's completely engaged. He selects a smallish, pretty bottle of lavender syrup, pulls a mason jar of cloudy liquid from somewhere under the counter—lemonade, judging by the seeds—plucks a velvety leaf from a bouquet of herbs, adds all the chosen ingredients to a silver shaker and shakes it with ice before pouring the concoction into the waiting glass and topping it off with two more syrups and bubbly water from an old-fashioned seltzer bottle. When he plunks the glass down in front of her, it's as solid as she is and sweating, and being Anna, her first thought is that she needs to tell her dad to get this place some coasters before they destroy the elegant old bar.

Her second thought, on the other hand is: Wow.

The drink is beautiful, a misty periwinkle on bottom with an ombré effect to the seltzer on top. Anna can smell the fragrance of the crushed leaf rising, sharp and herbal, over the floral sweetness. And she's pretty sure there's no alcohol in it, as the bartender didn't go for anything behind the actual bar.

"What's it called?"

"The Key to Enlightenment." He winks and goes back to polishing glasses.

Anna looks down at the drink, pokes her straw through the layers to watch them swirl. She realizes that she didn't drink anything at the wedding—or before the wedding—because she didn't want to leave Emily alone long enough to use the restroom. That sort of clumsiness around health is very un-Anna, and she's anxious to rehydrate beyond her previous Shirley Temples. When the drink is mixed completely, she sips, and it's . . .

Oh.

Oh.

It's the Platonic ideal of an Anna drink.

Lavender lemonade, not too sweet, not too sour, not too perfumy, elevated by the crushed leaf and lightened up by the seltzer. It coats her throat as it goes down, reminding her of the bubblegum-pink medicine her mother gave her when she was little and had pneumonia. The drink isn't medicinal, but it feels . . . healing. Each sip gives her strength while relaxing her shoulders. She feels as if she's right where she's meant to be.

Now she just needs to solve the riddle, get out, and go back to Max. And then, as soon as possible, find the mysterious crypt girl's key and find her dad and get back to reality. All before midnight, of course. No big deal.

With the drink and the night halfway gone, Anna picks up the glass to inspect it. There are no designs on it, no maker's mark on the thick glass bottom. She looks at the straw, and as it's paper and starting to soften, she pulls it apart, making a long ribbon of pink and white. She doesn't want to be rude and walk around the bar to look at the other glasses, but she also doesn't have a lot to work with over here.

"Not a light bulb moment, eh?" the bartender calls from across the bar, but before Anna can respond, he's shaking something in a silver shaker, the ice rattling as the shiny metal sparkles with the golden light from all the bulbs overhead.

Wait.

*The Key to En*light*enment.*

Not a light *bulb moment.*

She looks up at the ceiling, dominated by hundreds, maybe thousands of Edison bulbs hanging from black cords. On closer inspection, they seem identical but are all hung at slightly different heights.

Anna takes a deep breath and focuses on the nearest corner, looking at each bulb carefully, hunting for anything unusual, counting it, and moving on. She works logically in lines parallel to the wall. It's time-consuming but almost comforting. Everything in this hotel changes, but numbers are still numbers; this is no dream. She longs to sip her drink but isn't willing to lose her place while counting.

When she hits bulb number one hundred eleven, she finds the first anomaly.

This bulb is out. It's right behind the bar, closer to the bottles than to her. She squints. Is there . . . something in the bulb?

Marking the bulb's place, she finally looks away from the ceiling and drains her drink until the ice nearly tumbles down her front. The bartender is cutting up lemons with a jackknife, but she can sense that he's keeping an eye on her, amused by her process. She steps around the bar, right under the unlit bulb—

And nearly falls down a set of hidden stairs.

"That can't be safe," she murmurs.

"Most interesting things aren't," the bartender agrees.

"What's in that bulb?"

The bartender walks over, but not too close. He looks up to where she's pointing, his arms crossed. "Huh. Never noticed that bit of flimflammery before." The ceiling is quite high, but he jumps up on the bar, lithe as a cat, and untwists the light bulb from its socket. When he lands on the ground, he holds it out to Anna, glass bulb up, as if offering her an idea.

Inside the bulb is a brass key that reminds her of the one on Max's chain.

"I guess this is for you, compliments of Blackstone's."

Satisfied that she now knows the speakeasy's name, Anna takes the bulb and discovers that the glass is still warm. "How do I get the key out?"

"Princess, there's only ever been one way freedom could be earned. . . ."

The bartender pauses, waiting for her to fill in the blank, but she just stares at him.

"By smashing the cage."

With a nod that seems quite final, he goes back to the other side of the bar and his pile of lemons. Bulb in hand, Anna walks down the stairs. There is no handrail to guide her down the stairs, no balustrade to protect the bartender. She has no idea how he hasn't fallen in and broken a leg. If this place was out in the real world, it would be a major safety violation that would put her dad in the news. But in the Houdini—whatever it is, wherever it is—this deathtrap of a stairwell is just another way to get from one place to another.

At least the stairs are painted bright red, and she can see another one of the flickering orange lights shining below. Thirteen steps down and she's standing on burgundy carpet in a tiny vestibule with nothing but an empty coatrack and a small antique table that holds a bowl full of matchbooks. Anna picks one up, surprised to find that it's real, that it isn't just something she's imagined. It's black with an ornate gold foil birdcage and the name BLACKSTONE'S on the front. Scrawled on the inside of the cover in emerald ink is a single word: *glow.*

She tucks the matchbook into her pocket with the pack of playing cards that should be her wallet and faces the door. When she turns the knob, she's momentarily frustrated that it doesn't open. Ah, yes. The bartender already told her: she needs the key.

The bulb is heavier than the ones back home. It looks like a work of art, like something made with love and expert craftsmanship, and Anna hates to break it, but she also doesn't plan to spend the rest of the night, or her life, in a bar talking to ghosts. When she shakes the bulb, the key rattles against the glass, and the feeling of claustrophobia falls over her. The room is too small, too pressing, too warm. She feels as if, at any moment, the bartender might lower a trapdoor, locking her out of the bar and leaving her in the airless chamber, in a place where she could scream until she lost her voice and there would be no one to hear it. This locked door is her only way out.

With a murmured "Sorry," addressed to whom she cannot say, Anna brings the glass bulb down sharply on the edge of the table.

It breaks like an egg, and the key falls onto the floor. Anna brushes the broken glass away before picking it up, grateful for the warm weight of brass in her hand. A long, lavender velvet ribbon is strung through the key, just the right length to slip over her neck. She wonders if Max's key came with its polished chain or if that's something he added himself. Does the hotel shape a person, or does it shape itself around them? Or is it some kind of symbiotic relationship?

And—wait.

Is this it? Is this the key the girl was looking for?

Could it really be that easy?

This key doesn't seem special in any way, just a simple thing of brass. The girl said her key would be near Phoebe and be special and magical, that it would glow. If that's true, then this key is not the one she needs.

"I found the key," Anna says to the room, as if speaking to the Houdini.

Nothing happens. Nothing shimmers or flickers. A rabbit doesn't show up to caper around in congratulations. Which means it's the wrong key.

And the girl never told Anna how to get back to her with the key, anyway. She'll start with that barrel upstairs, maybe. She could take Max's key, too. Ask him if perhaps he has a collection of keys. That seems like the sort of thing he would enjoy—an old jar full of skeleton keys. Not that she really knows him. Not that she knows anything about this place or what she's doing here. Not like back home, where she knows everything and constantly manages everyone.

There is one thing she knows, though: Emily would love the Houdini. She wouldn't care about how the magic works—she would quite simply accept it and follow her whims, flitting about, chasing shiny things. Just like she's going to do when she gets to New York, leaving Anna behind.

And it's not that Anna is afraid to be alone—not really. She has always been able to chart a path and follow it. It's just . . . well, maybe her confidence is because she's always had Emily nearby to support her. The worst day of her life was the day she went to that party as a kid, when Emily wasn't talking to her and the other girls were cruel. So maybe it's not so much that she's afraid to be alone as that she doesn't want to consider life without her best friend by her side. Surely that's not unusual? Things are good the way they are. They don't need to change.

Of course, that world is another world, far removed from the Houdini.

At least with Emily in New York, they could still text and chat and visit.

Wherever she is now, it's like her sister doesn't even exist.

Or maybe Anna herself doesn't exist.

A chill trills down her spine.

Enough of those thoughts, punishing herself with what-ifs in a glorified closet. She puts her key in the door and is entirely unsurprised when it turns smoothly and the door opens out onto a long hallway with numbered doors, all beginning with the number one. She closes the door behind her and notes the number: 111, the same as the bulb that held the key. She'll have to remember it and ask Max later if he's been here before.

The air is clearer in the hallway, the light better, and Anna takes a deep breath and looks ahead, to the elevator. Of course she tries her key in the first door she passes, but it won't turn in the keyhole. That's no great loss; she's just trying to learn the rules. As long as it works in the elevator, she'll be fine.

The hallway feels longer than the other hallways did, when she was with Max. There are none of the expected noises coming from the rooms, no comfortable burble of voices or hum of TVs or thumps of suitcases being moved around. The only sound is the continual music from the overhead speakers, a woman's smooth, yearning voice backed by a full orchestra, the words "sentimental journey" the only thing Anna can pick out. She feels weirdly, horrifically alone, and she wonders if this is how Max has felt his entire life.

There's a great and unspoken comfort in the ambient noise and energy of other people going about their own parallel lives. Anna misses the sounds that drove her completely nuts just a few days ago: her mother's blender in the morning as she makes a kale protein smoothie, her father's phone alarms buzzing endlessly, Emily's off-key singing to Taylor Swift when she has her AirPods in and is doing the dishes. Anna longs for the mundanity of a boring Sunday back home, with everyone where they're supposed to be, being exactly as annoying as people naturally are.

Reaching the elevator, she presses the button and waits for the machine to ponderously arrive. The door grates open, and Anna is a little disappointed that Max isn't inside, waiting for her. It's just as possible here, where the impossible is possible, right? She inserts her key in the keyhole, as she saw him do, and presses the button for the fourth floor to return to Harry's Hideaway. To her great pleasure, the elevator obliges.

The car trundles upward, and Anna holds her breath as the door slides open.

But Max isn't standing there.

Someone else is, though—in the foyer by the flowers.

It's an older man in a janitor's uniform, mopping the tiles.

And he's staring right at her.

Heart pounding, Anna hits the button for the fifth floor, but nothing happens.

"Hey, you! Come here!" the man shouts, dropping the mop with a clatter and walking toward her. She recognizes his voice from the basement.

This is the creep who chased her through the darkness.

Anna fumbles her key on its ribbon and struggles to get it in the keyhole and turn it as she frantically presses every single button and murmurs, "Come on, come on, come on."

"Stop! Get out of there!" the man calls. "I need to talk to you."

She can't let him reach her—can't let him in the elevator.

She doesn't know why, but she knows he means her harm.

Whatever Anna is doing must be working, as the elevator door begins to close—with painful slowness. The man picks up speed,

his face going from annoyed to angry as he reaches for the closing
door.

"Open the door!" he screams. "Hold the door, you—"

Anna doesn't get to hear what he was going to call her, as the
door finally snaps shut and the elevator rumbles downward.

She has no idea where she's headed, but at least it's taking her
away from the fourth floor. It's not that Anna has anything against
janitors—she knows they're the hardest workers in any hotel—
but there's just something wrong with that guy. He was so pale,
so sweaty, so needlessly angry. She's read *The Gift of Fear,* and she
is aware that on every level, that man feels like a threat. She hopes
she never runs into him again.

She wants her father so bad. Wants to hug him and feel safe
and know that no one can hurt her when he's around. If that guy
actually works for the Houdini, her dad needs to know that he's
a total creep.

But . . . does her dad actually have any power here?

Everything Anna has heard tonight and over the years suggests
her dad is a part owner of this hotel, along with Tony and Sebastian, but the Houdini she's seen doesn't seem like the kind of place
he'd care about, and there are clearly no guests and therefore no
revenue. He called it a dump, but that suggests it's a real place, not
a magical limbo place. So are there two Houdini hotels, like an
object and its mirror image, a person and a ghost? The girl in the
crypt said Phoebe runs the hotel, but she didn't say "owns." Can
this place even *be* owned?

Why didn't Max ever mention Phoebe? Anna mentioned her

own parents dozens of times while they ate, and although Max said "we" and "when I was young," he never said "my mom." He only said he knew two other people and tried to be unlike them.

If those other two people are Phoebe and the janitor, Anna can see why Max doesn't want to be anything like them.

She and Max will have a lot to talk about, whenever she finds him, starting with, "Why is your mom a Disney villain, and who is her creepy henchman?"

Every time Anna asks herself one question, it's immediately followed by a troubling flood of new questions. What is this place and where did it come from? What binds its denizens together? Is the girl in the crypt real, considering she straight up turned into stone?

Anna promised to find a key for the girl before midnight, despite the fact that she has no idea what she's doing here, what this place is, or even how to work a stupid elevator.

The Houdini is getting under her skin.

She is doing illogical things because in the moment, they feel logical.

And she doesn't hate that like she should—at least not when Max is there.

Anna pulls her key out of the elevator and twirls it a little like Max twirls his. It feels good, nicely weighted. It's a shame that it's not the one she needs. It was definitely hidden in a hard-to-find place. And yet the girl said the key would be near Phoebe, that it glows. Anywhere else in existence, Anna would wonder how a key might glow, but in the Houdini, she just assumes it's literal. This dull brass key is still a fascinating object, but Anna is fairly certain that the hotel wouldn't lead her directly to the thing she needed, moments after she was asked to find it. Which means Max's key can't be the girl's key, either.

So much for that brief flare of hope.

The elevator rattles to a stop, and Anna tucks the key inside the neckline of her dress. So far, besides Max, she's met an evil witch, a creepy minion, and a girl in chains. Maybe she'll find her dad on the third floor. . . .

Or maybe she'll find something even worse.

22.

When the elevator doors open on the third floor, Anna realizes she hasn't been here before. She steps off uncertainly into a hallway almost identical to the ones she has seen, except this one is decorated in deep peacock blue and silver instead of burgundy and gold. It feels quiet and serene, like a forest long forgotten by humankind. Key in hand, she steps down the long aisle of carpet, dainty and cautious as a fawn. She pressed every button, but the Houdini sent her here, to an unfamiliar part of the hotel. Why?

The seven doors along each side have the usual numbers and refuse to yield to her key . . . until she reaches a room whose brass sign reads MUSEUM OF MAGIC. Anna's heart lifts—Max mentioned this place as one of his favorites. There is no lock. The door opens easily, and she steps into an enormous and yet intimate gallery with focused spotlights drawing the eye along an array of exhibits so enticing that she doesn't know where to begin. Artful columns divide up the space, making each new turn feel like a fresh discovery. There are artifacts nestled on velvet cushions and in glass cases, colorful wooden pedestals of all sizes, paintings and photographs and even what appears to be a mermaid skeleton hanging from the ceiling, her bones an ancient shade of ocher and her hair as fine and light as spider silk. The walls are high, the ceiling painted indigo and covered in constellations—a running theme in the hotel, it seems.

As if on cue, a phonograph across the room starts up, its needle scratching lightly on the record as a man's melancholy voice croons about twilight and little stars and the memory of stardust. Anna is drawn to that corner, where she finds a child's storybook open on a bench, its cover cracked and worn, like it's been read over and over again. Glad to sit for a moment, she can't help but start reading.

Once upon a time, a star fell to earth. This doesn't happen as often as some might think, as most little stars can't help but burn up once they near the wickedness below. This particular star was very strong and kind, but when she landed, it hurt very much. She was stunned and could only lie back in the sand, gazing longingly at all her sisters still twinkling brightly overhead.

"Oho," said a voice. "What is this?"

"I am a star," the star said.

A woman reached down and picked up the star, cradling her in strong arms. The woman nursed the star back to health, bathing her and brushing her hair and wiping her brow with a cool cloth, for the woman had a soft spot for pretty, injured things. But when the star felt strong again and attempted to fly up into the heavens, she was jerked cruelly back to earth by a silver chain.

"What is this?" cried the star.

"That is an obligation," the woman answered. "For nothing on this earth is free. It is known that fallen stars can grant wishes, and I have decided upon my wish."

"And if I grant this wish, you will let me go?" the star said.

"I promise," said the woman.

"What will you have, then? True love, money, beauty, longevity?"

But the woman was more cunning than most, and she presented the star with a contract that spelled out all the magic the star must continue to perform for the woman while promising to never let harm come to her, a contract spanning much, much longer than the woman's natural lifetime.

"I wish you to sign this contract," the woman said, and the star had no choice but to agree.

But the little star was cunning, too. She read the contract well and saw many loopholes. For one, the woman wished to own a hotel so that she and her family would always be provided for, but she did not indicate the nature of the hotel—or in which realm of possibility it would reside. The star spun a place that had never existed before, one foot in our world and one foot in the spirit world, a place with a mind of its own powered by the star's magic. And thus was the wicked woman doomed to rule over a beautiful but impotent edifice of dreams instead of taking her supposed place of power in her own land.

For this cruelty, the woman's heart turned against the star, and they remained forever at odds, the star forever chained and duty bound to provide and the woman having received everything she thought she wanted yet still unhappy. Many lost souls found the hotel and became its silent denizens, but none of them knew to look beyond the surface. And then one day a new visitor arrived, a woman as broken as the star had once been, and the star thought she might find an ally in this tenacious soul. The star showed her the contract and told the woman how she might break that contract and use her wish to return everything to how it should be, the woman to her own world and the star to her rightful place in the sky.

But the woman was ruled by desperation and revenge, not kindness. She crafted another contract, even longer than the original one, and she chained the star more fully in hopes that no new visitor might set her free. She hid the key to the star's freedom that the star might never find it, nor tell someone else where it was kept. And thus did the cycle of servitude continue, all for the wickedness of the human heart.

The star could only dream that one day, she would be free again to join her rightful place in the heavens among her sisters.

The book's illustrations are beautiful and haunting, the star depicted as a familiar girl with long blond hair in a diaphanous nightgown, always surrounded by an otherworldly white glow. When Anna sees the chain shackled to the star girl's ankle, a shiver skitters up her back.

This . . . sounds like it's describing how the Houdini came to be, and like the girl in the crypt is the star.

But that's completely absurd.

It's 2023. Science is real. Stars are perpetually burning balls of gas millions of miles away, not magical girls who fall to earth and sign contracts to build ghost hotels. Maybe it's a metaphor, but it's not one that suggests an immediate explanation. It makes no sense and answers no real questions. Anna still doesn't know how to find the key or stop the clock.

She stands and replaces the book where she found it, as gently as if it were made of spun glass. She inspects the paintings hung in this corner, each somehow connected to stars and the heavens: gods, chariots, glowing orbs, even Van Gogh's *The Starry Night*, which is either the real thing or a cunning fake, with thick daubs of paint that look wet and juicy. Each work of art has a small title placard, but there is nothing that adds to the star's story.

Moving to the next exhibit, Anna is delighted to find it's on spirit photography, the very topic Max said he'd enjoyed. But as she looks closer at each image, she notes something shocking: she is in many of them.

As a ghost.

There's a photo from Harry's Hideaway, of her and Max, except she's as see-through as everyone else in the restaurant and he's reaching for her like she's disappearing before his eyes. Another photo shows her in the dessert lounge, barely visible, sunken in sadness, as Max sits across from her fully formed and eating affogato as he stares into space. In the one that disturbs her the most, she's in the hotel lobby, standing directly under the brass clock, barely visible. The clock's hands are at midnight. Her father is beside her, likewise invisible. She is dressed in formal Victorian black, in mourning, as if witnessing her own erasure.

A clock chimes in another corner of the room, startling Anna out of her transfixed horror. Seven chimes remind her she has only five hours before checkout time. With one last, longing look at the photographs that are clearly threats, she heads for the door with the same sort of purposeful, furious determination she felt going a second round with the SAT.

The warning is clear. Whatever is really happening, Anna is unwilling to become just another memory in this hotel. She's going to find a way out.

23.

Max has been studying the map for so long that he's nearly cross-eyed and he's definitely furious. The hotel generally feels like a kind but no-nonsense babysitter, but tonight it seems to be constantly defying him, and he's not sure why. It brought Anna to him, and then it took her away. It's not cruel, whatever magic runs this place, but currently, it's not helping.

There's a sharp knock on the door, and although Max's heart lifts with the thought that it might be Anna, he knows that knock. He hurriedly shoves the map back under the couch and composes himself with the nearest book before shouting, "Come in!"

His mother steps into the room, surreptitiously sweeping every crevice with her clever eyes.

"Good book?" she asks.

Max looks down. What book did he select? Huh. Something

he hasn't seen before and didn't request. *I Know Why the Caged Bird Sings.* He'll read the back cover later.

"I was just starting it."

"Have you seen any unusual men around the hotel?"

Because this is how they speak now, call-and-response.

"No. Should I have?"

Phoebe shrugs. "I'm sure I've no idea. I noticed we had some guests and just wanted to check in and make sure they weren't bothering you."

How he hates it, this strange facade, these lies.

"Mom, what year is it?"

She looks around the room in surprise. "It's every year here, pretty much. You know that, Max."

"Stop lying. There's another world, a real world, and it's not at all like this."

Phoebe draws herself up, tall and imperious. "Oh, you know things now, do you? You take some strange girl out for dinner and suddenly you know things?"

Max goes still, like a rabbit in the shadow of a hawk. "You know about that? You know about her?"

She looks at him like he's an absolute idiot. "Sweetheart, I know about everything in this hotel."

"Then why do you hide it from me and pretend that this is all there is? Why don't you let me know anything about—about what it would be like to live in the other world?"

"Because then you would want to go there!" Phoebe shouts with a stamp of her foot. "And we can't. We can't go there. The other world is a hideous place these days, darling. Ugly and dirty and cruel." She looks down, dabs at her eyes with the sleeve of her robe. "I never wanted that for you."

"Anna said—"

"Anna will be gone by midnight," Phoebe snaps. "You know better than to get attached."

"But why? Why does that happen? Can we stop it?"

Phoebe sighs and sits down beside Max on the couch. "I hate this old thing," she mutters, rubbing a hand on the worn seat. "You should ask the hotel for a new one."

"I love it, exactly as it is. Please answer the question."

Sitting side by side, his mother doesn't seem as tall and imposing. She definitely doesn't go with this room, in her silk robes and pearls. She usually wears pajamas and soft sweaters, only dressing up for trips to the ballroom. Tonight, however, she looks like a movie star, and he wonders what's so special about the hotel's current guests—about these men she doesn't want him to see.

"We can't stop what happens here, Max. It works how it works. The real world has gravity and physics and economics, and the Houdini has its own magic. I'm as much a prisoner here as you think you are."

"Then why aren't we ghosts? Why not Colin?"

Phoebe looks down, worries at her lower lip. Then she smiles a sad, fond smile, and puts a hand on Max's arm. "My beloved, precious boy," she starts.

"Sleep."

Max slumps down, eyes softly closed, and Phoebe sighs and rises to standing.

That trick has helped her immensely since Max reached teenagerhood and started asking questions she couldn't answer.

Something catches under her kitten heel, and she looks down to find a piece of paper sticking out from under the couch. She pulls it out to reveal a childish but very detailed map.

"Fascinating," she breathes, because Max, it seems, lives in an entirely different version of the Houdini. He knows secret passages she's never seen, uses rooms that she's never found. One of his secret rooms is quite near, actually. Phoebe walks over to a section of the bookshelf that is apparently hiding a door, but no matter what she does, she can't open it.

"Rude," she says, either to Max or the hotel.

She'd like to take the map, but Max would surely notice and he would never forgive her. Phoebe recognizes layers of his handwriting, all the way back from when he was tiny and got *b* and *d* confused. This map is a work of art, a globe in a new realm of unknown places. She loves this boy, loves his earnestness and diligence and tenacity, and she doesn't want her world, the real world, to rip him apart.

When she crafted her contract with Arielle over sixteen years ago, she added even more clauses than Celeste had. But she forgot to give herself a way back home. She was too hurt and scared and stunned at the time, and she knew that if she did go back, there would be nothing there for her. No money, no home—she'd be a single mother with a baby and no support.

If she set Arielle free, perhaps Phoebe could go back, but then she would lose all her power, all her magic, all her luxury. She would live a life of violence and uncertainty and doubt, a life of scrabbling and desperation, and as soon as he was old enough, Max would leave her.

She has chosen her cage, and she has chosen revenge, and it is all coming to fruition.

The girl will fade away, Max will forget, and all will be as it was.

As she looks down at her son, for the briefest moment, Phoebe considers what it might be like, standing in the halls of the real Houdini back in Las Vegas. No magic, no mystery, just a cruel world that would destroy her boy as it destroyed her. Smiling softly, she pulls a rainbow-colored afghan over Max, a thing she crocheted when he was just a baby. She likes that he keeps it here, likes that he isn't the sort of boy to throw away sentimental things. That's one benefit of the Houdini—he didn't have to grow up too fast, not like she did.

She wanted these particular men in her clutches, but in her excitement, she messed up. She gave Arielle no directions about barring the Houdini's doors to anyone else who might've been in that limo. This is how the contract's loopholes work, Phoebe and Arielle locked in hatred like two eagles wrapped in one another's talons, willing to plummet to the earth before they'll let go.

And now the girl has polluted Max. And if Phoebe isn't careful, Anna will turn him against his own mother.

As she leaves, she closes the door softly behind her.

Five more hours, and the problem will solve itself.

Much like its namesake, this Houdini is good at making things disappear.

24.

Anna stands in an elevator, finally understanding that she has no control over where she lands. The Houdini will decide, and all the keys in the world won't change that. This time, it takes her to the sixth floor. When the elevator doors rattle open, Anna is grateful to find that this place, at least, has not changed. The hallway is the same as before—or it looks that way—and deep, sad, haunting music floats out the open door to the library. Anna is not the running type, but she runs to the door and all but leaps into the room. She doesn't see Max at first, and her heart just about plummets to her feet, but then she spots the lump on the old, squashy couch, gently covered with a colorful afghan as if someone has been here to check up on him as he sleeps. His dark hair falls over his eyes, long eyelashes casting shadows on flushed cheeks. Anna is certain she has never slept so deeply in her entire life.

She doesn't dare move. This is a rare moment to take in—well, everything.

She slips off her shoes, enjoys the heavy, plush carpet under her tender bare feet, finally free of those last remaining crumbs of crypt dust. She wonders if the Houdini is a self-cleaning organism, or if someone else has to constantly keep every surface tidy and dust-free. The janitor on the fourth floor looked like he was trying to make the beautiful floor filthy with his disgusting mop, but Anna is certain that when he's gone, it will somehow be spotless again.

She steps fully into the library, realizing it's a more intimate space than she originally thought. It's not just shelves and books. There's the couch Max is on—old, worn, soft, almost cradling him. There's a desk, a heavy wooden behemoth with deep drawers that she would love to rifle through. It's a messy workspace, with fountain pens in chipped mugs and a vase full of bright bird feathers, greens and reds and blues and even a few peacock curls. Spread out on the rug before the couch is a large map showing all six floors of the hotel, messy and layered, his handwriting childishly staggering downhill in some places and adultishly sharp in others, lines drawn by hand and then redrawn with a ruler and more confidence. There's a recent-looking addition by the sixth floor, where he's sketched in the barrel she was shoved into by Phoebe, and Anna realizes that this means Max was trying to find her, trying to figure out where that secret tunnel fits into the hotel he knows so well.

Max was trying to find her.

Her heart melts a little, and she moves to a precarious pile of books by a leather chair under a hanging lamp. The lamp is ancient and looks handmade, but the chair has a 1950s space-age look that her dad is putting in some of his hotels to appeal to hipsters. It's odd, how this place seems to span several decades. Anna gets straight As in history, but she doesn't feel especially drawn to it, in part because she hates the hindsight of past politicians' horrible decisions. Everything she knows of the aesthetics and culture of any given decade is more tied into the books she's had to read to get good grades and the old musicals that Emily adores. From what Anna can tell, the hotel seems to span the 1930s, '40s, and '50s, and she remembers that Max said there were books from the '60s, too. She wishes she could have brought him the storybook about the star, but she suspects the Houdini places objects exactly where they need to be. That book clearly belongs in the Museum of Magic. Perhaps she can take him there later, see what he makes of the story of the star—and of the disturbing spirit images of them together.

Anna tiptoes closer, silent, to see which book sits beside him on the couch.

It's *The Night Circus,* the one she told Max was her favorite, a special edition that she's never seen before in black, red, and white leather. The book looks like it's fifty years old instead of barely a decade, with deckle-edged paper and silver stamping, and she wants to snatch it up and run her fingers over the endpapers and bury her nose in the spine.

This book—it shouldn't be here. She told Max about it mere hours ago.

And yet here it is, further evidence of the Houdini's whimsical magic.

Despite the fact that her fingers itch to touch the leather cover, she forces herself to inspect the rest of the shelves. As she recalls from her earlier time here, there are all sorts of books, but now she can see that they are clearly organized. Nonfiction and encyclopedias on one side, along with the biggest dictionary Anna has ever seen, practically a solid cube bound in gold-stamped black leather. The other side is fiction, half of it yellowed, dog-eared paperbacks and half the kind of leather-bound tomes she would expect in a place like the Houdini, as if it's willing to cede some space to Max's personal favorites but must insist on overall domination by books that look the part.

"You're back."

Anna spins around, and Max is sitting up, hugging a pillow to his chest, smiling sleepily at her.

"I'm back," she agrees.

He stifles a yawn. "Where did you go?" His voice becomes softer. "Was it something I did?"

Anna wanders closer, her dress swirling around her legs. "Definitely not anything you did. This lady grabbed me and asked me for identification, but my wallet was gone, so she shoved me in a booth and . . . turned it around."

Max's face goes hard with anger as his eyes skitter away. "Do you know who it was?"

Anna gives him a measuring stare. "Your mom. Because your mom is Phoebe, right?"

At that, his eyes close, his jaw goes tense, his fingers curl into fists. "Of course it was her."

"So she's one of the other two people here?" Anna asks.

He nods in confirmation.

"And she's not very nice."

Max snorts. "Before today, I just thought of her as firm and no-nonsense, but now . . ."

"Now she's acting like some crazy witch, grabbing me and throwing me in a dungeon—"

His head jerks back. "Okay, that's a bit harsh—"

"Yeah, because it felt harsh!" Now that the danger is over, Anna's anger bubbles up. Grabbed by a stranger, thrown in a booth, walking forever in a crypt, almost attacked by some random man. It's been an awful hour, and Max needs to understand that. She holds up one foot. Her toes are gray with dust. "A pitch-dark dungeon, Max."

Max stands, his face a mask of confusion. "She's never done that before. I've never seen my mother as a villain. A little dramatic, maybe. But she's never hurt me."

The way he says it . . . Anna feels like it's partially a lie.

"Well, she hurt me. She dug her nails into my shoulders. I have bruises."

"Well, I'm just hearing about that for the first time!" He huffs a sigh and paces. "You don't understand. People come here, but she's never interacted with them before. She says they don't matter, that they're only here for a few hours, so what's the point? I've never seen her take an interest like she is right now."

"So why, then? Why us? Why now?"

Max sits back down on the couch, head in his hands. "I don't know! She never tells me anything about where she came from or how she got here. Everything I know about real life I've read about in books, and they're all apparently fifty years out of date. My mom is infuriating because she's so evasive and secretive, but she loves me. I know it. I've never had reason to doubt her motives before tonight."

"Maybe it's tied in with—" Anna almost mentions the girl but doesn't. She isn't accustomed to keeping secrets. "With my dad and his friends owning this hotel."

"Oh, no one owns the Houdini," Max says, as if it's a ridiculous idea.

"Well, in my world, there's a hotel called the Houdini that looks just like this one from the outside, and they own it. So maybe that's what's making your mom so weird." Anna takes a deep breath. It's useless being angry—especially at Max. His emotions are so clear, his arguments so reasonable. Whatever his mother's sins, he's clearly innocent.

Feeling awkward now, Anna picks up the copy of *The Night Circus* and does her own examination. A UK special edition, so it might actually exist in her world, which is comforting. As she admires the endpapers, which are just as delicious as she'd hoped, she realizes that she needs to figure out how to enlist Max's help to find the girl's key. She can't tell him about the girl—she promised she wouldn't. But he knows Phoebe, so he might know where she would hide something. Anna hates lying, but . . .

"I think your mom must have my wallet and phone. I had them when I was with you, and after she left, all that was in my pocket was a pack of cards. I really need to get my stuff back."

There.

Not at all a lie.

It's very true. It's just not the full truth. Sure, she needs her phone and wallet. And it stands to reason that Phoebe wouldn't hide things around the hotel like Easter eggs. If Anna can just get near Phoebe, she will likely find the glowing key as well as her belongings.

But Anna realizes something else, something slightly terrifying. What she wants the most right now—really wants—isn't necessarily to run mysterious errands for strangers or find her things or be reunited with her infuriating dad and his awful friends or even to escape the hotel. Sure, she's scared of what she saw in the museum and every new room seems to have a clock counting down the hours, but . . .

She wants to be with Max, wants him to keep looking at her like she's the rainbow he's been searching for all his life.

It makes no sense that the only other person in this mixed-up place is a boy who is also her age, and that she's fascinated by him and his strangeness, and that he seems to share this mutual fascination, but this is her current reality. It's not logical, but like everything else in the Houdini, it's happening anyway. And now, if she can convince him, they'll have a quest together.

"Will you help me?"

Max looks up from folding the afghan, eyes twinkling. "Of course. But . . . it's not easy, figuring out where Phoebe might hide something. This entire hotel is under her thumb. I'm guessing she would keep something like that in her suite, but I don't know how to get in."

Anna raises an eyebrow. "You . . . don't know how to get in your mom's room?"

A shrug. "I know how to get in when she wants me in."

Instead of mentioning how weird this is, Anna pokes the map with a toe. "Well, where is it?"

Max joins her, standing close enough for his fingers to brush the drooping ribbons at her hip, and then he kneels. He unfolds an addition to the map that was tucked underneath it and stands again. "The seventh floor."

"But the elevator only goes up to the sixth."

He grins down at Anna. She likes that he's a little taller than her, but not a lot. "I know."

"So how do you get there?"

"I haven't been able to get there on my own in a very long time—like I said, only when my mom calls me. I remember she used to do something unusual with the elevator, use her key and press a combination of buttons instead of just one. And then it went up. The entire floor there is hers. And she sometimes visits the ballroom on the second floor."

"So where do we start?"

Max rolls up both maps together, ties a bit of twine around them, and slides the bundle under the couch. Anna likes watching him move when he's not looking. He's muscular, but not too much, graceful but still masculine. There is nothing shy or awkward about him, nothing arrogant or shrinking. He is what he is, and he moves naturally and with complete confidence, and she's never met anyone like that in her life. Maybe it's because he didn't grow up with dozens of eyes on him, surrounded by kids hungry to pick him apart for fun, calling out anything that might be the tiniest bit unique. Maybe this is what a person can be if they aren't constantly judged and bullied and told what to be.

Whatever he is, despite everything that's happening, Anna is drawn to it and finds herself following a bit behind him just to be near him. It also helps that he's terribly good-looking, which she tried to ignore before . . . and, fine, she failed. Being separated from him in this topsy-turvy place has only reinforced that against all odds, this boy gives her butterflies. To her imminently logical mind, it is absolutely bizarre that faced with every worry and fear, she still can't think of anything but Max when he's this close.

"What do you need?" Max asks, his soulful gray-blue eyes searching hers. "Sleep, more food, a clean dress?"

At the mention of sleep, Anna yawns, jaw cracking. "Definitely sleep. But I don't think I could if I tried. Do day and night even exist here?"

That grin again. "No. But sometimes I pretend they do."

Anna knows as well as anyone that day and night don't really exist in any casino hotel, that the lights are always on and the doors are always open. As her father likes to say, the people may change but people never change. And this place is even more removed from time. Everything is in limbo, and her body doesn't know what time it is either.

"Coffee might help," she admits. "I never did get my affogato."

Max puts his hands in his pockets and rocks back on his heels. "Okay. So, yes, coffee. We can get that. And then we should try the ballroom, since it's easy to access, unlike Phoebe's suite. If we find her, we can follow her. And if we don't find her, let's go up to the roof. I think there might be a way down to the penthouse from there, but I've never wanted to get in badly enough to try."

He holds out his hand, and without really thinking too hard, without considering if it's awkward or weird or moving too fast or if he might break her heart or she might break his, definitely not thinking about the fact that they've only known each other a couple of hours and this is completely insane and in no way logical, and that she might disappear in a few more hours anyway, Anna takes it. Their fingers interlace, their palms pressing together like a prayer.

She has never held anyone's hand like this.

It is oddly intimate and thrills her to her very bones.

And because he's Max and not trained to act like something big is nothing, like it's uncool to feel things, he squeezes her hand and beams at her.

"But on the way, you have to tell me where you've been. And how you can possibly fit a phone in your pocket. I looked for you everywhere and left you a message and looked at the map but couldn't figure out where that booth might lead to."

Anna walks by his side, their arms swinging. She has forgotten her shoes. She doesn't care. This is the Houdini, where anything can happen, shoes or no.

She considers how to tell the truth while keeping her promise to the girl.

"Let me tell you about Blackstone's," she begins.

25.

Max's two favorite things in the world are finding new places in the Houdini and being with Anna. He's fascinated by the existence of a secret speakeasy, which he's never seen before and longs to find—he wants to see what the bartender will make for him and read every book on its shelves. And yet he can't stop drinking in the sensations of being in Anna's company. Her voice, girlish but firm and confident. Her accent and word choice, unlike anything he's heard in movies, as if the world has moved on and is constantly crafting new slang and idioms without him. The feel of their fingers entwined, their palms pressed together, another person's warmth altogether new. He's never known prolonged contact like this since he was a very small child, and he worries his giddiness will shine through and frighten her away.

He does not think himself a shallow man, but he can't stop looking at her. Every line of her face, the crooked beauty of her smile, the way she raises an eyebrow in judgment or amused doubt.

The way her hair moves, the way her dress moves, the way her hips move. He wants to look at her every day for the rest of his life.

And he knows he wouldn't get bored of the view because he's been looking at her every day for years without even knowing it was her.

After he pulled out the map and marked the turned barrel in the dessert room, before he fell asleep on the couch—which, how? Because he wasn't sleepy at all—Max went through the bookcase and into the small eggshell-blue room. He stood before the orange tree and touched a branch, inhaling hungrily as the flowers burst into riotous bloom and the fruits grew heavy and ripe. Through the leaves and flowers, he looked at the wall where he's been tacking up copies of the same pencil drawing for years.

It's Anna.

It's so clearly her.

Somehow, the automaton has been drawing her for him, each time he visits the ballroom.

The greatest mystery of his life has been solved, and yet he only has more questions.

Why her? How did the Houdini know? How did she come here?

Like Anna said—why now?

And considering that the hotel went to such trouble to announce her all those years ago and keep his hope for her burning, surely it wouldn't just take her away at midnight like the rest?

Surely she has to stay here with him, stay corporeal.

Won't she?

The Houdini, after all, has never been unnecessarily cruel.

Mysterious, yes.

Mercurial, sometimes.

Magical, always.

Growing up here, Max has learned not to get too attached to anything. The children he once played with stopped answering him as he grew older; now he can't see them, either, although sometimes he can hear their laughter and the sound of their leather ball bouncing down the hall. Certain rooms he found once when he needed them most, he could never find again. When he wrote in his diary about how much it hurt his heart to lose the things he loved, a curious new book arrived on the library shelves—*Archy and Mehitabel,* about a philosophical cockroach and the cat who teaches him to live without expectation. It changed Max's view on the ephemeral nature of beauty, and now he maintains a "come easy go easy" attitude. His conclusion was that the hotel was telling him that some things were beyond both of their control.

But even knowing that, even knowing everything he does about how the hotel works, he wants to be with Anna like he's never wanted anything before.

She is new, real, surprising, and yet entirely familiar.

He wants to hold her hand forever.

He will make every moment with her last, make every moment beautiful.

Knowing the Houdini, he can't help but believe that tonight might be all the time they have together.

The only thing he wants more than Anna is freedom—for them both.

Max has spent his entire life trying to escape this place. After crowbars, hammers, and explosives failed to open the lobby door, he got maudlin and desperate and wild and drank too much in the ballroom one night and tried to throw himself off the roof.

He woke up in his bed, lovingly tucked in, with the phonograph playing "Somewhere Over the Rainbow." His mother never mentioned it. He doesn't think she knows. He found a book about depression in the library the next day, and then the Houdini revealed the dessert room like some kind of clumsy but loving consolation prize. Max hasn't tried again. Failure hurt more than he'd expected it to.

If, after years of trying, he can't save himself, if he can't break out of this gilded cage, how the hell is he supposed to help Anna do it in just five hours?

26.

Yes, Anna is trapped in an exciting, terrifying, magical limbo hotel, separated from her father and worried about her mother and sister. Yes, she barely survived a tornado. Yes, she made a promise under impossible circumstances to go on a mysterious errand for a peculiar person who may or may not exist, an errand for which she has less than five hours, an errand she can't share with anyone, even the only person she currently trusts. Yes, she is exhausted and pushed to her limits. Yes, this is the most illogical day she's ever had.

But she has a really good latte in one hand and Max's hand in the other, and she doesn't think she's ever been this happy before.

Max is walking slowly, sipping his coffee, savoring it, but Anna saw the clock in Harry's Hideaway as Max politely requested their drinks. She has four and a half hours. Four and a half hours to find the key and free the girl—the star?—in chains in the basement. And yet . . . well, the girl has her reservations about Max.

But who should Anna trust more—the strange girl in suspicious circumstances who apparently turned into stone, or the flesh and blood boy making her pulse race?

That's it. She's got to tell him.

"Max, do you know about the girl in the crypt?" she asks.

He's just starting to turn around when the floor disappears, and Anna is falling again. Her hand slips out of Max's and she drops her latte and feels the hot burn of it down her chest as she hits bottom and slides, down and around and around like one of those tube slides at a water park, but dry. It's happening so fast that she can't scream, can't call for Max. All she can do is struggle to stay upright. It's pitch-dark, and her body is jostled from side to side, twisting and turning, until she's dumped out in a pool of water.

It's not deep, at least—Anna lands on her butt, and when she stands, the water is only up to her knees. The glow of an orange gaslight guides her way out, and there are steps leading out of the shallow, tiled pool. She's not in a hallway or a room, not a place that has ever been properly finished for public viewing. At least it's not the basement, no dripping pipes and puddle-dappled concrete and screeching, scary janitor. Wherever she is, it feels like an in-between place, an incomplete place, like the long passageway that took her to the crypt.

There is, of course, only one way out—a narrow stone hall.

"Hello?" Anna calls, hoping that a helpful rabbit will appear.

None does, but it was worth a shot. Dripping, feet squelching, she walks down the hallway surrounded by the scent of the coffee that spilled all over her once-beautiful dress. The stone turns to wood, the interior of a building's walls. She stumbles, and then she's walking on thin carpet.

Two tiny spears of light arrow across the darkness, and Anna hurries ahead to find a box at just the right height to allow her to look through the two perfectly spaced holes in the wall.

The library!

This must be the portrait she'd noticed—the queen with the weasel.

A creepy shiver runs down Anna's spine as she wonders if someone has been spying on her and Max in the library. She slides the door over the peepholes closed and wishes she could glue it shut. She's assuming it was Phoebe who was spying on them, but then she realizes that maybe it was the janitor.

Maybe he's . . . stalking her?

Something creaks near her feet, and she does the sort of dance anyone would do if they were being attacked by a large spider, but . . . it's a door. A small door in the wall just big enough to wriggle through has swung obligingly open. Dust plasters to Anna's wet knees as she crawls into the library. As she's standing up, grateful to be in a familiar place, the door slams shut. When she tries to find it again, it has disappeared or is so well hidden that she can't figure out how to open it.

"Is this the Houdini doing this?" she asks. "Is this . . ."

God, it sounds so stupid.

Logical, reasonable, type A Anna Alonso who doesn't believe in magic is *talking to a hotel.*

And what's more, she's expecting it to answer.

"Is this because I asked Max about the girl in the crypt?"

There's another creak as yet another secret door eases open, this one built into the bookshelf on the other side of the library.

"Okay," Anna says, now fairly certain that the hotel—or someone, or something—is listening. "I'm sorry. I need his help. I can't do this alone."

A white rabbit hops through the open door, nose twitching as it stares up at Anna and shakes its head. It turns and hops back out of the library, pausing to look back at Anna.

"Got it," she says.

On dusty, wet knees and coffee-covered hands, she crawls through the little doorway behind the rabbit. The door doesn't slam shut, at least; this is a smaller space than Anna would prefer. Is the hotel punishing her? Is it going to dump her in a dungeon or another dunk tank?

The rabbit is a soft white smudge in the darkness as Anna crawls through the narrow hallway toward the light offered by the next open door. This one is also small, cramped even, and she begins to wonder if the Houdini has a sense of humor. A slide? A pool? Forcing her to crawl around on hands and knees—almost like she's groveling?

She really must need sleep. This is absolute folly.

But light is light, and the hotel seems like it's trying to show her something, and she can't wait to stand back up again. The open door leads through some sort of cabinet and then she's on the floor of a small room with walls the blue of a robin's egg and a dead tree planted in a pretty blue-and-white pot.

Even before Anna is upright, she sees it—the wall.

It's covered in pencil drawings that make her feel like she's yet again surrounded by lightning strikes, every hair on her body standing on end.

All these drawings . . . are of her.

Her face in a dozen different moods from laughing to serious to crying.

The drawings aren't very detailed. The pencil lines are light and sketchy, more like they've been produced by an app that purports to turn a photo into a drawing. They don't seem like the work of human hands.

What . . . is this?

Has someone been spying on her? Were all these images—dozens of them!—produced in the last few hours? Why would someone do this? Is she in danger?

She's breathing fast again, her hands shaking. She wants to run, but there's nowhere to run. No one to tell. No number to call and report that she has some sort of freaky stalker. The room seems to shrink like a funhouse chamber designed to make her feel claustrophobic, as if the entire world is falling down around her. As if it's a trap.

She swallows hard, shakes her head, tries to refocus.

She is Anna Alonso, and it's going to take more than some weirdo's creepy evidence board to stop her.

She has to get out of here.

There is absolutely nothing she can do but try to get back to Max, because he's the one thing in this hotel that feels safe.

There has to be something here the Houdini wants her to see. Anna knows by now that nothing that happens within these walls is random. She steps closer to the jumble of portraits.

The only thing tacked onto the wall that's not a drawing of Anna is a playing card in the very center—an extremely familiar playing card. It's the king of hearts—the suicide king—but instead of the traditional stylized man with curly hair, it's a white rabbit in a vest holding up a pocket watch.

She's seen this card before. As she lets memories of that night in the gazebo at the horrible party rush in, she reaches into her pocket and pulls out the pack of cards she found there when Phoebe asked for her ID. Although she was quite sure the cards were in a box when she found them, they are now in a waterproof silver tin. She cracks it open to find the queen of diamonds on top, that same canary she picked from the magician's fan. As she flips through the cards, she sees that the suits are canaries, white rabbits, monkeys, and poodles. The king of hearts is missing.

"What are you trying to tell me?" Anna says to the room as she pulls out the pushpin and reclaims the king from the wall. It fits the deck perfectly. The cards are thick, waxy, and detailed; their backs match the ceiling of the foyer outside Harry's Hideaway, with golden constellations against an indigo backdrop. She closes the tin on the complete deck and puts it back in her pocket with the matches from Blackstone's.

The hotel offers no answer to her question, and Anna begins to see why Max thinks of the Houdini as having a mind of its own. It reminds her of a wild horse that might come and go as it pleases, as eager to stand for a nose rub as it is to snatch a carrot from your back pocket and run. She next turns her attention to the small tree in the center of the room, but it just seems an elegant but long-dead thing, and when she touches a branch, she wonders why someone bothered to bring a tree into a room with no sunlight and then left it there after it succumbed to its inevitable doom.

When Anna investigates the china cabinet she crawled through, she finds a strange array of mementos squirreled away behind plates and in tureens—marbles, a black silk mask, a hippopotamus carved out of wood, a child-sized top hat, a leather ball, a book of poetry about a cat and a cockroach named Archy—but no obvious, glowing key, of course. The door through the back of the cabinet no longer opens, so she won't be exiting the way she came. There doesn't seem to be anything else in the room except for a full-sized door, and when she opens it, she finds the usual red-carpeted hotel hallway. The placard says this is room 603. Anna wonders if it's on Max's map or if she's discovered something new.

Well, maybe not discovered. She was led here after she got unceremoniously dropped through a trapdoor, where she fell into a curly slide and was dumped into a pool.

Oh!

Poor Max must be freaking out. Her fingers slipped right through his, and then she was gone. That's the second time she's straight up disappeared on him through no fault of her own.

Or, yes, maybe it actually is her fault this time, because she broke her promise to the girl in the crypt and was immediately punished.

Anna checks the library, which is still empty, then hurries to the elevator. When she puts in her key, it obliges her by taking her to the fourth floor. As it rattles downward, two important things occur to her. First, that she's a damp, coffee-soaked wreck, and second, that the curly slide somehow took her from the fourth floor to the sixth floor, which makes her brain hurt. She felt the gravity, felt like a kid on any normal slide going down, except she went *up*.

"This is so weird," she mumbles. "What am I supposed to do next?" The bland music tinkling away on the speaker stops. A record scratches, and someone starts singing about rocking around the clock tonight. Anna snorts. "Yeah, I know. Thanks for the reminder."

When the elevator doors open, Anna rushes out . . .

And runs directly into Max.

"Are you okay? What happened to you?" he asks, holding her by the shoulders and looking her up and down.

Anna winces. "Shoulders. Your mom clawed me, remember?"

He lets go but looks no less concerned. She's used to people asking "Where did you go?" (her father) or "Why did you leave me?" (her mother), and notes the difference; Max was worried about her, not annoyed that she was missing. It's nice.

"You were right there, and then you were gone," he says.

"Trapdoor. Second time tonight. It's odd, to go your whole life without ever encountering a trapdoor and then suddenly—bam!—you're falling. What's next—quicksand?"

Max nods. "No quicksand, but the trapdoor thing has happened to me a few times, too. Usually when I was misbehaving or getting into something I wasn't supposed to be. You were asking me about a girl in a crypt, I think?"

Anna's eyes dart to the floor; she doesn't want to go through this again.

But she also isn't really big on lying, and the cat is out of the bag.

This place—it has its own set of rules. The book in the Museum of Magic talked about an intricate contract, and contracts, no matter how intricate, always have loopholes. Anna can use loopholes, too.

The girl made her promise she wouldn't *tell* Max, that she wouldn't *say anything.*

But there are other ways of communicating.

Anna holds a finger up to her lips, then reaches for Max's vest. His eyes fly wide and he goes very, very still, holding his breath as she reaches into his pocket and pulls out his notebook with the little pencil stub stuck through its coils. She flips to an empty page near the back to avoid his personal notations and starts writing.

After the barrel, there was a passage to a crypt with the grave of someone named Celeste who owned the hotel before your mom. There was a girl chained to the crypt who made me promise to find a key that would free her. I think she's the fallen star from the book in the Museum of Magic. Know anything?

And then Max—the boy out of time who lives in a magical hotel—looks at her like she's sprouted a second head. He takes back the notebook and writes,

None of that makes any sense whatsoever. There is no crypt in the Houdini. There's no girl here. I've never heard of Celeste. And there's no book about a fallen star in the Museum of Magic.

Anna snatches the notebook, frantically scribbling,

There is, there is, her name is carved in stone, and there is, Anna writes, then underlines it all.

She steps backward into the elevator, pulling Max with her by the vest. The music switches to someone crooning, *"I put a spell on you."*

"Can we talk now?" Max whispers.

"I think so. There are just some things I can't say. You can probably say whatever you want, though. You didn't make any promises."

Anna holds up the notebook and writes,

The girl made me promise not to tell you about her. So I can't "tell" you, but I guess I can write whatever I want. Loophole! She said the key will be near Phoebe, and that it will be special and maybe glow.

"I've never seen a glowing key before, although Phoebe has a whole ring of them somewhere. But what about this book? How have you seen something in the museum that I haven't?"

"Let's go find out."

Max sticks his key in the elevator and presses 3, and then they're headed to the third floor and down the hallway toward the Museum of Magic. When they arrive, however, there's a beautifully lettered sign hanging on the door that reads Closed.

"It's never been closed before." Max flips the sign over, but the back also says Closed. He turns the crystal doorknob, but the door refuses to open.

"Let me try."

Anna pulls out her own key, but it doesn't work either.

"Where'd you get that?" Max asks.

"Blackstone's."

"Very interesting. Does it work most of the time?"

He holds up his key, and Anna holds up her key. They're both old-timey skeleton keys, absolutely identical. Max's key, Anna realizes, doesn't glow either.

"Mostly," she admits. "I've only used it a couple of times. Oh! And there was this creepy janitor guy mopping on the fourth floor earlier? Please tell me he's not your dad."

"What? Ugh. No!" The disgust on Max's face mirrors how Anna feels. "That's Colin. He's awful. And before you ask, I don't know where he came from, just that he's been here since before I was born and my mom bosses him around. He tried to kill her once, apparently."

"And she just . . . let that go?"

"I wouldn't call forcing him to be a janitor and eat rotten chowder and sleep on the wet basement floor 'letting that go,' but there isn't much you can do to someone here. The Houdini . . . is very secure, let's say."

Anna looks up and down the hall. "I'd prefer it if we could avoid him."

"Agreed. Where next?"

"Blackstone's, maybe?" If nothing else, they can interrogate the bartender together.

Max bows. "I'll follow wherever you lead."

But even with both of their keys, the elevator won't take them to the first floor, where room 111 is. It won't take them to the fourth floor, where Harry's is. It won't take them to the lobby. There are, Max tells her, no stairs. In fact, the only floor the elevator will take them to is the fifth floor.

"Why this floor?" Anna asks Max.

He steps out. "I can only think of one answer: the Wardrobe.

I'm pretty sure I know where we should look next, and it involves a fairly drastic costume change."

"Why?"

"Well, you need to find this key, and you said it's near Phoebe, and her favorite place, besides her penthouse is"—Max twirls his key and grins—"the ballroom."

27.

Anna is not so easily swayed; she is on a mission, and time is running out. "But why do we need a costume change?"

"Because it's a ballroom, and there's a ball happening there."

"There's a ball happening tonight? Right now?"

Max starts off down the hall, walking backward to make sure she follows. "There's always a ball happening. That's why it's called the ballroom."

This statement makes as much sense as anything else in the Houdini, and Anna's heart speeds up with unexpected worry. She hasn't been to a dance since the catastrophe that was the eighth-grade formal. Despite all her careful planning, her just-so dress, Emily's perfect work with her hair and makeup, it turned out that her date didn't really like her and his dad just wanted to grill her on her dad's next project from the front seat of his Land Rover.

Once they got to the dance, the guy abandoned her and danced with pretty much every other girl there.

But worst of all, the thought of a ball, of people in formal attire celebrating and dancing, forces Anna to think about Emily's wedding. Emily's perfect wedding, which should have gone exactly as planned but instead became, for Anna, a tragedy. If only her dad hadn't given Emily that apartment in New York. If only Emily hadn't wanted it in the first place. Anna's been squashing down her feelings, but now they erupt like a shaken bottle of champagne, her stomach roiling. If perfectly designed plans can fall to pieces despite all her hard work and best intentions, then it begins to feel like her entire life might be as precarious as a house of cards. What if none of her plans comes to pass?

Well, if she can't figure out how to find the key and escape the Houdini by midnight, her future is over, anyway.

And won't dressing for and attending a ball just waste valuable time?

"Can't we just go as we are?" she asks, stopping.

Max stops, too, and shakes his head. "Anna, you're soaking wet and covered in coffee. You're beautiful, but you can't be comfortable."

She huffs a sigh. "Fine, but we need to hurry."

Anna should know better by now, but still she is surprised when the Wardrobe's door opens to reveal a room subtly changed from when she first found the dress she's wearing, which, as Max pointed out, is embarrassingly stained, wet, and limp from her journey. The walls have the same wallpaper—big, blowsy flowers sprinkled with doves and bees—and the curtains and carpet are still that delicious deep burgundy, but the offerings showcased within are different. There are no pajamas anymore, no drop-waist shifts or forgiving trousers. Now the racks are dominated by gowns and suits. There are short, beaded flapper numbers with swaying fringe; long, elegant dresses in translucent layers of chartreuse and mauve and amber with delicate beading; giant, floofy princess dresses in candy hues with bedazzled bodices and puff sleeves. Anna runs her fingertips over sumptuous velvet, nubby silk, rich satin, tiny pearls, glittering embroidery, slinky chiffon, sequins like cut diamonds.

She looks at Max, who's selected an old-fashioned tux with tails and a pair of shiny shoes and is headed for the door. Guys have it so much easier.

"What's the dress code?" she asks.

He gestures around the room. "Anything on offer will suit."

"But . . . what are the others wearing? What do they wear generally?"

He chuckles. "Who cares? They're not real. You are." Anna must look confused, as he walks back to her, considers the rack in front of her. "Everything you see here is mirrored there. Anything in this room will fit in fine. I'm wearing this." He holds up the crisp black tux with tails, an elegant thing from another time, utterly lacking the awkwardness of JJ's suits in Emily's old prom pictures. "And I can be dressed in five minutes. I'm a whiz with a bow tie."

"But what's the ball like? What kind of music? What styles and colors—" Anna shakes her head. She just wants to know the right answer—she *always* wants to know the right answer. This place is beyond that sort of certainty. She can't even do her usual research—she just has Max. "There is no right answer here, is there?"

"More like, there's no wrong answer here." Max walks to the door and looks back. "Find me in the library, when you're ready. I'll be waiting." The door almost shuts, but then he pokes his head back in. "And don't forget a mask."

When Anna is alone in the room, her immediate reaction is her usual reaction: stress.

Fashion is not her forte. She didn't even know how to help Emily select bridesmaid dresses until she'd read twenty different wedding magazines that explained the process. And it seems, yet again, like the clothing here spans multiple decades, from the slip-like embroidered gowns of the 1920s to the ones with big tulle skirts from the '50s. She doesn't know when Max's tux is from, so she doesn't know how to match it, and—

Well, he said it, didn't he?

There's no wrong answer.

There's no one else here to impress, no one to make fun of her fashion sense, no one to take a hundred bad photos of her and Max standing awkwardly on the stairs while he stabs her with a corsage.

Max is the only other person, and Anna gets the feeling that he'd honestly be just fine if she actually went with the pajamas.

She doesn't have time for this—for all this wondering and floundering. She needs a plan. She needs just the right dress—

No.

It comes to her slowly, like a cat waking and stretching from a very long nap.

What if . . . she just . . . went ridiculous?

Not perfect, not subtle, not exactly what's expected.

What if, instead of trying to guess just the right thing, instead of picking a simple black dress to make sure that she fits in anywhere, instead of doing everything she can to appear normal and focused on her goals like she always does, she instead selects the biggest, most fabulous, most glamorous thing here? Just like she did when she picked out the dress she wore to the ill-fated princess party, all those years ago?

The idea is delicious, a forbidden fruit she's denied herself for too long.

Anna's life is a tightrope, a carefully planned path to hit all the right notes, check off all the right boxes, never stand out, never make a splash, unless it's by winning too many certificates of recognition at the end-of-the-year assembly. Since that party, when she saw the truth, she has hated the fakery and frippery of her father's version of Vegas. She doesn't want to be just another spoiled brat inheriting a legacy—she wants a life of her own choosing, a legacy of her own making. She has always felt eyes upon her, whether those of her peers; or her father's, sharply detecting anything that might embarrass him; or her mother's, hypercritical of anything that doesn't reflect their social standing.

But now . . . well, it's just her and Max, looking for a key, right? And if they don't find it, it won't matter anyway.

She plunges her hands into the racks of gowns, hurriedly pulling things out and shoving them back. She rejects the narrow, gossamer slips and somber chorus concert A-line gowns. She wants floof. A Disney princess gown. A big, bizarre, impossible, incredible gown that would make jaws drop on the Met Gala red carpet and tongues wag at a high school prom. If she's going to give in to the magic and go down this road, she's going to stomp on the gas pedal.

It happens like lightning—her eyes land on deep turquoise, dotted with embroidered flowers, and she knows that it's going to be exactly what she hopes for, whether because the hotel is truly magical or she just has good taste. The ball gown has a swooping, fitted, halter-neck bodice and a spun sugar skirt of three luscious layers of beaded and embroidered tulle that, yes, hearken back to ten-year-old Anna's rainbow skirts. It's heavy on the hanger, as if it's somehow more real than anything she's ever worn before. All her other clothes were made in factories, purchased online or at the mall, worn for a year and then stuffed into garbage bags to donate. This dress looks handmade, loved, someone's dream made reality. It's thick and complicated and insists upon itself.

This dress feels worthy of who Anna wants to be, just now. If she's going to be trapped in this hotel forever, she's going to do it in style.

She takes the dress into the powder room and changes, loving how it zips up as if tailored just for her. The skirts hang from her hips, swishing artfully with each step, and she wonders if this is how Lizzie Bennet felt before dancing with Darcy—the pride minus the prejudice. She dabs jasmine perfume on her pulse points, unwilling to spritz the gown and ruin it, but isn't sure what to do with her hair. Combs and pins are laid out alongside the brush, but she doesn't know how to use any of them and time is of the essence, so she just brushes it back in a low bun, pulling out a few artful pieces to frame her face. Her lipstick and mascara are still holding up, but she swipes on a layer of sparkly rose-gold eye shadow, something entirely new for her. Anna is plain and simple. Anna never glitters.

Until now.

She selects a pair of low heels that she can dance in—and, knowing the Houdini as she does by now, run in—and finds a little clamshell purse that can hold her key and the matchbook and the pack of cards that appeared in her pocket when her ID and phone disappeared.

The back of the Wardrobe room door is covered with golden hooks, which Anna is certain weren't there earlier today—or is it tonight? Each hook holds a mask, and each mask is different. There are big ones and small ones, simple ones and ornate ones, satin swatches and full-face Venetian masks surrounded by feathers. She selects a simple but elegant mask in gold and ties it behind her head to make sure it suits.

It does. Of course it does.

Everything here does.

She hurries out the room and down the hall and only realizes as she steps into the elevator that she was scared to run into Colin, who thankfully didn't appear. The elevator accepts her key, and the sixth-floor button lights up politely. At the library door, she stops and knocks, waiting for Max's response. She takes a deep breath and smooths her hands down her bodice, nervous. When she was getting dressed, she told herself that she didn't care what anyone thought, but now she cares what one boy thinks.

"Come in," Max calls. "Some Enchanted Evening" from *South*

Pacific is playing as she opens the door, and Max stands right across from her as if he's been waiting for this moment all his life.

He looks amazing, and she's not surprised. His tuxedo is immaculate, his black hair brushed back. But what really strikes her is the look on his face, soft and open and filled with wonder.

Because of her.

Because he's looking at her.

"You look stunning," he says, a little breathless.

Anna looks down, blushing, pleased that her new strategy is having an effect. No one has ever looked at her like this before, like she's precious and special and resplendent. People look at Emily like that all the time, and sometimes at her mother, but never really at Anna—because she knows she's a dove among flamingos. Before, she never wanted to be looked at. Now she finds that under the right circumstances, she doesn't mind it.

"You look wonderful, too." She looks up. Her teeth feel dry from smiling so wide. "So this is okay?"

"Very. Very okay. Perfect. Incredible. Astounding. Spectacular."

"I'm not a circus."

"You're better than a circus."

It's ridiculous, but she's beginning to like ridiculous things.

There's something about knowing you might disappear at midnight that changes everything.

Max holds his arm out, and Anna takes it, enjoying the heaviness of the cloth, the sturdiness of his forearm, the proud, formal way he leads her along, the music swelling as it plays them out of the library. She's never really heard a record player before the

Houdini, but it's growing on her, the mellowness and scratchiness of it, like every time a record is played, it's a unique experience that can never be repeated.

They're suddenly shy as they wait for the elevator, and Anna isn't certain whether she should keep clinging to his arm or not, but his arm stays there, so her hand does, too. When the door opens, Max slips his key from the pocket of his jacket and pushes the button for the second floor. Anna likes the aesthetics of the Houdini better than any hotel she's ever been in, but she misses the convenience of an elevator made of mirrors, how grounding they are.

Look, there you are, the mirrors say.

There's spinach in your teeth, but you definitely exist.

This is not some sweet, random dream where nothing makes sense but you never want to wake up.

Without mirrors to show the truth, anything could be possible.

Here, there's only Anna and Max and the rattling descent and a tentative silence that isn't uncomfortable at all. Even the speaker overhead is quiet for once, as if the Houdini is holding its breath. They step off on the second floor, and it looks like the other halls she's seen, except she can hear music floating along like a caress. Not the tinny speakers, not a record player, but what sounds like a full orchestra. Anna's blood is full of champagne bubbles, and her soul is standing on its tiptoes. There's a sense of expectation in the air, and Max thrums with it, too. His arm is tense under her hand, his eyes alight and his breathing quick. He takes out his pocket watch, fiddles with it, and hurriedly shoves it back in his pocket without checking the time. It's nice to know that whatever this is, this excitement, he feels it, too.

"I should put on my mask," he murmurs. He pulls his arm away reluctantly and reaches into his interior jacket pocket, retrieving a familiar black mask that reminds her of Zorro or the Dread Pirate Roberts. When he ties it on, it lends him the air of a rogue, for all that he's the purest person Anna has ever met. Then he grins, and she sees that there's been something dangerous and seductive underneath, as if waiting for the right moment to awaken.

A brief flash: if she gets stuck here at midnight, she'll be here forever, just like Max. He can still talk to the ghosts a little, sometimes, he said. He keeps distracting her—with food, with coffee, with fancy ball gowns and dances. What if, deep down, he *wants* her to get stuck and stay? Friends can leave you. Girlfriends can leave you.

Ghosts can't.

28.

Max and Phoebe aren't the only people who possess a secret knowledge of the Houdini. Colin has lived here longer than either of them and was the golden boy long before Max existed. The speakers used to play Colin's favorite songs. The toy store was always open, once upon a time. There was even a candy store that somehow never gave him cavities. Colin's mother, Celeste, was beautiful and glamorous, much prettier than Phoebe, and she doted on her son and promised him he would one day inherit this palace of wonders. As Colin grew into manhood, he wooed the occasional women who stumbled into the hotel, went to the ball to dance with and dip beauties whose eyes flashed behind their masks. No one ever told Colin no.

And then Phoebe showed up and ruined everything.

First, she killed his mother.

Or, perhaps more accurately, caused her to disappear.

Colin wasn't there for it; he only had Phoebe's word and a pile of ashes on the floor. Celeste was all he'd ever known, other than the hotel's infrequent visitors who never stayed, and he mourned her death and struggled to find his place in a world without his life's only constant companion.

As he began to piece himself back together, he thought he and Phoebe might make a good match, that together they would enjoy all the fine things the Houdini had to offer. But Phoebe spurned his advances, lashed out and punished him.

She had powers over the hotel, he quickly learned.

The last sixteen years have been absolute hell. With one word from Phoebe, the Houdini brusquely closed its wonders to Colin, cold as a cheating lover. Instead of a posh suite, he has a dank basement with perpetually wet floors. Instead of the finest steak and wine, he has iron-tasting water and maggoty bread. Instead of an array of haberdashery, the Wardrobe only offers him slightly damp versions of his janitor's uniform, and his name is always misspelled on the embroidered tag.

Colon.

Collin.

Corlen.

And, one time, Clump.

He has gone from king to peasant, and he wants nothing more than to end Phoebe's reign. The thought of it consumes his every waking thought, but when her knowing, all-seeing minion is the very building in which he lives, how can he ever bring his plans to fruition? His mother once told him there was a well-hidden key he would inherit one day, that she would teach him about a contract, but she was gone before she offered any details. After Phoebe took control, Colin took a sledgehammer to the walls of Celeste's old bedroom, desperate to find whatever she might've stowed away, out of sight. Phoebe didn't take that well; she brings it up constantly, as if he were some idiot child randomly destroying things instead of a man hell-bent on taking back what belongs to him.

He did try to hurt Phoebe once, when he couldn't take it anymore, watching her swan around. After that, she told the hotel to never let Colin harm her or Max, and now he *can't.*

Except . . . he can harm *other* people, can't he?

He can harm this foolish girl.

Phoebe might not know about her, but Max does, and the thought of causing Max the same pain Colin has felt all this time is delicious. Colin hurts the girl, and that hurts Max, and that will hurt Phoebe. And although Phoebe has commanded him not to approach the men, Colin has his ways of listening in, and he knows that these men believe they own the hotel, and that one of them is Anna's father. So if Colin can just get his hands on Anna, he can hurt Max, hurt Phoebe, and possibly have a bargaining chip if the men should take over the hotel. It's a perfect plan.

Well, except for the fact that Max is besotted with the girl and rarely leaves her side.

There is one chance, though. Colin knows that they're going to the ballroom—he was watching from under the door of the fifth-floor janitor's closet as they walked past in their finery. Oh, how he longed to take a girl to the ball, a real girl with soft hands and warm skin, a girl who would look into his eyes and laugh at something clever he'd said. He's visited the ballroom frequently for most of his life, but lately it has depressed him. Phoebe has forbidden him from tasting the hotel's delicacies and drinks, and so the ball is just a reminder of all that he has been denied. A man cannot live on air, no matter how beautiful the glass cup.

But Colin still has an old tuxedo squirreled away in one of the closets, just in case. It's a little snug across the belly and sags across the shoulders, but he can squeeze into it. Perhaps the Wardrobe won't help him, but he can still help himself. He doesn't have to look young and handsome, he just has to blend in with the throng, and only for long enough to snatch the stupid girl when Max isn't looking.

Tonight Colin will take back this hotel, his birthright. And he doesn't care who gets hurt along the way.

29.

Anna and Max step off the elevator and onto the second floor. The colors here recall Cinderella's castle, light blue and gold and gleaming crystal. When Max holds out his arm, Anna takes it, and there's something serious and heavy about their promenade.

Halfway down the hall, two French doors stand open on a scene straight out of one of Emily's favorite period pieces—which, yes, fine, Anna can now admit that she's grown to love, and not just for Emily's sake. The ballroom is absolutely and impossibly enormous, like a cathedral mixed with a warehouse, dominated by a grand chandelier in the center. The floor is polished wood the color of honey, and the back wall is papered in iridescent white like the wings of a moonlit moth. An orchestra plays on a dais opposite the doors, two dozen men in black tuxes entirely focused on their instruments with occasional glances at the madly waving conductor. Down both sides of the room and framing the dance floor, tables covered in white cloths present a mouthwatering array of foods punctuated by glass punch bowls. The walls behind the tables are divided into niches, each one partially hidden by velvet curtains of dove gray, giving a private air to the spaces beyond.

But what's truly arresting are the people. Hundreds of them, dancing and laughing and drinking punch. Max was right—Anna sees flapper dresses and ball gowns and sequined frocks, every iteration of every dress in the Wardrobe in a rainbow of colors, with masks to match. The men wear suits and tuxedos in dark colors and even white, their cuts as varied as their wearers. Every face is masked, which only makes their eyes shine twice as brightly. These people—they have more substance than the diners and bargoers; they're more like the bartender and the waiter, seemingly solid. As Anna and Max stand in the doorway, drinking it all in, she realizes that while she's staring rudely . . . no one is staring back.

"Can they see us?" she asks quietly.

"Not until you get quite close. I've probably talked to, and danced with, all of them over the years. Some of them will reply, but they never remember me the next day. If you bother the orchestra too much, the conductor will smack you with his baton, and you'll definitely feel it." Max says it lightly, a joke, but Anna can detect undercurrents of sadness.

She tries to imagine visiting this ballroom for the hundredth time, finding it entirely unchanged as you, yourself, grow and change. What must it feel like to establish a rapport with someone, make a connection, and know that you'll be entirely forgotten the next day? When Max told her the children in the hotel once played with him and then ran away, he neglected to mention that each day he had to reestablish himself with them, repeat the same introductions, just to get to whatever games they played in their doomed loop.

It's heartbreaking.

And yet he wanted so badly to bring her here.

For Max, this night is a first. He's here with someone who will remember him.

This is not something Anna knows how to put into words, so she settles for getting back to business, because that's what Anna Alonso does.

"So where do you think Phoebe is?"

Max snags both of her hands and faces her. "Anna, look. Just enjoy yourself for five minutes, okay? You have three hours left." As he says it, she sees a clock on the wall, big and bold as the moon, over his shoulder. "Please. For me. For both of us. This might be all we have."

Anna hates that line, the way it's used in songs to talk girls into giving up more than they're willing to; she doesn't like hearing it from Max. "But if I can't figure out how to leave by midnight, you can dance with me here every night, can't you?"

He drops her hands, and his head jerks back like she has slapped him. "Do you think I want that? For you to be a ghost who doesn't remember me? Do you think there would be anything for me in that situation besides sadness? That's not what I want."

"Then what *do* you want, Max?" Anna feels the burn in her cheeks, knows she's ruining everything but can't stop herself.

"I want you to find what you need and escape, but I was hoping there might be ten minutes where you just stopped and enjoyed yourself. It's selfish, I suppose. I've always wanted to dance with you."

Anna goes very still. "But you just met me."

"I . . . I . . . um . . ."

Anna lets him stumble. She needs to know if her assumption is right.

"I've seen you before," Max finally admits, blushing ferociously under his mask. "There's an automaton here that does drawings, and she always gives me a drawing of you. I, um, keep them in a secret room. I didn't know if you were real, but I always hoped I'd meet you. You looked nice."

Oh, the relief that flows through Anna as she learns the truth and all the little pieces click into place. It's still freaky, but there's an innocence about it. That's why Max looks at her the way he does; that's why he acted so strangely when they first met. But why would the hotel do that—how did it know she would arrive one day?

As always, every new revelation in the Houdini brings a new question.

"I've been there," she tells him. "In that room. The hotel sent me there, I guess. The blue room with the dead tree."

Max finally smiles again, and that, too, is a relief. "Oh, it's not dead. When you touch it, it comes to life. White flowers and oranges. An old magic trick."

"Not me. I touched it and it did nothing."

At that, he looks genuinely surprised. "That's strange. Maybe we'll go try it later."

There won't be a later, Anna wants to tell him. Either she's a ghost or she's gone. Thinking Max might selfishly want her here as a faded version of herself—that was silly. She wasn't thinking clearly because, if she's honest with herself, she panicked. Having such strong feelings for him is a little scary. It was easier to turn it back on him, to give him a reason to step away. Anger and accusation are easier than letting someone in. Of course it would be upsetting for him, to see her as a ghost. She knows that if their roles were reversed, wherever she found him, half-see-through and laughing, she would never go back again. It would hurt too much.

And that's when she decides she's not going to be scared. She's not going to hold back. She slides her hand into Max's and pulls him toward the buffet. "The food's real, though, right?"

"Very real. I can especially recommend the petits fours."

Anna is a very serious person, but she has never been this serious about protecting her clothing at all costs. To spill chocolate on this dress would be blasphemy. She darts here and there around the table, nibbling, realizing that it's been several hours and several thousand steps since they had dinner at Harry's Hideaway. She might almost forget that they're here for a mission if not for yet another stern clock face set into an ornate decorative birdcage in the center of the buffet. It's past nine o'clock. She doesn't have much time left. So thoughtful of the Houdini to keep reminding her of how the minutes are slipping away.

Anna dabs at her lips with a napkin, hoping the chocolate-covered strawberry is all gone.

"Okay, I indulged for ten minutes. Now, where is Phoebe? Or where would she hide a key? You said she had a whole ring of them. . . ."

Max looks around the ballroom briefly before refocusing on

her. He takes the napkin from her hand, places it on the table, and pulls her toward the dance floor.

"Come with me."

But instead of leading her toward, oh, some secret door or mysterious dumbwaiter, he swings her onto the dance floor, pulling her close—but not too close. Anna only knows how to dance because she learned from YouTube so that she could help Emily practice for her first dance with JJ, and even then, she led, not followed. Max knows what to do, though, and has his hand at her waist as he guides her into a waltz. At least this isn't Lizzie Bennet's time, when everyone had to memorize complicated country dances. If you can count to three and not stomp on someone's toes, you can waltz.

At first, Anna is uncertain, taking small steps, learning to move with Max, but his confidence and joy infect her, and soon they're sweeping around the room with the crowd, the world twirling around and around until she is quite certain she'd be dizzy—if she wasn't staring at Max.

It's intense—maybe too intense—what she sees in his eyes.

He barely knows her. She barely knows him. And yet—

"I don't think we're going to find hidden things by dancing," she says lightly, desperately clinging to logic so she doesn't just give in to her desire to kiss him.

"You can discover all sorts of things, dancing," he replies, his voice low and warm. The black of the tux makes his blue eyes glimmer, and in the candlelight, surrounded by glittering dresses, Anna sees a thousand colors in their crystalline depths. Still, this is her second time returning the topic of discussion to her quest and his second time distracting her from it.

She presses on. "In the niches, maybe? Under the buffet table? Do you think Phoebe might've given the key to one of these people to . . . hold on to?"

Max looks a bit disappointed to be called to task but answers nonetheless. "We'll check the niches. And, yes, I suppose a key could be anywhere on the tables or tucked behind something, although people here can't perform that sort of duty. If you try to hand them something, it just falls to the ground."

The song ends, and they join the crowd in clapping for the orchestra before a slow song starts up, and Max pulls Anna even closer, his hands sliding down to settle warmly on the small of her back. Her hands join behind his neck, brushed by the tips of his curling hair, her wrists light on his shoulders. He's so close, she can smell his cologne and the soapy, boy scent of him, feel his breath whisper past her hair. The other dancers surround them, brushing past like curtains in a breeze. She can hear murmurs but detect no particular words, hear their laughter but not their jokes. Although she would expect to smell a mélange of bodies, perfumes, and colognes, they don't seem to have a scent; all she smells is Max. It's the oddest sensation, being completely surrounded and yet utterly alone.

Their eyes meet and understanding passes between them like electricity. Max's eyelashes sweep down, and he leans in—

"Why does Phoebe come here?" Anna squawks, and he jerks back, frowning a little.

She's never been kissed, and she's not used to so many emotions, to this closeness, to the way he looks at her—

"Do we have to talk about my mom right now?"

"I'm trying to understand. Everything here defies sense." She can't fidget with her hands behind his neck, but she definitely got skittish when she saw that he was going to kiss her for real.

Max sighs, his fingers tapping along her back. "I would never claim to know her mind, but I suspect it's because when you come to the ballroom, at least for a little while, you can forget that you ever wanted to leave." He leans back in, mischief written across his features. "And the punch is quite nice. A few cups, and you forget a lot of things."

Anna draws back, laughing. "Why, Max, do you come here to get smashed?"

He shrugs one shoulder. "There's no one here to arrest me. Why not?"

She gets the tiniest, annoyingly welcome bad-boy vibe from that response and briefly considers trying a cup of punch, but . . .

The song ends, and before the orchestra can play something even more romantic, Anna pulls away, grabbing Max's hand and tugging him toward the niches set in the walls.

"Promise you'll dance with me later?" he asks.

"If we find the key, we can dance again."

And she does want to dance more—she wants to try the forbidden punch and nestle her head against his chest and hear his heartbeat during another slow song and have no worries and nothing waiting and no plans for the future. She wants to be kissed, she does. But this isn't some pleasant daydream—she's trapped here, and she needs to find her father and get out, and therefore she must find the missing key before midnight. The more time she spends here, the more certain she becomes that she won't escape the fate of the Houdini's other residents if she fails.

Magic can give her dresses and ice cream and drinks, but it can also spring traps and chain girls up and turn them into stone. Anna has been told that the Houdini is a gilded cage, and she does not wish to be captured. She does not wish to fade away.

Max follows as she floats from niche to niche. In one, an automaton plays chess with the audience, masked dancers stepping forward to move the game pieces and watch what the freckle-faced wooden boy will do next. In another, a woman's head seems to float in a crystal ball at a spooky séance. In a third, a somber clown clad in a baggy suit covered in stars holds up a hoop for a pink toy poodle to jump through.

"Fair warning: the dog is real," Max murmurs in Anna's ear. "And he's not friendly."

In the next niche, a crowd of people are focused on something within, whispering their excitement. Max moves ahead of her, gently making room, and the people effortlessly shift to oblige. Much to Anna's surprise, there's a robot—or what someone in the early twentieth century might consider a robot—sitting at a heavy desk. The robot is crafted of wood and metal in the shape of an elegant woman with a Mona Lisa smile. Although the desk is clearly a box that contains mysterious machinery, the woman's dress is quite real, down to its tiny buttons and delicate lace, and in her hand is a pencil. Her arm moves jerkily, the pencil lightly sketching on a piece of paper clipped to a drawing board.

"She's called L'Artiste," Max whispers. "An automaton. When I'm here, she only ever draws you. I've been watching her since I was ten and I still don't understand how she works."

Anna steps closer, mesmerized by the automaton's perfectly curled eyelashes, drawn low over downcast eyes. There's no way to get behind her—her desk blocks the crowd—which must be part of the trick. Her pencil scritches over the paper, a sound barely audible over the murmurs of the audience and the foxtrot playing in the room beyond. It's fascinating, sure, but Anna has seen many robots, and she has objectives of her own. She moves out of the crowd, checking the sides of the desk for hidden panels and running her hands over the frames of the landscape paintings on the pearlescent white walls. There are no cubbies here, no desk with locked drawers that might hold keys, no secret doors. Just a robotic wonder and her audience.

"She's done," Max calls softly, and Anna abandons her search and joins him.

L'Artiste bows at the waist, the movement somehow both graceful and jerky, and straightens back up, tilting her chin as if to inspect her work. Before Max can take the paper, Anna swoops in to grab it.

She gasps, and the world tunnels down to the piece of paper in her hands. It's a sketch . . . of Max. He's in his tux, tears running down his face. On one shoulder sits a canary. Over his other shoulder is the clock from the lobby, stopped at exactly midnight. His hands are over his heart, clutching something to his chest that's glowing from within.

"But . . . it's always been you," Max says, leaning closer. He seems perplexed, even a little upset. "That's . . . really odd. Her sketches are never this detailed. Why me? And why am I crying? The clock I understand, but why the canary? And what am I holding?" He looks up at Anna, confused. "What does it mean?"

"I don't know." She clutches the drawing in one hand, suddenly feeling very young and small and silly in the grand, heavy dress, like she's playing at someone else's life. "I don't know." She isn't aware of what she's doing until she's done it, but she steps into Max, one hand against his chest, her forehead to his cheek, knowing he'll wrap his arms around her and provide comfort that she's never before needed.

He obliges, because he's Max.

"Don't be frightened. We'll figure it out," he murmurs into her hair.

"But what if we don't?"

He rubs her back. "We will. We have to. We won't let it come true."

And they won't. She won't. Anna Alonso does not give up.

She swallows hard, disentangles herself from him. The drawing is limp and creased in her hand, and she folds it up until it's small enough to fit in her shell-shaped bag.

"Let's try another niche," she says, wishing her voice didn't wobble.

"Whatever you need." Max's voice is deceptively even as he holds open the curtain for her to leave, but before she can step through, his arm blocks her and he goes rigid.

"What—" she starts.

"Shh. Don't move." He looks at her. "It's Phoebe."

30.

Anna peers excitedly around Max, hunting for her prey through the crowd. This is exactly what she was hoping would happen.

Phoebe has no idea she's here, which means she can follow Phoebe, possibly to the key.

The ball beyond the curtains continues, merry and unabated, but a single figure moves through the crowd. The woman who shoved Anna into a secret passage behind a wine barrel is easily distinguishable from those who surround her. She wears the same sharp suit instead of a gown and is maskless, frowning as she pushes through the throng like a fierce ship bashing a path through a vast ice floe.

The dancers shift around Phoebe without stopping or showing any sort of surprise or outrage as she stalks with singular focus to a niche across the room, the one farthest from the door to the hallway.

"We have to follow her," Anna whispers.

"Give her some space. If she sees us . . ."

"What if she sees us? She's your mom. It's not like she can hurt us."

Max grimaces. "Just trust me: You can get a lot more done when she doesn't know you're around. If she has the key, she won't want you to have it."

Phoebe puts a hand on the velvet curtain and looks over her shoulder, and both Max and Anna duck down out of sight. When Anna risks another look, the severe woman is gone, the curtain gently swinging in her wake. Without consulting Max, Anna hurries after her.

"Anna, no—" he starts, but she's already committed.

She skirts the crowd, swaying to look like she's part of it in case Phoebe is feeling paranoid. Max grabs her arm and spins her around, pulling her close and into the dance.

"Just give her a moment before we follow," he hisses, hands clamped at her waist as Anna bares her teeth and nearly growls.

She jerks away, absolutely done with being restrained. "And what if she disappears through some hidden door and we miss it? I need that key. Before midnight. It's the most important thing. And we both know she's not here for the dance, so there must be another reason, and it's in that niche."

"Yes, but it's a very small niche. If we follow, she'll see us."

"And then what, Max? What if she sees us? What is an adult going to do to two teens in a public place?"

He looks away, brow furrowed. "All she has to do is catch us and lock us in a closet, and we'll never be able to find that key."

"Then I won't let her catch me." Anna turns and hurries to the niche where Phoebe disappeared. She hears Max curse behind her and knows he's following her.

She reaches the niche and hides behind the gray curtain, daring a quick glance within. A white-mustached magician in an old-fashioned tailcoat and top hat stands before a big red box on a wheeled stand. The box's top is open, and it looks unnervingly like a coffin. Across the top, *The Great Torrini* is painted in elegant gold.

The bottom drops out of Anna's stomach as she realizes she's seen this man before, long ago, when she was ten, at a birthday party she didn't want to attend. The magician hasn't aged a day.

And he's not completely see-through; he's more like the bartender and the waiter.

But how did he get here? Is he one of the random, occasional guests who wander in and become ghosts? Or did the Houdini let him out? Are her memories of the party flawed, warped by years of embarrassment and her sleeplessness in this topsy-turvy place?

Even having accepted the Houdini's inner logic, Anna can't make sense of it. The hotel seems to know things, seems to have an influence in the bigger world. How far, she wonders, does the star's magic reach?

"Might I have a volunteer?" the magician calls, and the woman who breaks out of the crowd to stand defiantly before him is Phoebe.

"I will now hypnotize this woman and, with the help of my assistants, saw her in half!" The crowd murmurs and claps politely, but Phoebe's high-heeled foot taps with impatience.

The magician gesticulates around Phoebe's head as if trying to draw ghosts out of her ears. Phoebe looks deeply bored. Two younger men in tailcoats arrive. One of them stands behind Phoebe and the other behind the magician.

"Abracazam!" the magician cries, and Phoebe falls backward into the waiting assistant's arms. Together, the assistants lift her into the box by her shoulders and her feet.

Anna risks a glance at Max, who is utterly transfixed and also . . . disgusted? He looks as if he's discovering an unpleasant secret, but the whole thing feels as impossible as everything else in the hotel.

"I didn't know you could just push your way to the front," he mutters. "He's never chosen me, even though I volunteered."

Once Phoebe is in the box, the assistants make a big deal of putting guards over her feet and neck while the magician makes dramatic flourishes to the tune of a hurdy-gurdy played by a tiny monkey in a fez. If what was happening didn't feel like a life-and-death situation, if this was a show she was witnessing in one of her father's more reliable hotels, Anna would be charmed and taking photos to show Emily. She would know it wasn't real, that it was interesting and carefully crafted. As it is, she inspects every aspect of the scene, knowing there's some trick at hand, some hidden but very real magic, and that Phoebe isn't here to have fun with the ghost of a magician.

The music speeds up as the magician fusses with the box. Phoebe's head sticks out one side, her feet out the other. The assistants spin the box around, showing that it is indeed moving freely. When the magician picks up a shining silver saw with two handles, Anna feels a bone-deep runnel of fear. The magician is corporeal, and the saw looks very real, and Phoebe is trapped. Even if she is cruel and a thief, she doesn't deserve to be slowly sawed in half through the gut. With plenty of flourishes, the magician inserts the gleaming metal blade into a special slot in the box and begins sawing.

When the saw is halfway through, Anna is surprised that Phoebe's only reaction is a bored little sigh. Otherwise, she simply lies there, staring at the ceiling. Finally, with much grunting and groaning on the magician's part, the saw is through, and the assistants slide in panels to hide what should rightly be Phoebe's bleeding insides.

"We don't wish to disturb the ladies with such gore," the magician intones solemnly as the assistants pull the boxes apart, allowing enough room for Torrini to stand between them. Much to Anna's surprise, he looks directly at her and winks.

The crowd gasps and claps and murmurs, and Anna looks at Max.

"It's just a trick," he whispers, but he sounds worried.

After twirling the individual boxes around to prove Phoebe has truly been cut in half, the assistants push the boxes back together, pull out the center panels, and struggle dramatically to open the top, which appears to be stuck.

"A bad fit," the magician tuts. "Perhaps I can speed the process along."

He walks to Phoebe's head and pushes it gently into the box, then does the same with her feet. Nothing of Phoebe is visible now.

"That's better, isn't it?" The magician flips open little windows on the sides and top of the box, revealing that it is now completely empty. The crowd gasps in surprise before a thunderous applause.

"What the hell?" Max murmurs.

He pushes past Anna and into the room, shoving through the crowd. It parts for him, Anna following in his wake.

"My good sir, if you are amazed by this miracle, perhaps you'd like to pick a card, any card," Torrini begins, producing a deck of cards that Anna recalls with perfect clarity. But Max just shoves past him, feeling around in the box and squatting to look under it.

"Clever," Max mutters as Anna joins him. This close to the wall, she can see it, too—a carefully hidden panel in the wainscoting, just the size of the box, with no visible way to open it.

"How does it open?" Anna asks the magician.

"How does what open, miss?"

"The secret panel that woman just went through."

Torrini smiles at her like he's just walked out of her memories and says, "We think we know what's possible, but the role of the magician is to prove otherwise."

"That's not an answer."

He tips his hat. "Some things are more stubborn than others, wouldn't you say?" He bows, whipping off his hat to show that it's empty before producing a cottony white rabbit with curious pink eyes from its black satin depths. He places the rabbit on the floor, and it gives Anna a significant look and lollops off toward the dance floor, but Anna isn't taking the bait.

"How are you here?" she asks Torrini. "Did you stay past midnight?"

Torrini looks as pleased as a mall Santa, his eyes sparkling.

"Logic only gives a man what he needs. Magic gives him what he wants."

"Spouting quotes doesn't answer the question."

"Then perhaps you asked the wrong question."

Max reaches out to grab the man's lapels, but his hands go straight through him.

"Don't believe your eyes, kid," Torrini says, waggling his eyebrows.

Fairly certain that they're not going to get anything more out of the magician, Anna wedges her fingers into the seams of the panel on the wall and fusses with it until she snaps a nail.

"How do I open it?"

Torrini ignores her, ignores Max's questions. He starts pulling familiar handkerchiefs from his pocket, and they mound on the floor in crimson and goldenrod and emerald and indigo, rich and silky and useless. The crowd claps and the show goes on, oblivious to the two people trying desperately to open the secret panel.

The panel, much like a magician's mouth in regard to his secrets, refuses to open.

31.

Elsewhere in the Houdini, three childhood friends face off in an empty casino, the air thick with cigar smoke and long-simmering rage.

"Are you threatening me?"

Daniel directs this to Tony, but it's clearly meant for both Tony and Sebastian. This is not an equilateral triangle; Sebastian and Tony have subtly arrayed themselves against Daniel. He's seen flashes of their dissatisfaction with their arrangement lately, looks exchanged when signing contracts or hammering out new acquisitions. He always assumed this was just how business partnerships worked, that sometimes he would come out on top, and sometimes he would compromise, and the end result would be a general rising of the tide that would raise their communal ships.

But something about this place—about the storm and the smoke and the drinks and the gambling—has brought out the worst in his friends. Tony's temper and greed, Sebastian's tendency to be sneaky and dishonest. Daniel doesn't feel that he's asking too much to leave the casino. He knows his business partners both have gambling problems, but it seems obvious that finding a missing child should be more important than collecting pennies in a bucket.

It would appear the other two men disagree. Violently. Daniel's eyes shift around the room as he looks for a weapon.

There are none. Other than Sebastian's bottle, there's nothing but slot machines.

There are no people here. No guests. No employees.

No witnesses.

"Let's be reasonable," he says, having found no weapon and realizing that it's two against one. "You can have all the coins you want. I'll help you carry them. I just want to find my daughter. Hell, I'll leave you guys here alone to gamble and go find her myself. I don't want to fight with you."

"Who said we wanted to fight?" Tony says, weaving back and forth like the boxer he used to be. "Who said it had anything to do with your dumb kid?"

Daniel doesn't take the bait. "I'm just trying to find a way to move past . . . whatever this is."

For a long, tense moment, the three men just stand there, eyes flitting back and forth.

And then Tony straightens up and grins, arms out wide. "It's nothing," he says. "Come on, Daniel. You're worried about your kid. I get that. I guess the champagne just went to my head. Maybe you're right. Let's gather up the winnings and get the hell out of here."

Daniel's body relaxes as the tension drains from the room. "Yeah, let me help you. Thanks, Tony." He goes over to a janitor's closet and pulls out a bucket. It's not clean, but it's not wet. "How about this?"

"That'll do. Let's start with the quarters."

But Daniel is Daniel, so first he upends Sebastian's bucket of pennies into the bigger bucket, then heads over to the machine that spewed quarters. This happens every few years—Tony gets riled up and acts threatening and then comes to his senses before they all cross a line that can't be uncrossed. Usually Sebastian de-escalates the situation, but not this time.

As the three men squat to collect the money, Daniel runs after an errant quarter and Sebastian's eyes meet Tony's and ask a silent question. Tony's answering grin is a dark and promising thing.

He puts his thumb against his neck, draws it across in a gesture that Sebastian understands completely. When Sebastian taps his watch, eyebrows raised, Tony nods.

It's got to happen soon.

32.

"So you had no idea?" Anna asks Max. They've moved out of the niche and back into the main ballroom.

"That there was a secret compartment in the wall that can only be accessed from inside the magician's box? No." Max's face is red, his hands in fists. "I've watched that trick dozens of times, but I've never seen him push the girl inside the box. They usually just help her climb back out. Phoebe disappearing—that's not part of the trick. I thought she just liked to come here for the same reasons I did. Guess I was wrong."

"What's on the other side of this wall?" Anna puts her hand against the glowing white wallpaper, which is solid under her hand.

"A smoking lounge. Now I'm guessing there's a hidden passage between them, one I've never found." Max's eyes meet hers, and he seems lost at sea. "I've read enough to know that yardsticks and rulers exist, but do you know that I've never seen one?

Phoebe must go to great lengths to keep them out of the hotel." He knocks his forehead softly against the wall. "Because if I could measure things, I would know where the numbers don't add up. Where there are empty spaces between the walls, hidden places I'm not allowed to find."

"Maybe we could wait awhile, then try to open the passage? Or look from the other side, in the lounge?"

Max shakes his head hopelessly before looking up at Anna. "No. Not that. If she's in there, we don't want to be trapped with her. We should do the opposite."

"The opposite?"

He perks up and grins. "Try to break into her penthouse from the roof. Because we know where she is right now, and the seventh floor is about as far from here as you can get. Come on."

Max takes her hand, but Anna pulls out of his grasp.

"I know that I'm the first person you've really met," she says carefully, "but you can't just keep grabbing me, like you did on the dance floor."

"I was trying to stop you—"

"And that's not your right. Things in my time have advanced from"—she waves her hands around at the ballroom—"whatever times you're used to. Guys can't just grab girls like that."

Max looks mortified. "I'm so sorry. It won't happen again."

Instead of touching her, he gestures at the door and follows her out of the ballroom, and she gives one last, fond look to the buffet table. Outside, Max unties his mask and tosses it on a divan as they pass, and Anna follows suit, glad to feel air on her face again. Poor Max looks a little shell-shocked, like he's been overwhelmed by too many emotions in a short amount of time. Happiness, then sadness, then frustration, then mortification.

It's the same cycle Anna went through from the beginning of the wedding to her dad announcing Emily's wedding gift.

In the elevator, she's surprised when Max selects the fifth floor.

"I thought we were going to the roof?"

He twirls the key's chain around his finger. "We are. But you can't climb down a building and through a window in that dress, so we're hitting the Wardrobe first."

"I wasn't aware adventures required quite so many costume changes."

He grins. "Just think of it like a play, then. Or like we're spies. Or detectives."

Anna likes that his excitement is back, but she's uneasy about how much time they're taking. The next clock they pass suggests they only have two hours until midnight, two hours to find the key. Every costume change, every dance, every trip to the buffet bleeds time that Anna doesn't have. And she's worried that they haven't seen a single sign of her dad or his friends. Even in a much larger hotel, with no other denizens, they should have found a soggy footprint in soft carpet or heard her father's raised voice echoing down a hallway. Anna had half hoped she'd see her dad at the ball, but it's very much not his scene. He hates parties— unless there's a business aspect. He spent most of Emily's wedding reception sitting at a table in the back, scrolling through his phone while Uncle Tony hit on all the widows and divorcées.

Then again, perhaps the Houdini is keeping them separated on purpose. Max mentioned it earlier, and Anna has had plenty of evidence that it's possible. And that makes her more anxious to get into Phoebe's suite and find the key. If the hotel won't let her see her dad until she's fulfilled her promise, then that's got to be her priority.

They grab dark, sensible clothes in the Wardrobe, and Max goes to the room next door to change while Anna uses the powder room. She's all business now, braiding her hair to keep it out of her face . . . but she leaves on the eyeshadow, just because. When she emerges in the hall, someone grabs her arm.

"Max, I said—"

"I'm not Max."

She gasps and shudders when she realizes that it's Colin.

She immediately tries to wrench her arm away, but his fingers are dug in deep enough to leave bruises. He's in an ill-fitting tuxedo now, stained and wrinkled, tailored for a smaller man and reeking of years of nervous sweat.

"What do you want?" Anna growls, fighting him as he tries to drag her down the hall, away from the elevator and toward an open door. "Max!"

Colin's other hand clamps down over her mouth, and she gags at the smell of bleach and something so rotten it can't be bleached away. "None of that, now. Come on." His voice is rough and ragged.

Like he's got nothing left to lose.

He's bigger than her, taller than her, a fully grown man. He's willing to do damage, and no matter how she twists and stomps and tugs, his grip doesn't loosen. Furious and terrified, Anna collapses her legs and slumps on the ground, and it takes him a minute to get a better grip, now that she's dead weight.

"Just do as you're told!" Colin hisses, dragging her down the hall as she tries to dig in her toes, her heels, anything to keep her out of that yawning open door to what looks like a janitor's closet but is probably a dark, dank passageway that leads somewhere much worse.

Anna knows, on some instinctual level, that if Colin manages to get her through that door, all chances of escape are over. From him, and from the hotel's magic.

"Anna!"

Relief floods her chest as Max appears. Colin releases Anna's mouth but not her arm and flails at Max with an animalistic scream. With a powerful yank, Anna tears herself from him, his nails scoring her forearm as the power of her desperation lands her on the floor. She skitters backward on her rump, trying to get away from the two men squaring off in the plush hallway. Young and fading, clean and filthy, kind and cruel, they circle each other like dogs as she stands and puts a hand against the wall to steady herself.

"You took it all!" Colin growls, throwing a punch that goes wide.

"Not on purpose!" Max growls back, ducking out of range and socking Colin in the stomach.

"You don't deserve it! You and your bi—" Max's next punch catches Colin in the jaw, silencing the last word.

Anna wants to help, but she isn't sure how. She's never been in a fight in her life, never even practiced throwing a punch. There are no weapons, no cameras, no management, no police. They could fight to the death here and there's nothing she could do.

Colin throws another punch, which misses Max entirely and

sends the bigger man stumbling off balance. He backs up and tries to tackle Max, but it ends up an awkward hug, as if Colin weighs nothing and has no strength. He's grunting and growling like a little kid grappling with an adult; apparently nothing he can do has any effect. Max throws him off, and as Colin staggers backward, punches him in the ribs. With a gasp of pain, Colin doubles over, clutching his side.

He looks up, glaring hate, and barks, "I'll kill you!"

But then there's a real bark—and a low, deep growl.

The men part, and they all stare down the hall toward the open elevator. The toy poodle from the ballroom's clown act stands there stiffly, its cotton candy puffs of pink fur quivering as it pulls back its lips and growls.

To Anna, it's almost comical—this poodle couldn't bite higher than her ankles. Much to her surprise, Max stands protectively in front of her, while Colin gasps and stumbles away, his back against the wall.

"No!" he yelps. "No! I'm sorry! I'll stop, I'll—"

The poodle, which doesn't even come up to Anna's knees, stalks down the hallway toward them, teeth bared, still growling, its black shark eyes pinned on Colin. He backs down the hallway, hands up and breathing heavily. He looks like he's being threatened by a lion, not a lapdog.

"Don't move," Max whispers to Anna through clenched teeth. "Not an inch."

Her back against the wall, Anna holds her breath as the poodle barks like a dog ten times its size and runs directly for Colin. He spins around, stumbles, and takes off for the open door he was dragging Anna toward, the poodle snapping at his tux jacket and flinging foam from its lips. As it gallops past her, close enough for her to smell its baby-powder perfume, Anna realizes that somehow, impossibly, the dog has become the size of a pony. As soon as Colin and the poodle are through the door, it slams neatly shut. Max sags in obvious relief.

"What just happened?" Anna asks, rubbing the scratches on her bruised arm. "That was crazy. How did the poodle grow? How can it use an elevator?"

The look Max gives her is wry, almost pitying. "The elevator has a mind of its own. You know that."

"But that doesn't explain how—"

Max exhales and begins to roll up the sleeves on his black button-down. "I told you in the ballroom—the poodle is not friendly. It doesn't age. It changes size. I don't know if it's my mother's pet or her . . . guard. Sometimes I wonder if it's some kind of demon. She uses it to torture Colin. And sometimes me, if I've misbehaved."

"I'm pretty sure that poodle just saved my life."

Max raises his chin, puffs out his chest a little. "I was holding my own."

Anna can't stop staring at the door to the janitor's closet. She's still trembling. "My hero. Now can we get out of here? I never want to see that guy again. Why did he even do that? Like he was trying to kidnap me." She takes a shuddering breath, her hands in fists. "Oh God. He was . . . he really was trying to kidnap me."

Max takes Anna's shaking hands in his, then pulls her to his chest, his chin over her head. "It's okay now. He can't hurt you.

If the poodle is involved, Colin is probably going to be too busy running all night to mess with you again." He plants a kiss on the crown of her head. "Come on, now. You're safe. We have work to do, right?"

"You said Colin tried to kill your mom once. . . ."

"A long time ago." Max strokes her back, again and again, and she begins to calm down. "He can't hurt my mom or me now, but I guess he's allowed to hurt you. Did you notice how his punches couldn't touch me? Maybe he thought you could be a bargaining chip."

"Gross."

"Very gross. I'm not leaving you alone again. I can't believe he dared."

Normally, Anna wouldn't want someone to suggest they weren't leaving her alone, but in this case, she'll allow it. She doesn't want to be alone. She doesn't want to give Colin any more chances to corner her or pull her into a dark closet. It was strange, how every punch or kick Colin attempted on Max failed with the clown-like flair of professional wrestling, whereas Anna can feel bruises everywhere he touched her.

Her shivers have finally stopped, and Max unwraps himself from around her and gives her an encouraging smile. They walk side by side to the elevator, as if he understands she won't tolerate being grabbed and pulled around but knows she wants him to stay close. As Anna waits for it to open, her eyes don't leave the door Colin wanted to drag her through. If she was to design a magical hotel, she wouldn't include places like that or the crypt, dark and empty and sinister.

When the elevator doors open, Max pushes the button marked *R,* and the car rattles upward, playing a jaunty song about swinging on a star, the man's voice as smooth and sweet as caramel. They're standing side by side, their backs against the polished wood and their shoulders almost touching as Max fiddles with his pocket watch. Anna is rattled, and she hates that the intimacy they'd developed at the ball has been eroded by . . . well, Colin's attack and attempted kidnapping. Yes, Max comforted her—in just the right sort of way. But she doesn't want him to touch her out of pity or mercy or kindness. She wants him to touch her because it makes him feel alive. She wants him to touch her because he can't not touch her. Right now it's like he's scared to touch her at all.

The elevator bings and the doors open on the roof. Before Anna can see what's outside, she can smell it: flowers. Surprised, she steps out into a forest, or possibly a jungle.

It's nighttime and the sky is perfectly clear and spattered with stars. What she can see of the rooftop around her is bordered by tall walls of greenery bursting with vines and flowers. Strings of round white light bulbs glow like icing on a cake and candles glitter in dark corners, leading the way through what feels like a hedge maze. A chorus of birds sings and chirps—and screeches?—nearby. Max steps out of the elevator, and Anna looks around in total wonderment as her eyes adjust to the night.

"What is this place?" she asks.

She shyly holds out her hand, and Max takes it and leads her forward. "Let me show you."

33.

Their path winds among the hedges, the scents of jasmine and gardenia commingling. It's intoxicating, with a gentle breeze and the soft susurrus of leaves instead of the constant old-fashioned music Anna has grown so accustomed to in the past hours. Right when her eyes adjust to the light, the path opens up to an outdoor café with a wooden pergola covered in climbing flowers. Colorful round tables with spindly chairs are topped with candles in mason jars. Around the perimeter, wooden troughs and planters spill colorful flowers and fountains of grasses, and concrete statues of rabbits pose around a currently useless sundial.

The most arresting thing, though, is an open aviary that resembles a gazebo. The sides are an almost see-through net, and inside a flock of small birds chirps and twitters and sings. They are all about the same size and shape, ranging from yellow to red, orange, olive, and bright turquoise.

"Canaries," Anna murmurs, putting a hand to the net. The birds flock to her touch, curling their little claws into the net and plucking curiously at her fingers.

Just like on the card she pulled from the magician's deck as a child. Just like the card in the tin in her back pocket. Just like the automaton's most recent drawing, folded up and tucked beside that tin.

"Don't worry, they won't bite," Max says. "I like to bring them treats so they're not scared."

"Why canaries?" Anna asks.

He smiles and pokes a finger through the netting. The birds jostle to sit on it. "Lots of magicians use canaries."

Near the aviary, nestled in the shadows, there's a boxlike building that resembles an old train car with a half-moon serving window like the one in Harry's Hideaway.

"You don't think this is a house elf situation?" Anna asks. "Like in Harry Potter? Like, are the people producing the food doing it by choice?"

Max puts his hands in his pockets and gives her a confused look. "Who's Harry Potter?"

"Oh." She chuckles. "You're the only person on earth who doesn't know. He's a character from a book written in the nineties. A wizard. The books were great, but the author turned out to be a piece of work. Anyway, there was this magic school, and food just appeared all the time, and you find out in the second book in the series that all this time, what you thought was magic were enslaved elves producing food and cleaning up messes and carrying suitcases, and then you're supposed to believe that the elves are happy and love serving people. . . ." Anna sighs. "I just want to know how the magic works, you know?"

Max nods. "I've always wanted to know. I used to create complicated traps to try to catch someone moving my food trays or cleaning up my stray socks, but it never worked. Whoever or whatever it is, it seems . . . benevolent? It's always been kind to me. I hope it's not someone who feels like they're being taken advantage of." He glances nervously at the train car and shouts, "Hello there! Are you working against your will? Are you happy?"

Max and Anna stare at the dark, empty building for several long moments, but there is no response whatsoever, and their focus returns to the birds jockeying for their attention.

A subtle thump makes Anna look back at the serving window, and she's both startled and utterly unsurprised to find a silver tray sitting there with two steaming mugs of hot chocolate topped with swirling mounds of whipped cream. She walks over, and Max joins her. A small note in elegant pen reads, *Confined together, thee and we.* It's in beautiful cursive with a little heart over the *i*.

"So whoever's doing all the magic . . . is also trapped here?" Max asks. He hasn't sipped his hot chocolate yet, hasn't even taken the mug. He's staring at it like it might bite him.

Anna thinks about the girl in the crypt and the story of the star and wishes she could talk to Max about it without having to write it all down. The girl said Phoebe had trapped her, that she needed the key to escape. And then the girl turned to stone. And then the story suggested she's really a fallen star responsible for creating and maintaining the Houdini per some twisted magical contract. Is the note from her? And how can she leave a note or make a latte or pick up socks if she's chained up in a crypt? None of it makes sense. None of it is possible. And Anna is just a normal girl who ran inside to shelter from a storm, yet she's somehow supposed to fix it all?

Everything would be so much easier if she could just find the machinery at work. She doesn't see a door into the structure, so she goes up on her tiptoes to look inside the window. From what she can see, it's just wood, with no hidden doors or joints or hinges. It's almost as if it was built for effect rather than function.

"Anything?" Max asks.

"Nothing. Just a solid box." Anna feels a little silly, trying so hard to find an answer, but at least her curiosity is sated regarding whether a girl in a long white nightgown could silently get into and out of the booth without being noticed. The deeper Anna gets into the Houdini, the more she believes in something beyond reality . . . because magic is becoming the only possible answer for what she's experiencing.

At a loss, she picks up a mug and sips, noting that the hot chocolate is thick and rich and deep and just the right temperature and feels almost medicinal, as if someone, somewhere, somehow evaluated the situation and delivered exactly what she needed most right now. Max picks his mug up but doesn't drink.

"I never thought about that—that the magic might be powered by . . . something bad. My entire life, I've depended on it, leaned on it. When I had a stomachache or headache, I would ask for medicine, and it would deliver."

"Where was your mom?" Anna asks.

Max shrugs. "She was there when I was little, but as I got older, I guess we grew apart." He looks a bit sheepish. "I . . . had more stomachaches and headaches once I started going to the ballroom by myself. Too many cakes, too much punch. I didn't want her to know."

Of course this thought reminds Anna of the fact that throughout her childhood, her parents were often absent when she was sick, leaving Emily to act as nurse. Whenever Anna felt bad, her mother always felt worse and swore she was too ill to care for someone else. And her father was almost always at work. Thanks to Emily's presence, Anna didn't even notice their absence; she always felt cared for. She's never really considered that part before— she thinks of herself as taking care of everyone, but when she's sick, Emily's the one who takes care of her.

Emily, who is going away.

"What's on your mind?" Max asks.

Anna looks down, shakes her head. "Just worrying, as usual."

"Hey, now, this is no time for melancholy." Max steps closer and looks down at her, and she looks up at him. It's like the stars are caught in his hair. "I come here to see the sky. It's always night here. It's my only real connection to your world. I used to come up here and wonder about the girl in the drawings. Wonder what she was doing, and if she could see the same stars that I was wishing on."

His hand moves to cup her cheek, but he freezes.

"Is . . . is this okay?" he asks, uncertain.

"I—" Anna can barely breathe. "Yes."

With a little hum of relief, Max leans in, slowly, eyes open, giving her plenty of time to turn away or move, but she doesn't. She stands, frozen, excited but a little scared, hands wrapped around her mug, looking into his stormy eyes, and then his lashes finally sweep down and his lips just brush hers, the softest and warmest of flutters.

"There," Max whispers, his forehead against hers. "That's what I wished for."

Anna leans into him, likes their foreheads touching, appreciates that she doesn't have to worry about what she's doing with her hands if they're holding a mug, nor with her eyes if they're shut. For a long moment, she and Max simply exist, and she replays that butterfly flutter of a kiss over and over in her head, half terrified and half hoping that he'll come back for more.

Just as she's decided that she's going to have to be the one to lean in again, there's a loud screech overhead, and they break apart shyly. White wings flash against the night, and Anna watches an enormous cockatoo settle on a perch over the train car. More and more bodies flutter down, big wings beating the air, parrots and cockatoos and lovebirds squawking and trilling to each other, taking their places on perches that were, until now, almost invisible against the night-dark hedges and buildings.

Anna can feel the birds' bright black eyes on her. When they beat their wings, wind ruffles her hair. Now she knows where the feathers in the library came from.

"Forgot about them," Max murmurs.

"Checkout time!" the big cockatoo screams, yellow feathers rising on its head.

Anna flinches, feeling like an absolute idiot. There are no clocks up here in the wild night, just a useless sundial, and she definitely wasn't thinking about her goal.

It's Max. She keeps letting him distract her.

If it wasn't for the threat of fading away, she could be having the best night of her life.

"We have to go." She takes a last big sip of the cocoa and melted whipped cream, sets her mug down, and looks around the space. It's beautiful, and it's definitely romantic, but Max is right—there are no obvious trapdoors or hatches to the floor below. Everything seems solid and settled. "What's the plan?"

The look Max gives her is measuring but also excited. He walks into the hedge maze and leads Anna to a waist-high wall. The sky is still clear, the stars dancing, but when she looks out at the horizon and down, hunting for the familiar lights of the Strip, there's . . . nothing. The night sky goes starless and then merges with that odd, solid gray she saw from the Wardrobe window, like smoke or clouds.

Max steps right up to the wall and leans over, and even though it feels dangerous, Anna joins him. There's a spindly fire escape of black metal that spiders down the side of the building.

"We climb down," Max says.

34.

Phoebe stands in her office and pats at her hair. So undignified, the whole sawing-her-in-half thing. This is so Arielle, Phoebe thinks—doing what she's asked, what she *must,* but making it so inconvenient as to almost be a joke. Phoebe built her loopholes into the contract, and Arielle . . . well, she's found some loopholes of her own.

Phoebe requested a secret space that Max couldn't access, and this is what Arielle came up with, this ridiculous, uncomfortable farce in the ballroom niche. Phoebe despises the way it feels when those ghoulish ghost hands grasp her shoulders and feet to lower her gently into the box. She hates the way the assistants buy time and cause a theatrical distraction by fussing around unnecessarily, pushing down this and centering that. She especially hates the part where she's sawn in half by a saw that's only half there.

As far as she can figure out, there is no trick.

She does not put her legs in a secret compartment. The

ghosts—or memories, or whatever the hell they are—saw her in half, and she feels a cool breeze through her middle, and when they push her halves back together, it feels warm for a moment, like drinking hot soup.

And, yes, she also hates tugging her head and feet into the box and edging out the chute that feels just an inch too small in every direction until she falls with an always-startling plop onto the rich pile of sultan's pillows and blankets she keeps ready in her office.

Phoebe is fairly certain Arielle set it up this way to goad her. Yes, the spirit has done exactly as she was bid, and yes, there's no way Max will ever find this hidey-hole, despite his snooping, but still, it puts a sour taste in her mouth, every time she strides into the party that is always occurring and that originally felt fun and new to her, when she was a much younger woman.

Now it feels like they're all having fun and she's the one who's a ghost.

She hates everything about this charade, and yet she knows that since the contract can't change, whatever she requests of Arielle in this regard will be just as needlessly, foolishly complicated. She needs a safe, secret place, and she's willing to go through this inane rigmarole to get there. Because of the annoyance, she doesn't come here often. Only when it's absolutely necessary.

Once Phoebe is in her hidden office, the room is without reproach. Nestled between the ballroom and a lounge, it should be only a few feet across at the most, and yet it's probably eight feet, wide enough for Phoebe to sit in a Herman Miller chair, facing an enormous secretary desk with dozens of cubbies both visible and hidden. After checking that the room is completely empty, she unlocks a drawer and removes her MacBook, placing it on the pull-down desk.

She's been trapped in the Houdini for over sixteen years but has kept up with everything in the real world. Politics, culture, art—she's watched all of it unfold, bit by bit, right here in her hidden room. It's funny how Arielle can provide Wi-Fi and Phoebe can surf the internet to her bored heart's content, and yet . . . she's never been able to contact the outside world.

She's tried to create email addresses, but every combination of letters and numbers has been taken. She's tried to craft social media handles, but the activation emails never arrive because she has no email account. Phoebe knows people all over the world can now order anything they want online—not that she needs Amazon when she has Arielle—but without email or a credit card, she can't enjoy that little pleasure, either. Asking Arielle just isn't quite the same. Her laptop is a window, not a door.

She's kept such modern inventions away from Max, for his own good. If he knew what he was missing, being born here, he'd be a lot harder to deal with. A kid who doesn't know cell phones and tablets exist can't get addicted to tiny, portable screens, much less video games and inappropriate content. Max has an entire hotel to himself to explore, his every move safely watched. He has books and records—just supply an array of anything PG-rated up to 1970, Phoebe told Arielle. But the older he gets, the more restless and melancholy he grows. When he was younger, he would cry over how his only friends were ghosts. No wonder it's made him odd.

Not too odd for Daniel Alonso's daughter, apparently.

For years, Phoebe has tracked the progress of her enemies, scouring the internet for any mention of Daniel Alonso, Anthony Pappas, and Sebastian Williams. She's seen their successes reported in local papers, their awards and speeches lauded on the websites of various organizations. She even watched Daniel's local TED Talk on how to turn a hotel around, seething at the way he left out the story of his most significant hand up, the hotel he helped steal from its true owner.

She is all too aware that there's another Houdini out there, the real one, a hopelessly out-of-date but successful hotel full of real people with real money who come and go in the real world.

All the people in her hotel, this tragic mirror hotel, are just memories. Or ghosts.

Ghosts, of course, don't pay, not that Phoebe needs money as long as she has Arielle.

It was the internet that gave her the idea that finally delivered her enemies to her doorstep. When she found out Alonso's older daughter was getting married, she knew exactly where the three men would be and banked on them sharing a car—she'd seen enough pictures on Instagram of them partying in a limo or on a boat or a plane to know how they would celebrate.

Phoebe knew they'd be together near the Houdini before it happened, and thus did Arielle's storm deliver them directly to her. She can't contact anyone on the other side, can't command anyone but the spirit. But the spirit can make a storm, and Arielle was happy to help, once Phoebe dropped an innocent little mention of how she might free her sooner rather than later if her three enemies were driven directly into her hands.

Daniel's daughter is simply the cherry on the banana split of her revenge. Phoebe will make sure he knows what his daughter's fate will be before he fades away.

The cuckoo clock on the wall tells her these most esteemed visitors don't have much time left.

Midnight checkout is one of the hotel's constants. When Celeste found Phoebe pregnant and broken and bleeding on the floor all those years ago, she didn't explain the deadline; in fact, she went out of her way to avoid talking about the future at all. She was kind and doting and brought Phoebe up to a cozy room as if this was a regular hotel and gave her a key and told her how to press the button on the wall for room service. Phoebe begged for a doctor, for an ambulance, but Celeste simply shrugged and said that if Phoebe could find either one she was welcome to it.

Phoebe was furious and desperate that night, aware on an animal level that two lives were on the line, and as she tore her room apart looking for a phone, she found a book in the bedside table—a book about a star.

It was so strange that she sat and read it, still in a state of shock, and when she hobbled across the room and pressed the button for room service, she didn't ask for lobster or caviar. She asked, "Where is the star?"

And then the gramophone in the corner of the room started playing "When You Wish Upon a Star," and Phoebe followed the sound and found her first hidden door, slightly ajar in the wainscoting. She crept through the darkness, trailing blood, terrified she might lose her child and half-mad with pain. She found a girl chained up in a crypt.

There was no hidden key back then; Celeste thought her contract was watertight. Phoebe's room key opened Arielle's shackle easily enough, and the girl thanked her profusely and told her long, boring story and asked if she might be free after she granted a wish. Instead, Phoebe snapped the manacle right back on and drew up a contract of her own. She spent hours writing and crossing things out and rewriting as she gritted her teeth through early contractions, and then she presented the contract to the star. She considered going back to her world, but she didn't know if it would be too late to save her child, and even if he was born safely, she knew that her life there was already doomed. Her future had been effectively stolen, and so she dreamed up a new future, one where she and her child would be healthy and safe and want for nothing.

Only much later did she begin to plot her revenge.

The contract worked. Her contractions stopped, Max was born safely on his exact due date, and the hotel has been under Phoebe's control ever since. The moment she unlocked Arielle's shackle, elsewhere in the hotel, Celeste aged a hundred years in seconds and fell away to dust. Phoebe didn't know Colin even existed until she heard him screaming. By then, it was too late to include him in the contract, and so he has remained here to torment her all these years. At least Celeste's spirit isn't here—and Phoebe has looked for it in every room.

The other residents—be they ghosts, shades, memories, whatever the people of the Houdini are—they once walked in through that rotating door. Unlike Phoebe, who arrived in a far more unconventional and dangerous way. She doesn't know when new guests will arrive or why, and when asked, Arielle shrugs and says the

Houdini gets lonely. It has a will of its own, Phoebe has learned—apparently, magical places in spirit realms grow as strange as people left alone too long. So guests randomly, accidentally arrive, and they can't check out at midnight because there is no way out. The Houdini has been collecting them for over a century.

If Arielle can just keep the three men running around like fools until their time is up, there will be four new ghosts, and Phoebe will have her ultimate revenge.

They, like her, will be stuck here forever, except they'll be fully in her power. . . .

Because she lied to Arielle. She's not giving the spirit her freedom.

Why should Phoebe give up the source of her magic so readily? Her enemies certainly didn't cede any of their power when they took what they wanted and left her to rot.

They're going to pay tonight. She's stealing their futures as they once tried to steal hers.

But it's not enough, just sitting back and watching them fade away.

First they need to suffer.

They need to *know*.

She pushes a button on the desk. "Oh, Arielle?"

"Yes, boss?"

"How would you like to have a little fun with our guests?"

Arielle gives a sigh so tiny it could almost be imagined. "I'm all yours until it's time to scram."

"Lead the group of men to the Levitating Lady. And then here's what I want you to do. . . ."

35.

 Daniel, Tony, and Sebastian are yanking on doorknobs.

They have attempted to enter hundreds of doors, and yet there are still more doors that will probably refuse to open. Once they left the casino, they entered this hallway, and they have been traversing it for hours. When it appeared to go nowhere, they turned back to retrace their steps, but they have not yet returned to the casino. Against all logic, the hallway is endless, and behind those doors there are no sounds of movement, no murmuring voices, no annoying blare of the news channel turned up too loud on a TV. The whole world seems to revolve around just three men, one of whom is desperate to find his child and two of whom are desperate to be rid of him. And, of course, the overhead speakers have seen fit to play one song on repeat, a man crooning that he's got you under his skin.

"Getting real sick of this song," Tony growls. He looks up at the nearest speaker and then glances around as though he might find a convenient mop with which to disembowel it.

"The music will change," Daniel says, exhausted and still suffering a headache from . . . whatever happened with the smoke. "So first we find Anna. Then we find whoever is in charge. We get rooms. We sleep this off. We wake up and immediately call the decorator and start knocking out walls. And speakers."

"There's something to be said for a bespoke hotel these days," Sebastian notes gently. "You can't buy ambience like this. It would cost millions. Which"—a small cough—"it's my job to protect. So let's let this old girl be and just sell her to someone who cares."

"I don't see any sprinklers." Tony stops to inspect a crystal doorknob that sparkles like a diamond even though it must be at least a century old. "I'm surprised this rat's nest hasn't gone up in flames yet. With so much wood, it wouldn't take much. . . ."

"I'm not hearing that!" Sebastian puts his hands over his ears. "La la la!"

Tony yanks on the doorknob. It doesn't budge. "I'm serious. This place—it needs to go. Especially after tonight."

Daniel shakes his head at their bickering and speeds up. He's got to get out of this never-ending hall before he faints. Whether it's from the long day—Jesus, what time even is it?—the smoke, or low blood sugar, he'd kill for a glass of tap water and a bag of chips. "Now's not the time to make any rash decisions. If we could sell it, we would. You know the contracts have been a problem. But we're not going to resort to—"

"Shh! Don't say it out loud. There could be cameras," Sebastian hisses.

Tony kicks the door. It's so solid it barely shakes. "There aren't cameras because we don't put money into this pit. It needs to go. Permanently."

Daniel puts a hand on Tony's shoulder; Tony looks at it like he's thinking about biting it. "Look, Tone. It's a rough night for everyone. Let's not make it worse. I know this was our first place, and I know it's what kicked us off and got our business going, but it gives me the creeps, too. Whenever we talk about it or drive past it, I just think about your poor sister—"

Tony's jaw tightens. "Forget about her. She made mistakes of her own. Good riddance to bad rubbish."

Daniel squints, and finally, finally, there's something besides more emerald-green wallpaper and burled wood doors. No wonder Tony and Sebastian are acting strange. Looking at wallpaper like that for too long would drive a person insane.

Just ahead, the hallway opens up into an atrium, which has an old-fashioned toy store on one side and, wonder of wonders, a restaurant called the Levitating Lady. The polished wood double doors, with the name beautifully painted in old-timey script, are fronted by a plush red carpet and flanked by tall white columns. Instead of a pediment, the form of a woman stretches between the columns, her head supported on the left and her feet on the right as if she's floating in midair. Her long hair hangs down, as does her dress, all of it carved and painted as if by a master, as if she might wake up and tumble down to smash on the floor.

"That wasn't there last time I was here. It better be Styrofoam," Tony growls at Sebastian, who bristles.

"Do I look like I would green-light large, heavy, dangerous, unnecessary artwork?" He touches the trailing dress. "So tacky."

Daniel steps forward and pulls the door handle. He's surprised at how easily the door swings open—if everything else is closed and locked up, why would this place be open and available?—but hopeful that there might be food within.

The Levitating Lady is the sort of posh restaurant that high rollers favor—a buffet in a horseshoe shape, plates and bowls aplenty, offerings starting with soup and salad and transitioning through sushi and prime rib and chilled seafood towers, ending with an epic dessert selection. Amid all this glorious plenty wait baskets of golden rolls, cruets of dressing, and silver platters of chilled butter in the shape of stars.

"Now, that's more like it!" Tony crows. He puffs out his chest and struts around, head cocked like a rooster. "But where's the staff? No one's greeted us. Hello? Anybody?"

Sebastian sighs and bustles over to the door that must lead to the kitchen. He pushes it open and looks back at his friends, frowning. "There's no one there. And it's spotless."

"They must be sheltering from the tornado," Daniel says, half to himself, half to the others. "They got the alert, they rounded up their guests and went to the basement until the all clear. It's the only thing that makes any sense."

Tony laughs and cracks his knuckles. "Well, boys, I see a buffet with food that needs eating. Hell, they'll probably have to throw it away when they come back upstairs anyway, seeing as how it's been sitting out."

"That prime rib smells amazing," Daniel says. He hovers by the plates as if unsure, but Tony swoops in and grabs two.

"One for meat, one for seafood. I don't like it when they touch." Tony loads up on bread and butter, picks through the chilled seafood tower, and hacks away at the prime rib until he finds the pink center.

Sebastian starts building a salad, and Daniel fills his plate with fried chicken and mashed potatoes.

"That fish, at the wedding? It wasn't good," Tony says, popping a chunk of prime rib in his mouth with his fingers.

"It's wedding food," Daniel admits. "It's not there to be good."

"What's this?" Tony plucks a boiled egg off Sebastian's plate and inspects it like he doesn't know what an egg is.

"My doctor's attempt to keep me from dying of a heart attack, you ignoramus," Sebastian shoots back. He turns away from Tony and grabs another egg.

They set down their plates on the nearest table and head back to the buffet, but . . .

"Where's the drinks?" Tony bellows, as if the waitstaff will appear from the basement just because he's being denied something.

"Probably in back. Come along, Tony. We can serve ourselves." Sebastian waits, eyebrows up.

At first, Tony glares at him like he's lost his mind, but then he nods. "Yeah, sure, me and Sebastian'll get the drinks. Whaddaya want, Danny boy?"

"Cola," Daniel says. "Sugar and caffeine."

Sebastian leads the way through the swinging door into the

kitchen, a sea of gleaming white tile and polished steel. Tony looks back to make sure the door is closed and they're alone.

"What's the deal?" he says, voice low.

Sebastian steps close, picks up a glass, and starts the rattling ice maker.

"If you want to continue our earlier plans, now might be the time. What if something ended up in Daniel's drink?"

Tony raises an eyebrow, his lips twitching with a smirk. "A little something, sure. But what?"

After digging through a few cabinets, Sebastian holds up an ancient canister of concentrated industrial drain cleaner.

Tony grins fully. "And to think, you look so harmless."

Sebastian pours the cleaner into Daniel's glass. It's clear and thick, and he finishes off the glass with cola, as requested, then stirs it with a spoon until the liquids are mixed. After Tony adds the ice in by hand so it won't splash, Sebastian sniffs his concoction and holds the glass up to the light.

"No odor, luckily, and I can't see anything. Can you?"

Tony shakes his head. "Just dollar signs."

Knowing what Sebastian wants to drink, he fills Sebastian's glass with sparkling water and his own with acid-green soda; he needs caffeine and sugar as much as Daniel does, but he wants to be utterly sure he can't possibly mix up their drinks. The men nod at each other and paste on smiles before returning to the dining room.

"Smart that they keep the drinks back there," Tony notes as he hands Daniel his cola. "Makes the customers ask for stuff, makes 'em remember they have to tip. And we save a little."

"Not as much as we'd save if we took the lobster off the seafood towers," Sebastian notes, sipping his water.

Daniel picks up his glass—and stops.

He holds it up. "To my beloved Emily and her new husband."

Tony and Sebastian share a nervous glance and hold up their glasses.

"Here, here!" they cry.

But as they bring the glasses to their lips, the door to the kitchen bursts open with such ferocity that it bangs off the wall. A chef appears—a big, bald man in his sixties who looks like seven hams strapped together with rage, all muscles and barrel chest in his flawless chef's whites. Startled, Daniel sets down his glass on the edge of a plate, spilling the cola across the table.

"What's this?" the chef shouts, charging directly at them, hands in fists. The other two men put down their drinks, and Daniel and Tony push their chairs back as if ready for a fight. "You people think you can just come in here and steal food?"

Tony stands and faces the chef head-on. He's shorter and less muscled but looks like he's ready to start punching. "We're the hotel owners. Care to explain why you left your restaurant unattended? Give us one good reason, then apologize for this accusation, and you might still have a job on Monday."

The chef steps closer, sneering. "Wait. I know you. You're the Pappas kid—the younger one. Rude, spoiled little brat. Gimme gimme gimme, every time your folks brought you in here. Now, they were good people, and so was your sister, Phoebe."

At the sound of her name, Tony goes stiff and begins to sweat and snort. Sebastian and Daniel finally stand and move away a bit, giving each other the same look they share any time Tony loses his temper—this could go very well for them, or they could end up having to call their lawyer.

"Oh, you don't like hearing her name, huh?" The chef leans in, and Tony leans away. "Phoebe. Phoebe Pappas. Sweet kid. She was supposed to inherit this place because you were younger and a wild card who couldn't be trusted, always in trouble. But then she disappeared, didn't she? Poof! Not a sign of her. How very convenient for you, *Anthony*, you and your buddy Sebastian, and I guess that other guy, too. You got to inherit everything."

Tony is breathing through his nose like a bull. He gets up in the chef's face, pointing a meaty finger. "Yeah, that's how inheritance works. My dead parents made this place, and now I own it. So I'm sorry if you didn't like me as a kid, but that doesn't change the fact that I'm your boss."

"Oh, I don't work for you, you twerp." The chef steps past Tony, smooth and sudden, grabs the table, and flips it over. The plates of food and the drinks crash to the floor in a shower of glass and ceramic and sauce. Leaning in toward Tony, the chef adds, voice low and sinister, "*I know what you did.* And you don't get to eat my food."

With that, the chef looks down at the food and sauce melting into the carpet, nods decisively, and strides back into the kitchen, the door swinging in his wake.

"Screw that guy," Tony says, but not too loudly. "I'll eat whatever I want."

Sebastian is frozen in place, aghast, probably calculating the price of the wasted food, but Daniel and Tony head back to the buffet.

"What the hell?" Tony drops the tongs and knife he just picked up and backs away.

A foul smell fills the room, wet and heavy as death. The salad is liquifying in its chilled bowls, the lettuce melting like it's been in the fridge for half a year. The rolls are crusted in fuzzy white-green mold. The meat has shriveled on its cutting board; it looks more like jerky now. The fruits are rotten and pinched, the cheesecakes caved in. The seafood tower—well, no one even wants to look at it.

"It's been five minutes," Tony says, appalled and mystified.

Sebastian looks down at the mess on the floor and staggers away, knocking over his chair and holding a hand over his mouth. Roaches skitter among the wreckage as it seeps into the carpet, a mélange of brown garbage festooned with mold.

"Let's get out of here," Tony says, and the others follow him to the door, all of them trying not to retch.

Before they reach the hall, Daniel pauses and glances back at the kitchen.

"What?" Tony growls.

"I'll be back in a minute." Daniel jogs to the swinging door and, after taking a deep breath to center himself, opens it just a few inches.

The chef looks up from where he's deboning a chicken with a gigantic knife. "What?"

"My daughter Anna. She's sixteen. Have you seen her, or do you know where the rest of the staff might be? She's somewhere in the hotel, but I can't find her—"

The chef snorts. "Yeah, well, sounds like lots of young women get lost in this hotel. As you know."

"As I know?"

The chef slams his knife into his cutting board. "Well, don't you? Didn't Tony and Sebastian tell you about their little scheme back then?"

"No. What scheme? Did . . . did they do something illegal?"

Daniel is completely lost as he stands in the doorway, and whatever the chef sees on his face, he must believe it.

"You may not know the truth, but you still benefit from the deception, pal. Ask Tony and Sebastian what happened that night, the last time it stormed like this. Maybe if you can find one missing girl, you can find the other."

"What does that mean?"

The chef picks up his knife and gives a half shrug. "Ask them. And, hey, maybe you should keep better friends." He buries the cleaver in the chicken meat, and Daniel's throat rises at the wet, juicy sound.

"Whatever happened, I'm sorry," he says softly. "I didn't know."

He closes the door and looks around the restaurant, holding his breath and willing his eyes to skip over the rotting buffet. He knows he's been in this hotel before, but he doesn't remember this restaurant at all.

None of it makes any sense.

And the chef didn't answer his question about Anna. Daniel opens the swinging door again, but the chef and his chicken are gone. All that's left is the knife, lying in a pool of blood on the cutting board.

36.

Anna has never felt as scared as she does swinging her leg over the roof wall and onto the rickety fire escape. When her foot lands on the first rung, the ancient black metal squeals and settles uncertainly. She can feel the emptiness under the rubber soles of her sneakers, and she looks to Max for reassurance.

"Are you sure it'll hold?" she asks.

There's worry in his eyes, his fingers clenched around the metal bars as if he can keep the flimsy structure in place through sheer force of will.

"I think so, but again, please let me go first."

She shakes her head. "No way. I told you: you weigh more than me. And I'm the one who's actually been dragged to a climbing gym by her overenthusiastic sister."

Max's brows draw down. "Are you saying I'm too weak?"

Anna takes another step down, and another. "No. I'm saying that I'm already doing the thing, so let me do the thing."

For an old-fashioned guy, he doesn't fight back like she expects, just firms up his jaw and holds on to the ladder for dear life. It feels like there's something he's not telling her, but she needs to concentrate on what she's doing, not ask him questions he doesn't want to answer.

Anna has never been on a fire escape before—she thinks of them as something quaint from New York, something mainly used to hold Instagrammable arrangements of potted plants or as a backdrop for romantic moments in Netflix rom-coms. But this thing—it's a series of balconies with railings linked by ladders slanted awkwardly. She doesn't recall seeing any fire escapes on the hotel when they drove up, but then again, the storm obscured everything, and she's never really paid much attention to architecture. She's doing her best not to look down, to focus on the rungs under her hands, but she can't help seeing that there is no "there" there. No ground below, no street, just the thick, gray cloud that obscures everything and seems to press against her back like a heavy blanket that doesn't quite exist.

The metal rungs hurt her hands, and each time her toes feel out a new foothold, she's not sure if it'll hold her weight. She only has to go down one floor, but it might as well be ten thousand feet.

Finally, Anna reaches the end of the ladder and steps off onto the landing—also ancient black metal, but a sturdier mesh instead of bars. She looks up, and Max is still holding the top of the ladder, watching her fiercely. She gives him a thumbs-up, and he hauls a leg over the wall and starts climbing down to join her. Anna is honestly more worried about him than she is herself—right up until the first time he steps down just a little too hard, his weight juddering the whole thing like it might rattle off into space if provoked. She flings herself toward the building, her back against the bricks. Did the storm weaken the already crumbling structure? Has anyone ever used this thing before?

As she watches Max descend, she has the unsettling realization that in a hotel with no indoor stairs, not even an emergency stairwell, it's a little convenient that there's a fire escape right when they need one.

Too late. Max steps off beside her, a finger to his lips. Anna is disturbed at how much she'd like to kiss him, how wild the whole experience makes her feel, as if anything could happen while they're out in the middle of nothing. Her blood is singing, the wind whipping her hair free of its braid. Max approaches the window and murmurs, "Huh."

It's not closed—it's open, just a few inches, held up by a woman's high-heeled, red-soled shoe turned on its side. The curtains within are pulled closed.

Max squats to eye level with the three inches of open window and carefully moves one of the curtains just enough to glance inside.

"Hello, Maximillian."

The voice from within is amused and all too familiar.

Phoebe has apparently finished her business on the other side of the ballroom wall and has returned to the penthouse.

Max silently, desperately points at the ladder and then up at the roof, and Anna's heart races as she puts a foot on the bottom rung.

"Please ask the young lady to join us."

Crap.

Phoebe knows she's here.

Anna stops and looks down at the swirling gray miasma below, uncertain. Max flaps his hands at her, urging her to escape, his eyes desperate with longing and worry. And so Anna climbs, but when she gets to the top of the ladder, it stops woefully short of the wall around the rooftop, at least four feet. There's no way Anna can keep climbing, no way to reach the safety of the roof.

The rest of the ladder has simply . . . disappeared.

The Houdini's magic strikes again.

Anna climbs back down, shaking, having gained new respect for what Phoebe can do. All along, she's been hunting for the hotel's internal logic, and it turns out that it can be controlled in part by Phoebe's will. Max fidgets, waiting for her to step down beside him. Anna's certainty is gone. She has no idea what might happen inside that penthouse, but she does know there is no other route of egress, other than jumping off the fire escape. The ladder that was beneath them just moments ago is also gone. She has never felt so trapped or hopeless.

"I'm sorry," Max whispers. Anna just gives a half shrug. They both know what they're dealing with, that the chips are stacked against them. The usual rules of reality no longer apply, and maybe Max is accustomed to that, but Anna is still finding her feet.

"Don't dawdle." The window grinds open wider, the curtains rustling.

Max extends one arm as if he's chivalrously inviting Anna to crawl into the open mouth of a shark. She shakes her head, and he ducks inside first. For just the briefest moment, alone on a fire escape that has become a balcony, Anna puts her hands on the railing and leans over, wondering what would happen if she jumped. Would she splatter on the ground of this world or her own, or would the gray fuzz just swallow her whole in an infinite fall?

"Don't even think about it," Phoebe says. Her face appears between the curtains, sideways and smiling, like she can't be bothered to squat down.

With a last, almost longing look into the gray void, Anna straightens her spine and turns to the window. She is not accustomed to being cowed; she's indulged in her moment of desperation and is ready to face the woman who most recently threw her into a dungeon.

Once inside, Anna finds Phoebe seated on a gorgeous chaise. She's draped in an old-fashioned ivory robe with feathers at the wrists and lapels, her white-blond hair in a chignon. She looks like she has stepped out of *The Great Gatsby*, but she's smiling like a cat with a mouse tail in its teeth. The room has been done in a hundred shades of pink, from peach to magenta, and is dominated by satin and mirrors and pearls and feathers. It's huge and aggressively feminine, and nothing about it seems personal. No photographs or tchotchkes, just a tall record player with a horn that resembles a pale-pink lily. The record on it turns rhythmically, but there is no music. *Kuh-bump. Kuh-bump. Kuh-bump.*

"Miss Alonso. I'd like to apologize for our earlier misunderstanding. It's been an unusual day at the Houdini."

"A misunderstanding? You threw me in a dungeon!"

Phoebe's lips pucker doubtfully. "A dungeon? That's a bit hyperbolic. We both know that barrel spins around into a perfectly safe, nicely carpeted hallway. The fifth floor may be boring, but it's in no way dangerous."

Anna and Max share a swift and knowing glance before Anna continues, not wanting to alert Phoebe to the fact that she absolutely did not end up in the fifth-floor hallway.

"I could've gotten hurt. I could've broken my wrist."

Phoebe smiles sweetly. "As I'm sure Max has told you, the Houdini has cures for all ills, my dear. We wouldn't want any harm to come to our guests."

Anna can't stand the fake sincerity a moment longer. "Where's my dad?"

Phoebe flips a hand. "Somewhere in the hotel. I'm sure he'll turn up soon." She stands, seeming so much shorter than she did in the restaurant, in those high heels. "Welcome, by the way. It would appear this is your first visit to our glorious establishment."

"What do you want?" Anna asks tiredly.

Max's eyes fly open wide, and he shakes his head at her in warning, but she sees no reason to play along with whatever Phoebe's game might be. Anna Alonso isn't about to clasp her hands and beg for crumbs from a monster.

Phoebe smiles, and now it's the scary smile. It does not touch her eyes.

"What do I want? To get you two scamps off that dangerous fire escape, for one thing. So rickety. You simply can't count on it." She swans to the window, pushes the curtains aside to show that there is no longer a fire escape there, yanks the shoe inside, and slams the window decisively shut.

"That's better. Now. I think perhaps we got off on the wrong foot. I'm so glad you're here and unscathed by the storm. I'm sure we'll soon see your father and his friends"—the word "friends" is spoken through clenched teeth—"but until then, I need to make sure you don't get into any more trouble—"

"How does it work?" Anna interrupts.

That catches Phoebe's attention, and it's gratifying to see her caught by surprise and breaking character, her face screwed up in a way that shows she isn't as composed as she pretends to be. "How does what work?"

"The hotel. The magic. I want to know."

Phoebe sighs through her nose, taps her long fingernails along the chaise. They were painted red when she and Anna met earlier, but now they're petal pink, and Anna can't help but wonder whether it's magic or if the woman spends all her time changing her appearance for such a small audience. She risks a glance at Max, who is tense and focused, his hands in fists.

"Miss Alonso, do you like coffee?" Phoebe asks.

The question makes Anna do a double take. "Yes. Why?"

Another villain smile. Phoebe is a bleached-blond Maleficent in a silk robe. "When you purchase a coffee from a café, do you ask yourself where that coffee came from?"

"Yes. I only buy fair trade."

Phoebe rolls her eyes. "But do you ask whose land it was raised on, who watered it, who picked it, who planted it, who sold the beans, who first cultivated that varietal? Do you ask how a seed grows, what makes that tender little green shoot decide to seek the sun? No. You do not. You merely pay your money and enjoy your coffee. And thus when I took control of this vaunted edifice, I didn't look too closely. Curiosity killed the cat, you know."

"That's not the whole saying. It's 'Curiosity killed the cat but satisfaction brought it back,'" Anna informs her, arms crossed.

Max stifles a chuckle, turning it into a cough, and Phoebe shoots Anna a death glare.

"Then perhaps you'll find some *satisfaction* in this locked room as we wait for the clock to strike midnight. I need to go find our other guests." Phoebe points at a nearby clock of crystal and gold, and while Anna stares at it, the older woman swiftly strides to the only door and opens it, revealing a marble foyer, the open elevator waiting enticingly. "Max, come with me."

"No."

Phoebe's head swivels around with the slow threat of a snake.

"What did you just say?"

"I'm staying with Anna."

Hands on her hips, Phoebe turns to face them both and seems to grow a foot taller.

"You know I can make you do whatever I like, Maximillian."

He reaches for Anna's hand. "And I also know that if you use whatever power you hold to make me leave Anna, I will never, ever forgive you."

The air in the room is as charged as it was in the middle of the tornado. Anna squeezes Max's hand.

"Fine," Phoebe finally snaps. "You can both stay here. Look all you like, but you won't find one of your secret doors."

She walks out, slamming shut the only visible door in the room. Anna looks at Max, and he groans, and when she looks back, the door Phoebe just slammed . . . has disappeared. There were several doors when they arrived, but now there are none.

"I'm so sorry," Max says, turning to Anna and pulling her into a hug.

Anna is glad for the hug but confused by everything else. "Sorry for what?"

He strokes her back and she melts into him. "My mom threatened you. And now she's trapped us in here."

Anna stills. "Trapped?"

"You heard her. There are no secret doors. No doors at all now."

Pulling back from the hug, she looks up into his eyes. "That doesn't mean there's not a way out. And besides, you're forgetting that this is where we wanted to be. Now we can look for the—" She mouths the word "key."

The look Max gives her is pitying. "If she left us here alone, it's not here. And she doesn't want us to escape, so we can't. No secret doors, no way out. That's the way it works."

Anna shakes her head and starts feeling along the wall where the door had been. "I don't accept that. There's always a way out. And I'm not ready to stop looking. We just have to get creative."

"Don't you get it? You can't get creative when someone like her is using magic against you. I've spent my whole life trying to get around her rules, and all I found was disappointment and punishment."

There is nothing but smooth wallpaper where the door was. There are no bookshelves, no wainscoting. Anna yanks back the thick shag rug, but there are no trapdoors. She pulls furniture away from the walls, opens every drawer, wrenches open the spines of the art books as she hunts for hidden treasure. Max watches her tear the room apart, wincing when she peels up a corner of the wallpaper.

"The Houdini won't like that—" he starts.

"Then the Houdini can offer me a better way to get out of here. We have to get back to the ballroom and see what's on the other side of that magic trick. We have to find that—you know what. Did you ever think . . . maybe the Houdini wants to be free, too?"

There's a creak across the room, and Anna runs to the window. It's open now, just a smidge, letting in an enticing breeze. She throws back the curtains and pushes the sash all the way up, but there is still a distinct lack of the previously existing fire escape. As she stares down into the swirling gray nothing, an irrational idea rises, a wave of dizziness making her head spin.

She turns to face Max. "What happens if we jump?"

"I—I don't know," he says, glancing away from her. He is not a good liar. And why would he be? How could he possibly practice, when his every step is watched?

Anna walks up to him and takes his hand. Looks up into his eyes. "You can tell me."

Max can't meet her gaze, a blush high on his cheeks. "I didn't— I just—" A sigh. "You don't know what it's like, being so alone your whole life, trying to get out of this place in any way possible. Nothing worked. I was being stupid, and it was a last resort." He swallows hard and finally looks at her. "I only tried it once, and I woke up in my bed."

"How much time had passed?"

His smile is sheepish and lopsided. "None, from what I could tell."

A wild hope rises in Anna's chest.

"Then we have to jump."

She turns to the window, hands on the sill.

"Anna, no. We can't be certain. What worked for me might not work for you. The rules seem to be different for you."

"We have to try—"

Max shakes his head. "Don't you understand? If it doesn't work, if you just fall, then it's all over, but you're gone. No key, no chance of a better life. It's just over."

"But my only other choice is to sit here and watch that ridiculous crystal clock count down, and I'm not willing to do that."

"Anna, listen." Max holds up his hands, and she sees scars on his knuckles. "I would tear down these walls for you if I could. I would pull out the bricks one by one until my fingers bled. But it *does not work.* Nothing does. This place can't be destroyed or altered by physical means. But that doesn't mean I'm willing to watch you risk everything—"

"You can't stop me, Max."

His eyes spark as he looks at her as if trying to commit every detail to memory. "I can damn well try."

His hands find Anna's jaw, lifting her face to meet his as his lips fall on hers. The delicate tenderness of their last kiss is replaced with fierce desperation, like he's trying to spill his heart into her body. She melts at the touch of his tongue, at his hand cupping the back of her head, her body pressed against his. His pocket watch ticks against her ribs, a reminder that she ignores. Her fingers find his neck, tangle in his hair. For a boy who has spent his entire life alone, he seems to know exactly what he's doing—but then again, he is an avid reader, and you can learn a lot about kissing from books.

Anna is lost in sensation, something that has never happened to her before, lost in his hands and his warmth and the hungry demands of his mouth . . . until she feels a breeze whisper over her back, where Max's fingertips have edged up the hem of her shirt.

She takes a step back.

"Checkout time!" calls a cockatoo from somewhere on the roof.

Anna looks away, looks down, looks anywhere else but at Max's eyes as she tries to catch her breath. His hand is still on her back, idly stroking her spine as he watches her with the wariness of a cat.

"Okay, then," she says, a little shyly. "I guess you can stop me for a little while. But I'm still going, and that won't work twice."

His grin flashes, cocky. "Are you sure? I could try—"

"Jump with me or stay behind, Max." Anna holds out her hand.

For a long moment, he considers it, then snorts and takes her hand. "If those are the only choices, of course I'll come with you. Why not? What's the worst thing that could happen? We could—"

Anna goes up on her tiptoes and kisses him, effectively silencing him. "Don't give the Houdini any ideas. Come on." The window is wide enough for them to stand side by side, and Anna ducks under the sill, leaning out at her waist.

Max joins her. "See you on the other side, I hope." His smile is a new one, resigned and patient. He doesn't know if this will work, but he's willing to risk everything. For her.

Anna is scared—she can't deny that. But she's desperate, and she trusts Max—and even trusts the Houdini, a little. It won't let her come to harm.

After all, the girl in the box doesn't actually get sawed in half. It's all part of the show.

Isn't it?

"One . . . two . . . three!" she counts.

They fall forward.

37.

Phoebe sits in yet another hidden room, this one only accessible through a secret door in the seventh-floor foyer. She stares at a bank of monitors, each one showing a different part of the Houdini. She presses the button on the wall.

"Arielle?"

"Yes, boss?"

"Where are the men? I can't see them."

An exasperated sigh. "Check camera three, boss."

When Phoebe looks at that monitor, the grainy black-and-white picture goes from an empty hallway to an overhead shot in an elevator. The three men barely fit in the tiny space and are all conspicuously miserable. There's no sound in this system, but their facial expressions make it clear that they've been arguing again and each is trying to pretend that the others do not exist.

"How long have they been in there?"

A giggle. "Nearly an hour."

"And what are they trying to do?"

Arielle sighs. "Well, they're real mad. Tony and Sebastian want to cut this Daniel guy out—they got plans to do him in. Tried it a couple of times already tonight."

Phoebe leans back, considering the dozens of monitors before her. There are so many interesting places in the hotel, so many amusing ways to mess with three very greedy and impatient men.

It's almost checkout time, but there's still some room to make them as uncomfortable as possible, to bring their true feelings to a proper boil.

"Lead them into my boudoir," she says.

"But, boss, what about—"

"I said what I said, Arielle. Just let them in, and the chips will fall as they may."

"You got it, boss."

Phoebe kicks one kitten-heeled slipper off her foot, letting it dangle from her toes as the most hilarious idea strikes her.

"Oh, and, Arielle?"

"Yes, boss?"

"Wouldn't it be lovely if the sprinkler in that elevator went off just now?"

"But . . . there is no sprinkler in that elevator."

Phoebe grins like a jack-o'-lantern.

"What's the point of magic," she drawls, "if you don't use it?"

Arielle is more than happy to oblige. If Phoebe is watching the men, she won't notice that the penthouse camera is on a loop, the two kids just innocently poking at the wall again and again. If Arielle can keep her occupied, Phoebe will never know they're gone.

38.

Three men stand in very close quarters.

"I thought these elevators were up to code," Tony growls.

Sebastian tries to edge away from Tony's belly, but the elevator is barely big enough for all of them and seems to shrink by the minute. "All our elevators are up to code." His voice goes softer, barely perceptible. "But, of course, they still have limits. This is significantly more poundage—"

Tony leans into him, crushing Sebastian's face against the polished wood of the elevator wall. "I'm sorry, what was that about poundage? I don't see one of those certificates with a weight limit. You not doing your job?"

With Tony focusing on Sebastian, Daniel has a little more elbow room, and he jams his thumb into the button again. Much to his delight, the elevator judders into motion.

"There we go—"

He abruptly cuts off as the elevator light goes out and freezing-cold water sprays from the ceiling. The music, which had bliss-fully been off, turns on despite the malfunction, screeching some stupidly childish, loud song about mairzy doats and dozy dotes.

"What the hell?" Tony roars.

"Is there a fire?" Sebastian bleats, clawing at the seam of the doors. "Why is there no emergency button in this death trap?"

Tony jumps, swatting at the ceiling in the darkness, aiming for the sprinkler or the speaker, whichever he finds first. He misses both, and when he lands, the elevator shakes in a very unhealthy way, making the smaller men cling to the railing along the walls.

"Don't jump, you idiot!" Sebastian shouts. "It's not safe!"

"What part of being stuck in an elevator with two idiots for an hour while being rained on feels safe to you?" Tony shouts back. "You did this! You're the one in charge of elevator stuff!"

"And you're the one who tells me to just bribe the inspector!"

"He tells you to do what?" Daniel barks, furious.

Finally, the elevator stops, and not gently. The men rattle against one another like bowling pins, and even before the door has finished grinding open, each tries to escape first. For a long moment, they flap and shout and slip and fall and grunt in a big tangle before they manage to squeeze out. All three men are soaked to the skin and furious, and wet coins litter the floor.

"What now?" Tony asks, hands on hips as he looks around.

"This must be the penthouse," Sebastian says, waving at the glossy white marble foyer. "I don't recall signing off on any renova-tions, but it looks classier than the rest of this dump."

"Finally, where we belong." Tony sloughs off his ruined jacket and drops it on the floor with a wet smack.

"Only one door," Daniel notices. "Do we have the keycard?"

"No, but we have my shoulder and I'm willing to knock down a wall if it'll get me into a king-sized bed." Tony strides toward the door and reaches for the crystal knob like he's expecting a fight . . .

But the door opens easily.

"What the hell?"

They were expecting a posh, sleek space with elegant seating, huge beds, a long conference table, and a view of the Strip.

But this room is stuffy and as feminine as the inside of a woman's mouth.

The walls are a vibrant, shiny fuchsia, and the carpet is patterned with roses and vines. White sheepskins and pearlescent afghans drape over pillow-mounded velvet couches, squashy chairs, and one curvy black leather chaise. There's a changing screen surrounded by racks of clothing, robes of silk and drapes of lace and net. And there's a bed—a big, heavy, dominating thing with four posts hung with swagged curtains.

"Okay, whoever *did* sign the reno papers is fired," Tony says.

"It's not tasteful. . . ." Sebastian runs a hand down the duvet. "But it's a bed." He looks at the racks of fabric. "And dry clothes."

"Does someone live here?" Daniel asks. "It seems so . . . personal."

"Well, it's our hotel, and we don't do leases." Tony strides over to the racks, nudges Sebastian aside, and pulls out a silk robe, red with a fierce tiger on the back. He doesn't bother going behind the changing screen, just shucks off his wet clothes, tosses them on the ground, and slips into the robe. Miraculously, it fits him perfectly.

"Now that's what I'm talking about," he says, throwing himself onto the bed. "I'm sleeping here. You guys can take the couches."

Sebastian finds another robe, gold with a dragon on the back. "I'm fairly certain that this penthouse is occupied, but they can send us a bill, if they're unhappy. They'll probably demand a comped night anyway if they spent the entire storm huddled in the basement." He changes behind the screen and collapses onto the chaise as soon as his robe is tied.

But Daniel doesn't select anything from the racks. "I'm not comfortable borrowing clothes from a guest."

Tony is busy arranging pillows, punching them into the right shapes. "So don't. No skin off my nose if you want to drip on the carpet. At least sit down. All this pacing around makes me nervous."

Daniel walks over to the mirrored desk and opens a drawer. It's empty. There are no papers, no purse, no briefcase. Pushing the heavy curtains away from the nearest window, he squints out into the darkness.

"Thick fog out there. You guys see a phone anywhere? I need to check on—"

"For the last time, give it a rest!" Tony shoves up to sitting and glares daggers. "This whole night, it's been nothing but orders and complaints. 'Wah, wah, my missing daughter.' I've had it, Daniel. I'm at the end of my rope."

Sebastian sits up, on the alert, and Daniel lets the curtains fall back and gives Tony a measured glare. "You've been out for a fight all night, Tone. Just say what you need to say."

Tony nods at Sebastian, who stands and picks up a heavy marble bookend.

"You've been dead weight for a while, buddy," Tony says. He stands and walks to the tiled fireplace, plucks an ornate metal poker from its stand.

"We've been friends for thirty years. Business is booming. You can't be serious." Daniel nervously glances from Tony to Sebastian to the door, calculates his odds, and takes a step backward.

"Oh, we're serious. You know how cutthroat real estate is. Margins get smaller every year."

Tony takes a menacing step forward, and Daniel takes another step back.

"I have a family—" he starts, still unable to believe this level of betrayal.

"We don't care."

Tony takes another step forward, Sebastian in his wake, and a low, long growl emanates from a pile of pillows on the nearest couch. All three men freeze.

"Is that a dog?" Tony asks.

In response, the pile of pillows shudders and erupts like a volcano. A huge pink poodle unfolds from the couch and leaps to the floor. It's as big as a wolfhound, lanky and spare, with ridiculous pink cotton candy puffs on its head, legs, and chest. Sebastian stumbles back, and the three men focus on the nightmare poodlewolf stalking stiff-legged toward them, jaws slavering and head low.

"Jesus, what is that thing?" Tony swings the poker at the dog, which leaps at him, grabs the twisted metal in its teeth, and tosses it aside like a used chew toy.

"That's a lawsuit waiting to happen," Sebastian mutters.

"Screw this!"

Tony bolts for the door, throwing it open and running into the foyer. Sebastian and Daniel follow, the monstrous poodle hot on their heels.

39.

Anna opens her eyes. She is on her back, spread-eagled on the floor of the library.

She was falling into the gray cloud, hand clasped in Max's, and then there was nothing—like being under anesthesia.

And now she's here.

Much to her surprise, there are no physical effects, no pain or drowsiness or strangeness. She sits up and looks around the room.

Max isn't there.

"Max?" she calls.

The library door opens, and relief flows through her chest, except . . . it's not Max.

It's Colin again.

His grin suggests that finding Anna alone is the best possible thing that could happen.

Her body reacts immediately, an antelope spotting a hyena. Her vision narrows, her hands go cold.

"There you are. And without a protector . . ." The way he trails off makes Anna's skin crawl. When Colin shuts the door behind him, there's a dread finality about it. He's back in his janitor's uniform, and there's something bulky sticking out of the pocket—a wrench.

"Leave me alone," Anna says as she stands up, glancing around for a weapon and finding nothing more dangerous than books and fountain pens. "Max is on his way."

His smile is cloying and greedy. "But he's not here now. I don't want to hurt you. Just come with me, and everything will be fine."

"No. Stay away from me." She takes a step back.

There's nowhere to go.

It's funny how Anna was warned about kidnappers and creepers her whole life and yet never encountered one until she got lost in a magical hotel where jumping out a window can't hurt her but a man's fingers can. Colin is walking toward her, his hands up like she's a loose dog he doesn't trust. He slowly pulls out the wrench.

"They've been lying to you, you know," he says, soft and urgent. "This place—it isn't some gift bestowed upon Phoebe and her precious son. It was stolen from my mother. My birthright. And if I can't have it, then I'll take what I can get."

"Max!" Anna shouts. "Help!" When Max doesn't respond or immediately appear, she desperately adds, "Please, Houdini. Help me."

It feels very silly, begging a hotel to save her . . . until she hears a familiar creak behind her, close to the ground. Without another word, she spins and dives for the secret door. It seems smaller this time, a tighter squeeze, and she wriggles in on her elbows.

Fingers grab her ankle, hard. "Got you!" Colin cries. "Come on out—"

But Anna is not about to do what he says. She kicks as hard as she can, gratified to feel her foot connect with something fleshy and hear a cry of pain. As soon as he's no longer touching her, she drags her legs inside and kicks the door shut.

"Sorry," she mutters to the hotel. Because she kicked it.

Mere inches away, Colin scrabbles against the door that was recently a wall, shouting some very colorful expletives. Something slams into the door—the wrench, probably. Anna hears the disturbing sound of drywall breaking.

"Anna?"

The moment she hears Max's voice, a sob breaks free from her throat, and then she's crying. He crawls toward her in the dark, muttering about the tight fit. Anna can't see him—it's pitch-black—but she knows in her bones that somehow, impossibly, he's here. When he reaches her, he shuffles his hand along the floor and finds hers, and she throws herself into his shoulder. They're both on their bellies, and he's hugging her to him, her face buried in his neck.

"He was going to hurt me," Anna snuffles. "He said he didn't want to, but he was."

"Who?" Max's voice is a dark, furious thing.

"Colin. He's in the library. That's where I woke up."

As if in response, Colin kicks the secret door, startling them both. Max exhales hard and rubs his cheek against Anna's hair. "Come on. Let's get to the blue room. Can you follow me?"

She can only nod. She can't stop shaking and feels like she might fly apart into a thousand tender pieces.

When Max backs away, she crawls in his wake. "That's good," he murmurs. "Almost there." It's awkward for him, backing into the blue room through the cupboard, but he manages it. Anna speeds up as soon as she sees the light, anxious to be in a place that feels safe.

Max stands, and the moment she emerges, he helps her up and pulls her to his chest. "You're shaking," he whispers, brushing her hair back again and again.

"He was going to hurt me," she whispers. "No one's ever tried to hurt me before."

"He can't hurt you now. You're safe. I've got you."

Anna's sobs fall off to snuffles, and she pulls away from Max and dashes at her eyes with her hands. When she looks down, she's covered in dirt and dust from the narrow tunnel, and she's certain that if she had a mirror, she would look ghastly. Of course, there's nothing in this room but the wall of pictures, all of them of her—and all of them looking better than she does right now.

"So this is my secret room," Max says, clearing his throat. "Which I guess you already found. How'd you get in this time, by the way?"

Anna walks over to the tree and puts a hand on its trunk, but nothing happens. "I called for you, and when you didn't come, I asked the Houdini for help. It opened the door."

Max joins her, and when he puts his hand on the tree, the strangest thing happens. White blossoms sprout, filling the air with sweetness, and fat oranges appear as if from nowhere, heavy and glistening.

"How'd you do that?" Anna asks. "Is there a switch or something?"

He smiles and takes his hand off the tree, and the blooms and oranges shrink back as if withdrawn into the branches. "A magician never reveals his secrets. But just between us, the secret is that I have no idea. It's always done this. I once read an article in the museum about a mechanical tree created by Houdini's spiritual mentor, Jean Eugène Robert-Houdin—the Marvelous Orange Tree. It did something quite similar."

And yes, Anna was recently traumatized and is on a deadline and just snuffled snot all over this beautiful boy, but she is still Anna and part of her longs to inspect every inch of the tree, to dig down into its pot and see what's there and discover the trick. But part of her, the part that realizes she was just rescued by the whims of a benevolent hotel, is simply delighted by the magic and glad for something to concentrate on other than her shaking hands.

She reaches into Max's vest pocket, and he goes very still as she pulls out his watch.

"Thirty minutes left," she says sadly.

"And we're trapped again," he adds.

She tucks the watch back into his pocket and puts her hand on his chest, over his heart. "What happens if I can't . . . if we can't . . ."

Max puts his hand over hers, warm and sure. "It's not over. There's always a way out."

"But what if . . . what if . . ." A deep breath, a tiny whisper. "I become a ghost?"

Max pulls her close. "Listen here. All night, I've felt like every moment with you might be my last. Maybe you'll become a ghost, haunting me. Maybe you'll leave without me, and then *I'll* be like the ghosts. But this would be my moment, Anna, my little loop. This is what I would relive. I'd keep looking for you all through the hotel until I found you, in whatever moment had captured you, and I'd spend all my free time trying to get you to speak to me again."

She sobs a laugh. "Like it would be hard. I'd be on the roof. Waiting to kiss you."

"I don't want to lose you," he murmurs, lifting her hand to press his lips to her knuckles. "The real you."

"And I don't want to be lost." She pulls his hand toward her and kisses his knuckles in turn. "That's why we have to get out and find"—she clears her throat—"what we have to find. If we do, we can both be free. There's a whole other world out there, and you're going to love it."

"I would," Max whispers, putting his forehead against hers. "I've spent my whole life trying to get out those doors. I know I would love it."

Not *I will*, Anna notices. *I would.* Like he can't trust it.

But how could he? He told her himself: everyone here forgets him.

Everyone leaves him behind.

"We're so close, Max. I can feel it. We just have to find what we're looking for. We've got to get out of here—and use the magician's box in the ballroom to get to Phoebe's hidden room."

"But we can't leave now. Colin's waiting by the only door."

Anna steps away and scans the room to see if the Houdini has provided yet another helpful hint. When she sees the door she used to leave last time, she smacks her forehead and laughs.

"Oh, yeah. The cabinet isn't the only door. There's that big obvious one over there."

Max sighs like his heart is breaking. "It's a dead end. It's boarded up with old bricks. One of the Houdini's private jokes, I suppose. Always felt very 'Amontillado' to me."

Anna blinks at him, confused. "It's not bricked up. The hall is outside. This is room 603."

Now it's his turn to look confused. "I've opened that door a hundred times. Nothing but bricks. And 603 is at the other end of the hall. Believe me—I've mapped it."

With no idea what's going to happen, Anna walks to the door and turns the knob. When she opens it, they both gasp.

It's not a brick wall.

It's not the hallway.

It's another secret passage.

40.

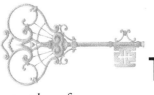The elegant marble hallway seems to stretch on forever.

Daniel, Tony, and Sebastian have been jogging, and staggering to catch their breath, and jogging again for what feels like an hour. At some point, the poodle gave up, but they can still hear it barking and growling, and thus they will not stop moving.

They've been in the Houdini for nearly twelve hours now without finding a single bite of food or sip of non-alcoholic beverage that wasn't there and then not, fresh and then foul. There have been no more restaurants, no cafés, no bars. They're so thirsty they drank from a fountain they found in a random lobby some time back, scooping up water with their cupped hands. It tasted like the old coins rotting on the bottom, green with patina.

"This crappy place," Tony grunts, stumbling forward, barefoot in his robe. "Gonna burn it to the ground."

"No, that's a waste." Even prissy Sebastian looks unkempt, his robe soaked through with sweat. "Gut it. Rebuild it. We can come in one day with sledgehammers and baseball bats. Spray-paint the walls. Shoot it with BB guns."

Daniel has no comment. These men, he knows now, are against him. He won't pretend that they're still friends.

They've been trudging in what seem like circles. Each long hallway of locked doors leads to a corner that promises something new, and yet the something new they keep discovering is another, slightly different hallway. Every now and then, they enter a new lobby with an unfamiliar configuration of wallpaper, tile, and uncomfortable but beautiful furniture, but every shop they find is firmly closed, the glass unbreakable. There's not so much as a dropped stick of gum in this bizarrely empty hotel.

"Wait. D'you hear that?"

Daniel cocks his head. The hallway they're in is seemingly endless—probably accomplished with all the mirrors—the black marble floors so shiny that it feels like a portal into Hades. The three men go still, listening, although Tony is still panting a bit.

Somewhere up ahead, they hear the click of high heels.

"Cigarettes!" a woman's sprightly voice calls. "Cigars! Mints! Candy!"

The men exchange excited glances like wolves scenting prey.

"The girl!" Tony splutters.

They take off at a wobbling jog.

"Chocolates for your best girl! Pretzels! Ice-cold cola!" the girl calls.

The men speed up, slipping on the tiles, clumsy with sleep deprivation and dehydration.

"I'd kill for a cola," Tony growls.

"You'd kill for a lot of things," Sebastian mutters, nearly delirious.

Tony giggles in a way that makes Daniel very uncomfortable.

They can see the corner that marks the end of this particular blasted hallway, and they slow down, preparing to turn in one big clot. Sebastian is the quickest and gets around the corner first, and that means he's the only one to see the elevator doors closing. He stretches out one hand and sprints, hoping he can snag the door or hit the button to make the elevator stop.

"Hold the door!" he cries.

But no one does. The elevator doors shut, nearly taking off his fingers.

"No!" Tony roars as he rounds the corner. "Why didn't you stop her?"

"I tried," Sebastian whimpers. "I tried."

He collapses against the wall, head hanging as he presses the call button again and again. "It'll come back. It's an elevator. But that girl is definitely getting fired." He turns to the others, his face twisted with rage. "She heard me, and she didn't hold the door!"

"Fired," Tony agrees. "Publicly. Embarrassingly."

They all lean against the wall now, pressing their faces against the cool white-and-gray marble, so welcome after miles and miles of mirrors and wallpaper prints: stripes and flowers and bees and snakes and cherries and an awful yellow one that showed an old-timey woman staring out a window, all in hideous shades of mustard.

When the elevator gears grind, the men perk up. Sebastian

keeps pressing the button, like it will quicken the process. The elevator doors open, and the girl is gone, but, well, it's an elevator. It will take them somewhere else, and chances are good that anywhere else will be better than here. They crowd in, with Daniel staying as far from Tony as possible. "Don't Be Cruel" crackles through the overhead speaker, Elvis's voice far away and scratchy, as if the record doesn't have many plays left in it.

Tony jabs his finger into a button, but it doesn't light up. He jabs another button and the doors slide shut. He goes up the column of numbers, cursing, stabbing angrily, but none of the buttons light up. The elevator doesn't move.

Instead, the doors slide open on an all-too-familiar foyer.

They are back in the penthouse, after they've been looking for it for what feels like a lifetime.

Oddly, however, there are now multiple doors instead of only the one.

"This was different," Tony says. "We were just here."

"I don't hear the dog at least." Sebastian looks around, nose twitching like a rabbit.

Daniel just stares at the first door, eyes narrowed. "Something very strange is happening."

As he stares, the door swings open, and a woman sings, "Come in," her voice significantly deeper than the cigarette girl's.

Tony shrugs and walks through the open door, leading the other two men back into the room the poodle had chased them out of so long ago. Directly ahead, a woman lounges on a chaise, a glossy book of black-and-white photos open before her as if she's been relaxing there all night. She watches the men, smiling, her lips painted the bright matte red of a screen siren from the 1940s, the kind of woman who can rip out a man's heart at forty paces.

"Hello, boys," she purrs. A pink toy poodle looks up from her lap and lifts its lip to show a fang.

Tony has gone completely still and paler than pale. "Phoebe?"

41.

Phoebe nods and closes the book with a bang. "In the flesh. Are you surprised, little brother?"

For once, possibly the first time ever, Tony is speechless.

"Phoebe," Daniel says, stepping forward as Sebastian subtly takes a step back. "Tony's sister who disappeared?"

"More accurately, Tony's sister who was *made* to disappear." Phoebe gently places the tiny poodle on the chaise as she stands. She looks as dangerous and elegant as a black widow spider in an off-the-shoulder black gown with a plunging neckline and a deep slit up one leg.

"Made to disappear?" Daniel puts a hand on Tony's shoulder and spins him around. "What did you do, Tone?"

"It was an accident!" Tony splutters, then pushes past Daniel and walks backward after Sebastian, who's nearly reached the door already. "It was Sebastian's idea!"

"Lies," Sebastian says. He grabs the door handle and yanks,

but the door won't open, which makes his timing comedic instead of dramatic. He and Tony push and scratch at the door like dogs who desperately need to go outside.

"You can't escape, fools." Phoebe throws her head back and laughs. "Because your little coup landed me *here,* in the other Houdini. Instead of a tawdry old casino that caters to the elderly and misty-eyed, you dropped me into Wonderland. Into Narnia. Instead of a magic-themed hotel, it's *real* magic." She snaps her fingers, and a jolt of electricity makes Sebastian and Tony jump back from the door with a cry, rubbing at their shocked hands. "So stop acting like you can escape. Because you can't."

"You've been here all this time?" Daniel asks, confused. "At the Houdini? Just . . . hiding in a hotel? But they said you were missing. . . ."

"Surely you understand by now that this is not the broken-down hotel you own back in Las Vegas? This is another place, a place out of time. A place where I have all the power." Phoebe cocks her head at him. "Daniel, did you really not know? You three have always been thick as thieves."

"I swear I don't know what's going on," Daniel says, desperate. "Tony told me you were dead. We stopped here because of the tornado. I can't find my daughter—"

"Ah, yes. Sweet Anna. Lovely girl. Pity what's going to happen to her."

Daniel storms across the room, stopping only when the poodle leaps in front of its mistress, growling with the fury and depth of a rottweiler.

"What about Anna?" Daniel shouts.

Phoebe doesn't respond; she merely stands there, smirking behind her poodle.

"You know, I'm getting ahead of myself." Shoving Daniel aside with a hand, she strides over to the button on the wall and pushes it. "Arielle?"

"Yeah, boss?" comes the perky answer.

"Let's have some refreshments for our guests."

"You got it, boss."

"Hey, was that the cigarette girl?" Tony says, turning from the door, which he's been ramming with his shoulder. "She's a real piece of work."

"Takes one to know one," Phoebe snarls before clearing her throat and smiling again. When they're both angry, it's easy to see that they're related, even if she has bleached her hair and eyebrows and dropped her Jersey accent for a posher one copped from old black-and-white movies. "Now, just give me a moment. Running this place is so very exhausting."

She swans over to a different door, which she throws open theatrically. "Well? Go on in. Or don't you trust me, brother dearest?" Daniel follows her into the other room, asking more questions about Anna.

As soon as Daniel and Phoebe are out of earshot, Tony grabs Sebastian by the front of his robe.

"What's she doing alive?" he rage-whispers.

Before Sebastian can answer, Phoebe calls for them. "Tony, Sebastian? If you're done blaming each other and ruining perfectly good kimonos, please do come join us. You must be dehydrated by now."

Tony tugs on the closed door once more, and Sebastian darts over to open the third and last door in the room, which leads to a closet full of cleaning equipment. There are no more doors, no possible way out. Reluctantly, they stalk toward the open one, through which they find a gleaming wood conference table covered in delicacies. There are cucumber sandwiches and tea cakes and crudités with dressing, as well as fruit and cheese and tall glasses of soda. Daniel is already seated. Phoebe is at the head of the table, elbows out aggressively like a queen on a throne. This room is decorated in a disturbing clown motif, with clown lamps on every table and oil paintings of sad clowns on every wall.

"You trying to poison us?" Tony says, picking up a glass and inspecting the liquid within.

Phoebe bites off the corner of a pimento cheese sandwich, chews, and swallows before saying, innocently and amusedly, "What do you think I'd do, dear brother—pour industrial-strength cleaner into someone's soda?"

Tony slams the glass down, making Daniel jump. He's already halfway through a cola and a sandwich, which is all the proof Phoebe ever needed that he had no idea whose pain their empire was born from. Daniel has no reason to distrust her, much less fear her. Whereas, like Tony, Sebastian abstains from the food and drink, for all that he keeps licking his dry lips like a lizard about to eat its own shed skin.

"So what's it going to take?" Sebastian asks.

Phoebe's perfectly plucked eyebrows rise. "What's *what* going to take?"

Sebastian steeples his hands as if he was in an Armani suit

instead of a sweat-damp silk robe. "What's it going to take to let us go? We are not without our resources."

But when he reaches into the robe's pocket for his wallet, much to his surprise he finds a pack of cards, still in their box. Phoebe takes her time eating her entire sandwich, watching him, smirking between bites. She dabs at her bright-red lips with a cloth napkin and grins.

"Is that not what you were looking for? How very odd."

Sebastian stands up and throws the box of playing cards on the table, then steps forward, hands in fists. "Where's my wallet, Phoebe?"

"I don't know, Sebastian. Did you perhaps drop it somewhere inconvenient? Maybe by accident?" She stands and slams a fist into the table. "Or did you toss it somewhere dark, where no one could ever find it?"

Daniel puts down his sandwich and looks at Sebastian and then Tony. "The chef said something . . ."

"The chef said a lot of things!" Tony roars.

Daniel turns to Phoebe. "Look, I want to know what's going on here, because I smell a rat, but I can't think straight until I find my daughter. If you know where she is, I need to know."

Phoebe steps around Daniel's chair. She picks up the box of playing cards from the table with one hand and spills them out of their box, facedown.

She plucks a card, holds it up so the men can't see the face.

"Once upon a time, there was a queen."

She throws the card on the table, revealing it to be the queen of hearts. But instead of a woman, there's a golden canary wearing a crown.

"She had inherited a great kingdom, and although she was sad about the tragic loss of her parents, she was hopeful. But then her brother saw a way to take her kingdom from her."

She pulls another card from the spread and turns it over: the king of spades, which is actually a pink poodle smoking a cigar.

"And of course, his little toady." She takes another card and flips it, showing the jack of spades—a cavorting poodle in a ruff and jester's cap.

She places both of the cards on top of the queen, then fans them out. Now the queen is in front, the canary trapped in an ornate gold cage.

"One day, in a hotel called the Houdini, she and the two men argued over who deserved to run the kingdom. Tempers were very high. The queen fainted, as she had an undisclosed health issue, a vulnerability she had not seen fit to share with the meddlesome men who wished to control her and her newfound power. And the would-be king and his toady took advantage of her unconsciousness. They dropped her down an old, bricked-in laundry chute while she was out cold." Phoebe picks up the queen and shoves the card back into the box all by itself. "And so the queen disappeared."

"This is bull—" Tony starts, but Phoebe puts a finger to her lips, and he goes instantly silent, gawping stupidly, his mouth open but emitting no sound.

"As I was saying. The queen woke up alone, in a dark place.

But she wasn't really alone, as she was pregnant. She hadn't told her brother yet, as he had thoughts about independent, unmarried women making their own choices. Luckily, she landed on something soft. Unluckily, the shock and injuries from the fall sent her into premature labor." She upends the box and the queen of hearts, still in her cage, tumbles out, along with a new card, the king of hearts. "She had arrived not in a blocked chute in the basement of the original hotel, not in her own kingdom, but in a new one. A place similar to the world she had come from but filled with magic and beauty. She found allies there and honed her powers. She took advantage of every resource offered. She bore a healthy son. And she waited."

Phoebe plucks up four cards. There are the king and the jack of spades again, but now there's another king in the pile—the king of diamonds. "Although the hotel changed her, she had patience. She had faith. She waited until she could arrange to have her enemies delivered directly into her hands."

Carefully, she puts the cards on the table, fanned out. She considers them before removing the new king. And then she picks up a cheese knife and stabs it through the stacked king of spades and his jack.

"That doesn't make any goddamn sense," Tony says as if out of breath. He still hasn't eaten, and his face is beet red, his hands fidgeting. "You're crazy."

Phoebe snorts. "Oh. Gaslighting. How very modern of you."

"We need to make this right," Daniel says, still seated at the table. "If you're saying what I think you're saying, the Houdini was supposed to be yours. I think that means we all owe you a portion—"

Phoebe shakes her head. "Oh, no. I've got something better in mind. See, everyone keeps trying to leave, and that's the thing: you can't. No one can. This place is a one-way street. You check in, and you don't check out."

"That's not how anything works," Tony growls.

"Really? Marvelous. I'd love to watch you stroll through any door, out of this establishment. If you can do so, I'll let you go, no hard feelings." Her smile curls in like a viper's tongue as her long nails tap the table. "But you've tried every door you've found, and by now you must know that none of them will open." She looks away and back, quickly. "It's a lesson I learned long ago."

"Then what's next?" Daniel asks, desperate to understand. "Are you saying my daughter is trapped here, too? How do you know she hasn't found a way out?"

"I really am sorry," Phoebe says, and she looks, for once, like she means it. "I never meant for her to get involved. But I'm afraid there is no hope. Perhaps you and Anna are innocent, but it's beyond my powers now. At midnight, those two will get what they deserve . . ."

She pauses, glancing at the clock, which reads 11:52 p.m.

"But I can't save you or your daughter."

42.

Daniel stands so quickly that his chair falls over. "You better find her!" he shouts. "You better find my girl!"

Standing, too, Phoebe swans over to another door—so many doors! "Or else . . . what? What more could you possibly do to me? I've survived multiple murder attempts, I've been robbed by my own kin, kept from my home and my family and my inheritance. I wish I could leave you out of this, Daniel, even if you did benefit from my disappearance." She snorts. "But you can't tell me what to do here. No one can. So you'd better find your manners."

Her hand is on the doorknob, her eyebrows up. She's waiting.

"I'm so sorry for everything that has happened to you, Phoebe. I wish it was in my power to help you. But it's not. I'm in your power now. *Please* will you help me find my daughter?" Daniel asks, his posture folding in hopelessness.

Tony sneers his disdain, as if there's something deeply wrong with surrender or basic courtesy. But Phoebe dramatically throws open the door, revealing . . .

An empty room.

Her jaw drops, and she looks more human than she has in ages. "They were here," she mutters. "I left them here. There's no other door. I made sure of it."

She rushes into the room, noting every overturned table, every rug tossed aside. She stands at the open window, staring outside in disbelief.

"Did they jump?" she asks no one in particular. "Did the love-sick idiots jump?"

As she stands at the window, hands on the sill, Tony and Sebastian share a very specific look and tiptoe across the room, their bare feet silent on the shag carpet. Daniel navigates around the table and rushes to follow them, calling, "Phoebe! Watch out!"

She spins and steps aside, right as Tony lunges. His hands catch at her shoulders, and it's almost comical, watching him try to shove her out the window like they're in some children's cartoon. Sebastian kicks the door closed and twists the lock, ignoring Daniel, who's pounding his fists on the other side.

"Arielle!" Phoebe shouts, hands clutching at the window frame. "Help!"

But she has pushed no button, and no help arrives.

There is nothing a hotel can do to stop what is already in motion.

As Tony, twice her size, pushes Phoebe with all his might, she loses her grip on the sill.

And falls.

43.

Anna and Max shuffle through a dark passageway, hand in hand, scurrying between the walls of a hotel that is, quite honestly, more secret passageway than anything else.

"It has to end sometime, right?" Anna asks.

"I usually bring a flashlight and some string," Max admits. "It's easy to get a bit panicky when the Houdini is in a mood and you're in a dark, tight space."

"I wish I knew what time it is. It's got to be getting late. . . ." Anna trails off. There is no satisfying way to end that sentence.

"I can help with that. Abracadabra!"

There's a click, and something vaguely green swims in front of their eyes. It's Max's pocket watch, the numbers and hands within glowing in the dark. The minute hand is so close to the twelve that Anna feels dizzy.

"Is it radioactive?" she asks, drawing back a little.

"What's that?"

The watch snaps closed, the numbers still dancing in her vision.

"My AP history teacher told us about these girls who worked in factories, painting the numbers on clocks so they would glow in the dark. They would lick their paintbrushes to get a fine line. But the paint was radioactive, and all the radium girls died."

"My goodness, that's grim," Max says, squeezing her hand. "I hope it's not—whatever that is."

"Me too. Although I guess I don't have enough time to get radiation poisoning before I just . . . disappear in five minutes. Why do all the passages here seem so endless?" Anna remembers the last few times she felt this way and says, a bit louder, "A little help would be good. A rabbit, maybe? Anything!" Hearing the frustration in her voice, she puts a hand on the dusty wall. "Please?"

There's a tiny noise up ahead, a wispy scratch like paper tearing, and two beams of light pierce the darkness of the narrow passage. Recognizing another set of peepholes like the ones she looked through in the library painting, Anna hurries ahead and stands on tiptoe, but she's not tall enough.

"If only I was wearing heels," she mutters. "Can you see anything?"

Max fits his eyes to the perfectly spaced holes. "Huh. What does your father look like?"

"Lift me up!" Anna squeaks. "Let me see!"

Max's arms curl around her waist, and then she's struggling to focus as the light momentarily blinds her. There's her dad, she's sure of it. He's standing at a closed door, frantically twisting the knob.

"Tony, don't you hurt her!" he shouts at the door, slamming one hand against it.

"Is he hurting my mom?" Max asks, holding Anna aside so he can see. She wriggles in his arms, trying to look through the peepholes again, and he loses his balance, and they both fall forward.

But they don't smack into the wall—they tumble through it, ripping a hole in what appears to be old canvas. Fortunately, there's a pile of sultan's pillows right where they land, with Max partially on top of Anna, who is already clawing her way to her feet.

"Dad!" she cries.

Daniel Alonso turns around, stunned, and runs for her, arms out. He hasn't hugged his daughter like this since before she hit puberty, cradling her close like she's the most precious thing in the world.

"Honey, are you okay?" he asks, pulling back to check her face.

"I'm okay. Are you okay? You look like you've got the flu."

He chuckles. "Oh, well, you know, wandering a hotel for twelve hours with no food or drink and soaked to the bone will do that to you. Have you eaten? Are you safe?" He looks past her, and it's like a stone wall comes down in front of his eyes. "Who's that boy?"

Max stands there, nervous but determined, like a racehorse at the starting line. "I'm Max. We heard you tell someone not to hurt 'her.' Is the her my mom? Phoebe? Where is she?"

Daniel shakes his head like this is all too much to take in. Anna glances back at where they came from. When she and Max fell, they ripped through a tall, creepy canvas painting of a sad clown. The frame is still there, tacked to the wall, but now there's just a big hole into the dark passage.

"Phoebe and Tony are on the other side of this door, but I can't get it open," her dad says, speaking to Max like he's another adult. "I think—I think he's trying to kill her. Can you open it? Maybe we run at it together?"

Daniel steps back, and Max whips out his key, but the door won't budge. Anna tries her key, too, but the door is stubborn. There are no sounds from the other side, no feminine screams or masculine shouts. It's utterly silent.

"Those keys won't work, I'm afraid."

Anna turns to find Phoebe sitting on the couch, legs crossed.

By now, she is incapable of being surprised.

"Mom!" Max runs to her, but he doesn't hug her like Anna hugged her father. He stops just short of the couch and nods. "But I thought—"

"That my brother had finally succeeded in ending me? Fortunately, he doesn't know much about how the Houdini works." Phoebe winks at him. "As I'm guessing you two recently learned, it would appear to be a very short fall even from the penthouse."

Max snorts and sits down like his legs have finally given out. "That's one way to put it."

"What about Tony and Sebastian?" Daniel asks. "Do we just leave them in there? What do we do now?"

"We wait," Phoebe says, pointing at a cuckoo clock that has appeared on the wall. "It's almost midnight, you see. I can't think of any worse punishment for my would-be murderer of a brother and that monster Sebastian than being forced to relive this moment again and again, knowing they've failed to get rid of me. But as for you and your daughter, I'm sorry you got caught up in the trap." She reaches for Max's hand and briefly squeezes it before letting go and looking directly at Anna. "I didn't mean for this to happen to you, dear, but I can't stop it now." Something like pity and regret shines in her eyes.

"Can't stop what?" Daniel asks.

Realization washes over Anna. She can't stop staring at the *tick-tick-tick*ing second hand of the cuckoo clock. They have three minutes.

Three minutes until midnight.

Three minutes until checkout time.

"It was already too late," Phoebe says. "Once you were in the Houdini."

Max moves swiftly to Anna's side, grabs her hand, and laces his fingers through hers. They're both staring at the clock as if they could stop the hands from moving if they wished hard enough.

A song quietly starts, trickling into the room from the tinny overhead speaker. It's a bluesy, soulful piano song, the record horribly scratchy. "I got the key to the highway," it begins, and the volume is turned by an unseen hand to an unbearable level that makes Anna's teeth grind.

Phoebe rolls her eyes and says, "Very cute, but you know it's too late."

The music stops, the record scratching, and Phoebe sighs in relief—until a new song starts up, a man crooning about a pocketful of dreams. Anna looks at Phoebe. This is part of her penthouse.

The key she's been looking for all night has to be here, somewhere. Phoebe doesn't have any obvious totem on her person, no glowing locket or broach. There is no conspicuous object in the room like the Beast's rose or Ursula's necklace.

Anna has to think about this logically.

What does she know?

The key will be near Phoebe. It will be magical and special. It will glow.

Anna thinks back to all the magic she's seen tonight. Food and drink appearing from nowhere. A room that changes its contents. Clothes and shoes that always fit. A library that delivers requested books that may or may not exist and creates secret passages out of thin air. An automaton that draws customized images. A dessert room that springs from nowhere to cheer a young man's heart.

A tree that blooms at only one person's touch.

All the magic . . . seems to revolve around Max.

But Max can't be the key. He is very dear to Phoebe, but he doesn't glow.

Not literally, at least.

And besides, a boy isn't a key.

"Lucky, lucky me, I can live in luxury because I've got a pocketful of dreams," the man croons.

A pocketful . . .

Anna turns to Max and reaches into his vest pocket. Her eyes meet his as she pulls out his pocket watch and pushes the crown to reveal the face.

"No!" Phoebe shouts, lurching up from the couch.

But Daniel moves in front of Anna, blocking her from Phoebe.

"Where did you get this?" Anna asks.

Max smiles fondly. "My mom gave it to me a long time ago. She told me to take special care of it and always keep it with me. Why?"

Anna pulls up the crown, and the pocket watch stops ticking. She holds her breath and looks at the cuckoo clock, but it's still going. Its hand moves one notch.

It's 11:59.

Maybe Anna is wrong, but she has to try one more thing.

"I'm sorry," Anna says, and before Max can ask why, she yanks the pocket watch hard enough to rip the chain off his vest. The watch is warm in her hand, heavier than it should be, and she places it on the ground and then brings the heel of her foot down on its open face with all her might.

The pocket watch shatters, glass and golden springs crunching into the carpet—along with a tiny silver key. Anna kneels and plucks it from the wreck.

The cuckoo clock stops ticking.

All the lights go out.

44.

"What have you done?" Phoebe wails.

"She pulled one over on ya, boss," someone says.

The voice is new, high-pitched and joyous, and they all turn to look at the rip in the wall. The girl from the crypt is standing there in her long white dress, glowing softly.

"Arielle, I command you to leave!" Phoebe screeches. "You are forbidden to access this floor!"

The girl flinches like she's been slapped. Her jaw tenses, and she pants, limbs moving slowly, as if she's walking through water. The chain drags behind her, trailing into the passage beyond. Step by step, chain clanking, the girl walks right up to Anna. She holds out a hand and smiles, although it clearly pains her.

"Can I have that key, kiddo?"

"Don't you dare!" Phoebe shouts. She tries to rise from the couch, but Daniel won't let her. "You don't know what she is, Anna! She's not human. You don't know what she'll do!"

Anna stares at Phoebe, then at Arielle. "No one should be in a cage. My wish is freedom. For you, and for us, and for the Houdini, if that's what it wants."

She puts the key in the girl's hand.

With a terrific boom that shakes the hotel, the girl disappears, leaving them again in complete darkness.

45.

The lights come on with a droning buzz. Their glow has changed from the warm, magical flicker of orange flames to the dull, urine yellow of cheap bulbs at too low a wattage. A new song sputters to a start from the speaker, a woman asking, *Is that all there is?* in an enervated, singsong voice, like someone who has lost something important but now knows better. The girl—Arielle?—is gone, along with the key. The food and drink that were spread out on the table are gone. The pack of cards is gone except for one lone card, a joker. It's not the usual jester, but a dancing rabbit capering away from a top hat. Anna snatches up the card and shoves it in her pocket. Her own tin of playing cards has disappeared, along with the drawing from the automaton in the ballroom.

"No," Phoebe moans. She stands and staggers to the table and sits, head in her hands. She looks ten years older now and utterly despondent. Black roots show along her hairline. "Look what you've done. You ruined it. You ruined it all."

"Maybe that's not such a bad thing. You and Max can leave, too," Anna says. She risks a glance at Max. He looks utterly shell-shocked, but whereas Phoebe is staring around the suite, no doubt noticing that it is smaller and shabbier, the walls faded and cracked and the carpet dusty and threadbare, rust instead of crimson, Max only has eyes for Anna.

Anna looks at him a little too long before she looks away, blushing.

"She ruined everything." Phoebe turns to look at her son, her eyes listless. "And now she's going to leave you. Outside of this place, we have nothing. We are nothing. The magic is gone with Arielle. It can't come back." She points a finger at him. "And you helped her. You helped her ruin our lives—"

The music stops with the zip of a record player needle being lifted.

"Hey, boss? One last thing." It's Arielle's voice, that saucy 1940s patter, peppy and clear.

Phoebe bares her teeth and looks up at the speaker. "What?"

"I want you to know that I forgive you."

Phoebe snorts. "Like that matters."

"It does. See, I've been imprisoned here for a hundred years. You came along, and you never even questioned it. You just signed that contract and took what you could. And then you made me bring you these poor people, knowing full well what would happen to them."

"They tried to kill me!" Phoebe hisses. "And Max!"

"Well, sure—two of 'em did, a long time ago. And I guess having me around made you feel real big and tough, but you're a welcher. You forgot that the whole point of having power is to help people, not harm 'em. No one deserves to be in a cage. Not you, not me, not Max, not anybody else. But it's easy to forget that. Maybe without magic, you'll remember. I've been watching people a real long time, and I figure living well is the best revenge. So go out there and live well, if you can. And, hey. You made mistakes, so did other people. Maybe you can forgive them, too. Not Tony and Sebastian and Colin, though—those guys were bad eggs through and through, and they weren't included in Anna's wish, so the Houdini took 'em out like the trash."

Phoebe looks up, hope flaring in her eyes. "They're gone?"

"They're wherever the magic went. Poof! But you're lucky. You get to go on. Take it from a star: everybody needs the chance to fall and get back up, every now and then." There's a pause and a sigh. "Max, you're a good kid. Keep that up. Anna, you're a good kid, too. Help him, okay?"

Anna can only nod.

"Abyssinia, dolls!"

They wait several long moments, but the speaker is silent.

Phoebe slams a fist on the table. "This is still my hotel, and—"

"No!"

Everyone looks at Max in surprise. He steps away from his mother.

"I want nothing to do with this place. Or with you. Who was that girl? You kept her imprisoned my entire life, hid her from me?"

"It wasn't a girl." Phoebe looks down, furious. "It was . . . some kind of spirit. A demon. Evil."

"She was a fallen star," Anna says softly.

Phoebe gives her a dirty look. "Whatever it is, it tells lies. It can't be trusted."

"And you can? You always told me I would inherit this place, but what was I supposed to inherit—an empty building, powered by someone else's pain, full of ghosts who can never leave? What kind of life is that? You kept me trapped in some ridiculous version of the past, when you could've given her that key and we could've left years ago. I can't believe I had it on me all that time and never knew. You told me to always keep it with me, that it was a gift, a sign of my maturity and responsibility. You made me culpable." Max shakes his head, pulls his elevator key out of his pocket, and throws it on the ground amid the wreckage of his watch. "If we really can leave, once I'm outside, I want nothing to do with you."

"I can't believe you're falling for all these lies—"

He throws his hands up. "Look around! This place is changed. The magic is gone. It's like . . . I've heard this hum all my life, and now that it's gone, the silence is deafening. The only lies I see are yours."

Phoebe stares at him, her mouth open, her lips quivering.

"Max, I—"

"Stop. Just . . . stop. It's over. It could've been over from the beginning, if you'd just let her be free. I could've grown up"—he waves his arms at the window covered with hideous paisley curtains and ivory-stained blinds—"out there. Where it's normal."

"Normal isn't better," Phoebe snaps. "The modern world is

terrible. I watched it happen, I saw the direction it was headed, and I made a choice. I wanted you to be free from influence—"

"So you caged me."

"I *protected* you. That's a mother's job. I did what I thought was right for us both. This place—I found it this way, I didn't make it this way."

Max pokes the remains of his watch with his foot. "Then you succumbed to it. Let it mold you. None of it is real."

"It's all real," Phoebe insists, desperate now. "Everything that exists here exists on the other side, in the past. You won't lose anything. I gave you a better world—"

"You'll understand if I prefer to discover that for myself."

"I—"

They all stare at Phoebe. She looks comical and ridiculous, as if all pretense has fallen away to reveal something cheap and tawdry. She steps toward Max, and his eyes are hard, his jaw set. When she reaches him, she puts a hand on his cheek, gentle and soft.

"Forgive me," she rasps.

Max just shakes her off and takes a step back.

"No."

46.

Everyone is deeply uncomfortable as Phoebe sobs in a chair, the only other sound now the harsh tick of an old alarm clock.

"So where are we?" Daniel finally asks.

"I think it might be the real Houdini." Anna runs a hand over an ancient avocado-green sofa with heavily dented cushions. "But I guess we'll know better once we try to leave."

Daniel walks to the door that he was struggling with when he thought Tony was going to finally succeed in killing Phoebe. He turns the knob, and the door opens to reveal a shabby bathroom with a flickering fluorescent light and a cracked mirror. "No sign of Tony and Sebastian."

Phoebe's sobs break into mad laughter. "Good. They deserve much worse."

"Did they really try to kill you?" he asks her.

She nods. "First them, then Colin. I wonder if he really is gone, too?"

"I hope so," Anna says.

The way she says it makes her dad stride over and ask, "Who's this Colin guy, and do I need to have a word with him?"

"It's a long story, and I'm too tired to tell it," Anna admits. "Can we leave? Please?"

With a decisive sigh, one Anna knows very well and thinks of as his Getting Down to Business sigh, Daniel goes to the last remaining door. "Okay. Here's what's going to happen. We're going downstairs, and if this hotel is, uh, real, we're getting the hell out and going to the Roosevelt. I'll call a car. Phoebe, I'll take care of all your necessities until . . ." He trails off and runs a hand through his hair. "Until Tony's estate is figured out. Whatever you did here tonight, you still get all of Tony's assets as far as I'm concerned. If you want me to buy you out, I will."

Phoebe nods decisively. "Until we can sort out the accounts, I want a suite in your nicest hotel." She has regained her regal bearing, for all that it's clear some of the magic that bolstered her beauty has fled. "For Max and me. And you'll help us reintegrate into life. ID, clothes, all that."

Anna is proud that her dad nods. "Of course. Whatever you need."

Because Phoebe may be a monster, but she is also a victim. Her own brother—Anna's supposed Uncle Tony!—tried to straight up kill her, and then Colin did, too, which Anna can well believe. She can't imagine what it would be like, to have someone you loved, someone you trusted, try to kill you for money. Anna loves her sister more than anything in the world, and she can't imagine either of them ever purposefully hurting the other.

Which—yes. Emily didn't mean to hurt her at the wedding. Anna has always known it in her heart, and now she's so desperate to talk to her best friend that she's ready to forgive anything. She needs to find a phone, but she can feel her body giving out. Whether time in the Houdini is real or not, she's been awake for more than thirty hours, and exhaustion is seeping into her limbs, into her head. She wants to sleep so badly. She wants to hug her dad. She wants to find out if Emily is okay and check in with their mom.

"Can we go now, please?" she asks again.

Her dad looks at her and nods, holding his arm out. She walks around the table and nestles under it, wondering why he smells like rotten garbage. Daniel leads the way out the door, looking as drained as Anna feels. She glances back at Max, who seems utterly lost. She wants to go to him, but she needs her dad just now, and Max's troubled eyes show that he's wrestling with problems of his own.

On the other side of the door, they find an entirely unmagical hallway. Ivory walls stippled with holes and cracks, carpet stained an unfortunate brown. The elevator is completely different, a much newer model, all flat silver that's been dented and scuffed. The elevator doesn't make that grinding, mechanical noise—it just appears, and when the doors slide open, it's a vast improvement, but still not on par with the hotels Anna has stayed in before. It's big enough for a dozen people and mirrored with a glossy marble floor with gold sparkles, and she has to turn away from what she sees in her reflection. She looks like a zombie Audrey Hepburn, her braid undone, hair covered in dust and cobwebs, big purple circles under her eyes like smears of old eye shadow. Her mascara and lipstick, insanely, are still in place, and she congratulates herself on finding a brand that would stay put not only through her sister's wedding but also through . . . whatever this has been.

The elevator's buttons go from 6 down to *L* for lobby and then *B* for basement. Once they're all in, Daniel presses the *L,* and the doors zing shut. Anna is trying not to look at Max because she wants to hug him and cry on him and kiss him all at once, but she can tell his heart and mind are all tangled up. The things he knows about his mother now—he must be, as Anna once assumed, an absolute mess.

When the elevator dings, Anna is prepared to step out, but they must have stopped on another floor. Two old ladies stand there in matching outfits of neon green shoes, fanny packs, hats, and T-shirts that say I'M WITH MS. MONEYBAGS. Seeing the motley crew already on the elevator, one of them steps back and says, "Uh, we'll wait for the next one."

But Anna's heart lifts. Judging by the custom tees and the giant cell phone one of the definitely not-see-through ladies is holding, they are back in her own time, in her own world.

The next time the elevator doors open, it's on the most blessed of sights: a busy hotel lobby.

Not a supernice hotel, but at least one filled with people and noise and suitcases on trolleys and the sound of far-off slots and the pervasive scent of stale cigarette smoke. There are nods to a magical theme here and there—posters for magic shows and wall-paper borders of card suits—but everything is completely different. The hotel shop is new and brightly lit, for one thing, and there are no rabbits visible. Signs point to restaurants, shows, and a pool. Business is brisk, even in the aftermath of the storm.

They unpile from the elevator, Anna staying close to Max but not close enough to touch. Daniel again takes charge, heading directly for a woman in a sharp burgundy suit behind the counter. "Hillary, how are you?"

She looks up, does a double take, and puts on her most professional smile. "Mr. Alonso, what a nice surprise. We didn't know you'd be stopping by or we would have had fresh cookies."

Anna's dad smiles in that way he has. "That's my mistake for not mentioning it, then. Look, we were just up on the top floor, and—"

"The top floor? Sir, we had to close that down. Water issues—Mr. Williams approved it. I'm so sorry you ended up there. I—we—didn't see you come in."

He waves it away. "A silly mistake. We were looking at what fixes need to be made to get it running again. If you could please call us a car, that would be fantastic."

"Of course, sir." Hillary hurries to her desk—which has a phone, thank goodness, and gets to work.

Within ten minutes, Anna and her father are pushing through the revolving door and finally, finally outside. The air has that marvelous fresh-rain smell—which is called petrichor, one of Anna's SAT words—and the storm has clearly ended. Anna turns to watch as Max pauses in front of the glass door. His mouth hangs open and his eyes are shining, whereas nearby, Phoebe's entire being is stooped and pathetic, suffused with regret. When the door moves under Max's hand, he walks through like a kid on Christmas morning and stares up at the Vegas skyline with wondrous joy. Something in Anna's heart warms, to witness this moment, and she wishes that she and Max could be holding hands while he makes this huge step.

He's spent his whole life trying to get through that door . . . and now, he has.

She can see the original white limo in the corner of the parking lot, its roof caved in and a downed telephone pole beside it. It's noon, and the sky is bright blue and cloudless. Anna has never been more grateful to feel sunshine. Max is standing a bit away from her, looking up and grinning.

That's right—he's never seen the sun before. He glances at Anna and they share this silent moment of wonder, and she wishes she could kiss him and feel the sunshine caught in his dark hair.

"See? It's not so bad out here," she says.

"It's beautiful," he answers, and she's aware that he's looking at her when he says it. "It's the most beautiful thing I've ever seen."

47.

The car arrives, and Max isn't quite sure what to do. Daniel helps him climb into the back row and get his seat belt on. Then Anna and her dad settle in the middle seats with Phoebe in front. Anna grabs a mint and leans into the armrest, slumping down. She's painfully aware of Max's eyes on her, keeps catching his reflection in the glass. She can feel his pain like a beacon, but she's too exhausted to do anything about it, and especially not in a car with both of their parents.

Her dad borrows the Uber driver's phone in exchange for a generous cash tip and starts texting with her mom. He learns that the electricity is out at their house, so she's staying with her sister and has been sleeping off a massive migraine. He calls Emily next, and Anna snatches the phone from his hand.

"So you're okay?" Anna asks anxiously.

"Of course I'm okay. I just had the best day of my life and I'm on my way to Bali. All I needed was to hear my little sister's voice to make it perfect. I was worried about you last night. I called and texted a million times and freaked out when you didn't respond. What happened?"

Relief floods Anna's chest, the tension that's kept her awake and anxious seeping away. "No power because of the storm, so my phone turned off. I was so worried about you."

"You don't need to worry about me, you goose," Emily says, laughing. "Let me worry about you for a change. I've got everything I want, so now it's your turn. And there's an extra bedroom for you in the new apartment, so you're going to have to come visit every single weekend."

"Maybe every other weekend," Anna says with a yawn. "Got a ton of AP courses next year. Lots of studying and clubs. And I think I might try out for the next play."

"I'm sorry, what? The wallflower is finally going to show the world her true colors?"

Anna catches Max still watching her in the window's reflection. "It might be time to try something new, you know?"

"Well, I've always known you're a star, and the whole world deserves to see you shine." Emily gasps. "Oh! I need to do a graphic for that. It would be so cute on tote bags. And phone cases. You're such an inspiration."

"No, you are." Anna yawns again.

"I mean, no wonder you're exhausted. You worked so hard for my wedding. You really are the best sister ever. I don't know what I'd do without you."

"No, you are," Anna repeats, and she feels all warm and glowy inside. Maybe it's the exhaustion, but she's starting to feel like even with Emily moving away, maybe everything will be okay.

Now that she knows her family survived the storm, Anna can relax and look around. She's shocked by the devastation in the streets, and every stoplight is out and blinking on the way to the Roosevelt. Anna loved the look and feel of the Houdini—the other, magical Houdini that disappeared—but there's something to be said for familiar comforts. She's looking forward to soft pajamas from the hotel shop and a hot shower with floral soap and a cold candy bar from the minibar. Only twelve hours have passed in the real world, for all that it feels like an entire week.

They stumble out of the car and into the Roosevelt lobby, where the manager is happy to arrange everything that Anna's dad requests. Without a word to anyone, Phoebe takes her keycard and disappears into the elevator; she can't even look her son in the eye. With a shy smile at Max, Anna heads straight for the shop to collect what she needs, noting that it's not quite as fun as the Wardrobe in the Houdini. Max follows her, and she helps him find a pair of pajamas and some toothpaste. Anna wonders briefly what they did for dentistry at the other Houdini but recalls that Max's teeth are nice and so is his breath, so maybe magic is better than science, sometimes. Max doesn't know what size he is, since the Wardrobe magically produced clothes that always fit perfectly.

In the elevator to the top floor, Anna's dad explains how room service works to Max, who assures him that he's well versed in this particular of hotel life. Anna can still feel their connection like a tether, but it's weird, talking to Max in front of her dad after all they've been through. When they leave for their separate rooms, waving sheepishly, part of her longs for a button she could push to hear his voice through a tinny speaker.

Cell phones, she reminds herself.

They will soon have functional cell phones, like normal people.

After she's checked in with her mom and gotten an earful about Aunt Debbie's new Chihuahua, Anna flops back onto the bed, loving the cool sheets, the puffy comforter, the array of pillows. At the end of the bed, something catches her eye. It's the joker she took from Phoebe's table, the last card in the deck. It's sharp and new but has that old-timey feeling, with slightly raised ink and a linen back. Anna turns it over and over in her hands, wondering what the Houdini really was, if it was in the world or something else. Was Arielle really a fallen star? Did the magical hotel disappear, or does it exist in some other realm? What exactly did it do with Tony, Sebastian, and Colin? And what about all the ghosts and the white rabbits and the shape-shifting poodle?

It's too much to take in, after what she's been through.

Anna falls back against the pillows, exhausted, and is soon asleep.

When she wakes, a full deck of cards sits on the pillow beside her. The box is black with a repeating design of silver stars and keys. She looks around the room as if she might find Arielle standing there, or maybe a trail of glitter or cockatoo feathers on the tile floor, but there is nothing else unusual. Is this a last gift perhaps, her final taste of the Houdini's particular brand of magic?

Anna opens the box and lets the cards spill out. The one on top is the king of hearts.

She has to go talk to Max.

48.

Oddly enough, it's just a little after midnight when Anna wakes up from the deepest sleep of her life. She checks the mirror and brushes her teeth with the rinky-dink hotel toothbrush before heading out in her wrinkled pajamas, fluffy white robe, and vacuum-packed slippers. She's a mess, but she's been a mess ever since she stumbled into the Houdini, so it's not like Max should notice a difference.

Anna's dad doesn't answer when she knocks on his door, but then again, he's a heavy sleeper. She doesn't know which rooms Phoebe and Max are in, but she's not willing to just sit in her own room, waiting for everyone else to wake up and move on. As she stands before the elevator, she thinks about what she knows of Max, about where he would go when faced with a situation this new and strange and impossible.

When the elevator arrives, Anna pushes the *R* and steps inside.

This elevator is swift and silent and smooth. When the doors open, she can hear the clamor from the rooftop bar, thumping music and laughter and the clink of glasses. It's amazing how things just . . . go on after a storm. The bar's violent neon decor has never been her favorite, so she turns away from it and heads toward the rooftop pool. It's quiet over here—not everyone knows about it, and the Roosevelt's clientele are all about noise, about loud bars and thundering slots and concerts so loud that tickets come with branded earplugs. On the opposite side of the roof, separated from the bar by a thick wall of tall cypress trees, the pool is lit from within, glowing crystal blue with rippling shadows from the tropical plants in giant planters all around it.

There's a shadow in a far corner behind a cluster of fan palms, and Anna knows instantly that she's guessed correctly.

Max stands at the wall, elbows on the stone, looking down at the glittering lights.

"I've never seen anything like it," he says as Anna approaches, his voice low as if he's worried about waking the city that never sleeps.

"I know. I grew up here. This is my kind of magic."

Anna sidles up beside him, their shoulders almost touching. She can see that he's been crying. He looks so different in modern clothes, even if they are pajamas.

"Are you okay?" she asks.

He chuckles ruefully. "I . . . might be a bit of a mess."

"Have you talked to your mom yet?"

Max looks away, raking his hair out of his eyes as they glow in the lights from the Strip. "I don't think I'm ready for that yet."

For a while, they just look at the sky, where the twinkling sparkles might be man-made or starshine or something in between.

"I think . . . she was doing her best," Anna says carefully.

"I don't think she gave any thought to what I might want."

Anna never wants to stop looking at him, but she has to look away to think through this, to find the right words.

"We're all victims, aren't we?" she begins. "Your mom—her brother tried to murder her. She found the Houdini and kept Arielle locked up, and then Colin attacked her. She was scared. She kept you in the dark and told herself it was for your own safety. She had poor Arielle deliver all of us into another world, knowing we might become ghosts. We're all victims of one kind or another, except Tony and Sebastian." Anna breathes out through her nose and corrects herself. "And Colin. Maybe he was a victim at first, and then he chose to be a villain. But . . . Arielle's right. It's all about forgiveness. About moving on."

She leans into Max, her shoulder more firmly against his, a welcome bolster. "Before the storm, I was furious with my dad. I thought sending Emily to New York was unforgivable. But underneath that, I was actually angry with Emily for leaving me. And underneath all that, I was still a little girl who never wanted anything to change because I wanted to feel safe. I wanted to control everything so nothing could ever hurt me." Her fingers brush the deck of cards in her robe pocket. "A bird who didn't want to leave her cage."

She looks at Max. "But I forgave my dad and my sister, and I even forgave that version of me that got so stupidly stubborn. You might want to forgive your mother. She was trying to keep you safe from the men who hurt her, give you a way to grow up happy and give you something to inherit. She did a bad thing, but maybe for the right reason."

"I'm not sure if I'm ready to forgive her. My whole life, Anna. My whole life, alone . . ." Max trails off, looks down at his bare feet poking out beneath his gray sweatpants; he must not have known about the slippers in the closet.

"But don't you see? You're free now. The only thing holding you back is all these feelings. You could dwell on them forever, like your mom in the Houdini. You could trap yourself like one of those ghosts in a loop. You could hate her, or want revenge like she did, or just simmer constantly, but . . . that's a cage, too." Anna puts her hand on his. "You're the only person who can set you free."

For a long moment, he looks away, and she studies his eyelashes, the planes of his cheekbones, the light stubble on his jaw. And then he turns his hand, entwining his fingers with hers.

"But . . . I don't know how to live this life. It's like I don't know anything here. Even the simplest tasks seem impossible. I can't even turn on the television."

"You just have to push a button."

Max chuckles sadly. "Well, you have to find the right button first, and I failed."

After a moment of thought, Anna puts her lips to his ear and says, "Once upon a time when I was a little girl, I went to a party." She has never told anyone this story, and her voice is barely a whisper. "I wore the prettiest princess dress, but the girls were mean and fake and grown-up, and they made me feel terrible. From then on, I didn't want to stand out or try anything new. I just wanted to be better than those girls. I focused on grades and accomplishments, on taking care of everyone and making sure everything was perfect. There were so many things I wanted to do, but I was too scared to try and fail and be laughed at again. And now I'm not scared anymore. You helped with that, back in the Houdini. You made the impossible possible. You brought the magic back for me."

"Yes, but . . . out here, there is no magic."

Anna smiles a Max-like smile. "There is when I'm with you."

With the closest thing she's seen to his old grin, he steps away from the wall and takes her into his arms like they're back in the ballroom. He leads her in a few steps, and it would be very romantic if they weren't wearing hotel bathrobes and couldn't hear a bachelorette party calling for shots at the bar around the corner while the music screams about a wrecking ball.

Max twirls her and laughs. "So this is the kind of music you like? It's hard to dance to."

"I never said I liked it. But waltzes are definitely not cool these days. The good news is that everything you had back in the Houdini—all the music and books—it's all available all the time. You can listen to music for free online, buy records or upload whole albums to your phone and carry them in your pocket. You can read books electronically or—"

Max is staring at Anna like she stared at him when he tried to explain the food at Harry's Hideaway.

"I'll show you," she says. "Food will help."

Max steps closer, looking down at her, but now it's not the lights of Vegas reflected in his eyes.

It's her.

"May I?" he asks.

She nods, and he leans down to kiss her, and her entire body comes alive.

The feeling is perfect and glorious and sparkling, too beautiful to be real.

Like magic.

ABOUT THE AUTHOR

DELILAH S. DAWSON is the *New York Times* bestselling author of *Star Wars: Phasma,* as well as more than twenty other books, including *Hit, Strike, Servants of the Storm,* and the Shadow series, written as Lila Bowen. Her comics include *Ladycastle, Sparrow-hawk, Star Pig,* and the series *Marvel Action Spider-Man, Adventure Time, The X-Files Case Files, Wellington,* and *Rick and Morty Presents.*

delilahsdawson.com